# DOLL²

## THE REVEALING

# MIRACLE AUSTIN

Wings & Fangs
PUBLISHING

# DOLL²

## THE REVEALING

Copyright © February 14, 2018 by Miracle Austin

ISBN-10: 0-9986182-2-5      ISBN-13: 978-0-9986182-2-7

Edited & Proofread by: Kitten Jackson
Edited, Proofread, & Formatted by: E & F Indie Services
Published by: Miracle Austin

Wings & Fangs
PUBLISHING
Published in (United States of America)
10  9  8  7  6  5  4  3  2  1

# DEDICATION

I DEDICATE DOLL 2: THE REVEALING to my mom, Eva Jackson, for providing me the initial inspiration to create and bring *Doll* to life for you. I also wish to thank and dedicate this sequel to a few of my amazing readers/supporters:

TRES KENNEDY

ELIZABETH WHITMIRE

MAUREEN BILLINGS

ETHAN COOPER

LAUREN AND LAURIE MURRAY

CHANEL HARRY

KIARRAH GUILLORY

JACOB HALL

YAZMINE

BRIANNA BEARD

LETHA HANOVER

MARTHA COTHRON

EMILY HERNANDEZ

ROSA CARAMAYA

SHAUN WHITEHEAD

*I appreciate each of you for your beautiful support.*

# FOR MY READERS...

I DIDN'T HAVE PLANS TO CREATE A sequel; however, my readers roared out loud, demanding more—and boom! *Doll 2: The Revealing* was born. Some readers voted for the first ending, while others voted for the alternate ending.

I utilized all the feedback and decided to pursue a mashup of both endings. I so hope that you enjoy it and share your thoughts with your friends and me. Thank you for choosing my book to read. Your support absolutely means so much!

*Miracle Austin*

P.S. A bonus short story THE HATCH is included. It first appeared in the *Ever in the After* anthology, which benefited Lift4Autism 2017.

Okay, ready, set, mark, and go!
Step into the world of

# DOLL²: THE REVEALING

# DOLL²

## THE REVEALING

# PROLOGUE

Reflect back to your junior year in high school. Bet it was pretty ordinary and normal, without any supernatural twists and turns, right? Well, mine was exactly the opposite. I have three words for you that describe that period of time at Frost High—*big unforeseen outcomes*.

I fell in love with my best friend, discovered unexpected and scary truths, befriended someone I should've dismissed, and attempted to reject my true identity more than once.

That year was magically complicated, but wait until you experience the events that took place the following summer…

I'm Tomie Dupuy—pronounced *Toh-me Due-pwee*—Teen Newbie Warlock, and this is the continuation of my story.

Let's jump back in.

# CHAPTER
ONE

Sari cried and buried her head in my chest as we sat in the church parking lot in my car, thinking about everything that happened the day of Pepper Fox's funeral. I rubbed slow circles along her back with my right hand. After a few minutes, she lifted her head up and stared into my eyes, not saying anything before quickly retreating to her safe place.

I looked out my open window and thought about how much had happened over the last few months. I knew that my entire life would never return to what it once was.

The sunset was approaching in the next hour or so.

Against my chest, Sari had fallen asleep as I stroked her hair. Just as I leaned down to kiss her forehead, my phone buzzed on the dashboard. Gently removing my hand from Sari's head, I reached over and grabbed it.

There was a text message from Mr. Ray.

> R: **Meet me at 7:30 tonight at the school gym**.
> T: **What's up?**
> R: **Have something I need to show you.**
> T: **All right. Sari and I'll meet you then.**

R: **No. Come alone Tomie!**
T: **Okay**
R: **See you soon.**

Glancing at my phone, I saw that it was already 7:00, as Sari squirmed a little and sat up.

"Who was that?"

She stretched her arms out towards the dashboard, pulled down the visor, and looked in the mirror to check her face. She grabbed a tissue from her purse on the floor to wipe off some smeared eye makeup.

"Mr. Ray needs me to meet him soon."

"Why?"

"He wants to show me something."

"What?"

"I'm not sure, but it sounds pretty important."

"Okay, let's go."

"Sari, he specified… just me."

"Oh."

Her chin flopped towards her chest.

"Hey, now, I'll call you later and tell you all about it, okay?"

Tilting her head up with my right index finger beneath her chin, my other hand fumbled for hers and squeezed it. She nodded, so I placed the key in the ignition and drove towards her house.

Once we arrived, I parked the car and left it running. I stepped out and walked over to the passenger's side, then opened the door for Sari, helped her out, and shut it behind her. She jumped up and wrapped her arms around my neck.

Pulling back a little, I asked, "Hey, what's wrong?" She held me even tighter. Lowering my head, I whispered, "Sari, I'm going to protect you."

With tears floating in her brown eyes, she released me from the hug and grasped my hands.

"Tomie, I know you will, but you can't always be with

me."

I took off the necklace that Lisette gave me and fastened it around Sari's neck. It shimmered as it touched her bare skin.

"This will protect you. Lisette told me so when she gave it to me."

"Oh, Tomie, I can't accept this."

"Yeah, you can."

She lifted it up and examined it closer.

"Thank you."

"No problem. Anything to keep my girl safe."

"What about you?"

"Don't worry about me."

Staring into my eyes, she said, "I do worry about you."

I scooped her up with one arm and whispered, "I know you do, and that's why I love you like I do."

After giving her a kiss, I watched her walk away from me, towards her house, as I leaned up against the car with my arms crossed in front of my chest.

Before she reached the door, she placed her hand up to her ear as if she were holding a phone and mouthed, "Call me later."

She blew a kiss at me. Reaching out, I caught it, pulled my hand back, and placed it over my heart with a grin. I threw one back towards her, and she grabbed it with both hands and smiled. She opened the door, went inside, and shut it behind her.

Her dad was staring out the window, with his hand holding the curtain off to the side, watching me. When our eyes met, he jumped and moved out of the way, while the curtain shifted back and forth in his absence.

After walking around to the driver's side, I got into my car and headed off towards Frost High School to meet up with Mr. Ray. I knew that he had something serious to share with me after everything that had taken place earlier.

# CHAPTER
## TWO

**A** black 1977 Cadillac pulled up next to me at a red light. I looked over and saw a dark-tinted window go down, and flowing smoke tumbled out. The driver, an older woman, glared at me. She pulled a cigarette away from her mouth, holding it with two fingers, and rested it on the steering wheel. I recognized her—Opal's grandmom, Verlinda Dawn.

She whispered in a dry, raspy voice, *"Beware... Tomie... Dupuy!"*

A stream of sweat rolled down the sides of my face, as she flicked her cigarette towards my open window. It landed on my right thigh, and I grabbed it and threw it out the window. Before I could reply to her warning, she sped off out of my sight.

Noticing a black spot of ash on my blue jeans, I attempted to wipe it off, but it was resistant. It was a circular pattern with three dots around it.

The light turned green, and I drove off. A few minutes later, I arrived in the parking lot and saw Mr. Ray's white Ford 150 truck. I stepped out of my car and walked up the curvy cement path. Just as I reached for the handle, the door opened, and I went inside. Then it closed, apparently of its own volition.

Half the lights were turned on in the oval-shaped gym, which had been remodeled a few months back. The bleachers on both sides were pulled in against the wall, and a few chairs rested on the shiny floor, where a huge Frost Polar Bear mascot, wearing our navy blue and gold, was painted.

Mr. Ray was sitting in one of those chairs in the middle of the room, so I approached him.

"I just experienced a strange encounter with Opal's grandmom on my way here."

"I know. I saw."

My curly, shoulder-length bronzish-brown hair bounced, as I shook my head.

"Wait a minute… never mind. I'm sure there's a lot you can do."

He agreed by nodding. "Come over here and have a seat in front of me."

After sliding a chair to where it was a few feet in front of him, so my long legs would have enough room, I sat down.

Mr. Ray noticed the black ash on my jeans and reached out to touch it. His index finger brushed over it, and he lifted it up to examine it closer.

"She left this on you?" I nodded. "Do you know what this is?"

"Just cigarette ash."

I stretched my legs out, placed my hands behind my neck, and laid my head back.

"Yes, but it's also something much more."

"What?" I asked in a low snicker.

"Tomie, it's time you start taking everything

seriously!" he yelled in a booming voice.

I straightened in my chair.

"All right, all right! What is it, then?"

"This is her coven symbol. She's marked you. Make sure you take those jeans to Lisette, so she can perform a special spell on them. Don't wash them!"

Leaning in towards him, I said, "Sure. But what do you mean when you say she *marked* me? What the heck are you talking about?"

"Verlinda Dawn, Opal's grandmom, is a Dark Witch. She practices the evil crafts. She's always enjoyed planting seeds of chaos and harm in the gardens of her enemies. I've known about her for a long time. She plans to wreak havoc in your life, as well as that of whoever else she perceives as a threat. Lisette will tell you more about Verlinda and her coven soon enough."

"But I've never done anything to her."

"Not to her directly. Yet, in her twisted mind, you're part of the reason Lisette, your cousin, placed a spell on Opal to prevent her from pursuing her evil practices. Plus, her dear Opal has been taken from her by Lisette."

"So, Lisette is in trouble, too?"

"Yes and no. Verlinda knows Lisette is a powerful Light Witch with abilities to transform into a Dark Witch if she wishes. She'll do her best to hurt Lisette, as well."

"Why didn't you tell me who you were before now?"

"It wasn't time for you to know. You wouldn't have believed me, anyway. You weren't ready to accept who you really are, Tomie."

"Yeah… I guess you're right. I wasn't until prom night. After I witnessed Pepper Fox's awful demise on the dancefloor, and then the way you showed me how to use my powers to save Sari… Am I a Light or Dark Warlock?"

"We'll discuss more when the time is right, okay?"

"Why can't you tell me now?"

"It's just best this way."

"Okay."

Mr. Ray smiled, leaned in closer to me, and whispered, "Tomie, there's something I need to show you."

"There's still so much I want to ask you."

"No time for that now. You'll be able to ask me all the questions swimming around in that inquisitive mind of yours soon enough. Now, follow my eyes."

While I did as he instructed, he peeled his glasses off, lowered his lids, and then opened them. His eyes transitioned into a reflective golden tint, and he turned his head towards his left. A bright light emanated from them, shining on the wall.

"Watch and listen carefully, Tomie Dupuy!"

He projected the image of *Pizza Beat's* parking lot, where I used to work before Pepper fired me. I saw Mr. Fox in his office, glancing down at his Rolex a few times impatiently, as if he was waiting for someone. He stared at a framed picture which I couldn't make out. A few teardrops fell onto his desk. He wiped his face with his hands and glanced back down at his watch, and then he lifted an oversized Frost Polar Bear-shaped coffee cup and took a few sips.

After a few minutes, he projected another image next to Mr. Fox. An older woman approached the glass door entrance and knocked. I couldn't make out who she was at first, because her face looked blurry.

As the scene panned back to Mr. Fox, I saw him rise from his chair and walk around his desk and through the restaurant, towards the entrance, and then the images merged into one. He welcomed the woman in, scanned the parking lot to his left and right, and locked the door behind her. He then closed the blinds, escorted her back to his office, and closed that door behind them.

When she sat down and began to speak, I knew it was Opal's grandmom, because her voice was raspy and loud. A cigarette levitated from inside her purse and landed between her crinkled lips, which were painted with nectarine lipstick.

I gasped, and she turned around and looked over her shoulder.

"Did you hear something?"

"No. We're the only ones here, Verlinda," Mr. Fox replied, sounding like he was out of breath.

She turned back around with one thin brow raised. With a snap of her fingers, she lit the cigarette. As Mr. Fox's eyes widened, he knocked over his coffee mug. Waving her finger, she stopped it and its contents in midair. She whispered a few incomprehensible words and then barked out instructions.

"Grab it!"

Mr. Fox retrieved it and set it back down on his desk, farther away from the edge that time, and took a few sips.

"It's still warm."

Her lips curled up to form a creepy, distorted smile.

"You shouldn't be surprised, Cage. Remember that night, when Resella almost experienced an unexplainable accident at the Frost Country Club? She was pregnant with your darling Pepper. My magic saved her from that near mishap." He nodded without uttering one word. "I know what you desire, Cage, and I need something from you in return."

He leaned in closer and asked, in a low growl, "What, Verlinda?"

After inhaling deeply from her cigarette, she dragged her chipped black nails across the desk, and a piercing sound echoed for a few seconds.

"I know who murdered your only child."

Mr. Fox jumped up from his chair and placed both hands on his desk, leaning over to the point where his face was nearly touching hers. She blew a thick swirling cloud of grey smoke into his face and flicked her finger three times, which pushed him back down into his chair. He squirmed around in an attempt to stand, but he was unable to move.

"I like my space. Listen up!" she demanded. "You know that boy, Tomie Dupuy, who used to work here?"

"Yes. From what I've heard, he's straight-laced and really smart."

"He told you that night at the hospital that he had no information about Pepper's terrible accident, right?" she asked with a smirk.

"Yes."

"Well, if you really knew *Mr. Perfect Boy Scout,* you would be aware of the fact that he's a liar and a murderer. He and his meddling cousin Lisette Laveau killed your precious Pepper and did away with my Opal, too."

"What?"

His calm face transformed into a bright raspberry tone, with throbbing veins along both of his temples.

"Listen, if you truly seek revenge, you have to do it my way, with no law enforcement involved. Understand?"

I clenched my jaw, digging my fingernails into my palms, as I balled up both of my fists and gritted my teeth. From the corner of my eye, I saw Mr. Ray raise his hands and lower them, gesturing to me to remain calm. Slowly, I relaxed my jaws and stretched out my fingers.

In the projection on the wall, Mr. Fox nodded, as one teardrop coasted down his cheek. He then pounded his fists on his desk.

Verlinda whispered, "Don't worry. *Bad magic always*

*wins, and I possess the perfect plan.*"

Their images faded from the wall, as Mr. Ray put his glasses back on and stared into my eyes.

"Ms. Dawn is a liar! Opal was the one who changed that spell and murdered Pepper, not Lisette and me! I tried to stop her!"

"Tomie, you and I both know the truth. None of that matters now. She's tricked Mr. Fox with her lies. She'll use whatever spells she needs to in order to keep him under her thumb until her purpose is served."

He stood and so did I.

"Mr. Ray, I know you said it doesn't matter; however, it does to me. I'm going to tell Mr. Fox everything. I should've told him that night at the hospital." As I walked towards the exit, I dropped my gaze down to the floor. I reached for the doorknob, but jerked my hand back upon contact. It was burning, red, and tender for a few seconds, and then it went back to normal. Turning around, I looked at him. "You really know how to stop a guy in his tracks, don't you?"

He walked towards me and said, "You can't go to Mr. Fox and tell him anything. He'll never believe you now. Verlinda won't allow it. She's probably already placed a deception spell on him to make him believe all of her incoming lies."

"Dang, she's really smooth and awful all at once. When did she put a spell on him?"

"Probably when she froze his coffee cup, and he drank out of it after, which gave her enough time to do it." Mr. Ray commanded in a firm voice, "We must leave soon and begin your training with Lisette!"

"When?"

"Tomorrow morning. I'll meet you at your house around 10:00."

"How long will my training take?"

"Probably most of the summer, and the rest will come over time."

After Mr. Ray walked near the switches, the lights turned off. We left the gym together, and the door locked when he touched it.

As we went our separate ways, headed towards our cars, he looked back at me and said, "I know this is a lot for you to take in, but I'm here to help you."

"Thanks, Mr. Ray."

As I opened my door, I watched him drive off. I turned the radio on and thought about how I was going to tell my dad and Sari about everything, especially about being away from her most of the summer.

I decided to text her before I left the school.

> T: **Hey beautiful.**
> S: **Hey there! How did it go?**
> T: **Lots to share.**
> S: **K**
> T: **Will call later tonight.**
> S: **Can't wait to hear more.**
> T: **Talk soon.**

While driving home, my mind kept drifting back to the meeting with Mr. Ray and what I knew I had to do. My mundane life ended the night I was told who I truly was, even though I attempted to ignore it. However, I knew that if Ms. Dawn marked me, she could do the same to Sari.

It was time for me to learn all I could.

# CHAPTER
## THREE

When I arrived home, I saw Dad's truck parked along the side of the road, and the lights were on inside the house. I figured he must've finished up his run to Oklahoma early. He wasn't due back home until Saturday night.

I turned the car off, grabbed the special book Lisette gave me out from under my seat, and locked the car. It was almost 9:00 when I walked towards my house and found the door open.

Dad was sitting on the couch, watching an Alfred Hitchcock movie.

After setting the book on a table, I said, "Hey, Dad," as I went over and wrapped my arms around him.

"What's that for? You're usually not much of a hugger—at least, not with me."

"Just really good to see you, Dad."

I held onto him for another few seconds.

"You okay? I know you went to Pepper Fox's funeral earlier."

"Yeah, yeah, Dad. Just a lot going on."

"I brought some Japanese takeout from *Orchid's Kitchen*. You hungry?" I nodded. "Figured you would be. I already ate."

We sat at the table, and he poured two glasses of ice-cold tea. He gave me one, and I began to eat, telling him all about the funeral and everything that happened later—including what Mr. Ray told me I needed to do.

Dad was silent for a bit, as he drank his tea down and poured it full again.

When he spoke, his voice was grave. "Tomie, I've harbored negative feelings about Lisette over the years, especially recently, but Mr. Ray is right about starting your training with her."

"Well, we're leaving tomorrow morning. I'm probably going to be gone most of the summer."

"What happened, son?"

"Verlinda Dawn and Mr. Fox."

"They're plotting something?"

"You could say that."

"Son, I had plans for us to travel up to Colorado and Nevada, but your training is way more important right now."

"Yeah, I know."

I looked up at Dad, wiping my mouth with a napkin.

"Hey, when you get back you can tell me about all of your adventures with Lisette."

I helped Dad clear the table, and then he washed the dishes while I dried them.

"Dad, can I ask you a question?"

He wrung the dishcloth out and pulled up the strainer from the sink.

"Tomie, you can ask me anything."

"Was Mom a Light or a Dark Witch?"

He paused and turned around to face me, hanging the

dishcloth on a metal hook on the cabinet in front of him.

"Why do you ask?"

I placed the last glass in the cabinet next to me, closed the door, and hung the towel over a bar on the stove.

"Just curious, because Mr. Fox said that Ms. Dawn is a Dark Witch. Kinda wondering what I could be."

"Well, your mom came from a very, very powerful witch line, as you already know. She was a *Gris* Witch." He spoke the term with a faint accent; from what I remembered of my year of French, it meant *grey*, but I wanted to be sure.

"What's that?"

"Both Light and Dark, with the ability to change from one to the other."

"So, there's a possibility that I could be a *Gris* Warlock?"

"Yes."

"When will I know?"

"Lisette or Mr. Ray will be able to explore more with you when it's the right time. Tomie, I want you to know that the Dupuy Silver Slayers haven't been in this area for many years, but with all that's happened recently, someone may have contacted a sector. They live to hunt down and exterminate witches."

"What does that mean?"

"One of them might attempt to track you down. I didn't participate in their missions, but I know how they work. It's good that Lisette is going to be training you. Not only will she prepare you to defend yourself from dark magic, but also from a slayer trying to annihilate you."

My head felt like it was spinning.

I still needed to call Sari and then get some rest before the morning, so after rubbing my hands over my face, I said, "Dad, I've heard and seen enough for tonight."

"Yes, I'm sure you have. You can call or text me anytime this summer, okay?"

"I will. Lisette and Mr. Ray will take good care of me."

"So happy that he was chosen to be your *Mega*, your wise guardian and protector. That makes me breathe easier."

"Me, too. I'll probably get out of here early, so I can see Sari before we take off."

"Understand." He gave me a hug. "I'm going to deposit some money into your bank account, which should get you through the next two months or so."

"You don't have to do that, Dad. I have a little saved up from when I worked at *Pizza Beat*."

"Tomie, I've checked your balance, and $200 isn't enough. You splurged on your junior prom. You need to give Lisette some money to cover expenses while you're there, and you'll need some to spend for fun. I want you to enjoy your last summer before your senior year as much as possible. You're still planning to apply to the Falcon Air Academy, right?"

"Well, I know how you originally felt about me pursuing the academy over college, so I haven't yet, but I want to."

"Like I've said before, it was *my* dream for you to attend an Ivy League college, not yours. You should live *your* dream. I love you, Tomie."

"Love you, too, Dad."

After showering and brushing my teeth, I slipped on my *Blade* pajama pants and a blue t-shirt. Grabbing my phone, I jumped into my bed to call Sari. I figured that talking to her about my leaving the next morning, though it wasn't in person, would come across better than just texting her.

As I dialed her number, I looked up at the ceiling and noticed something that wasn't there before—a mobile with fighter jets on it—that made me smile.

Her cell phone rang a few times and went to voicemail. It was after 10:30, so I figured she was in the shower or had drifted off to sleep.

After scanning some movies, I clicked on *Jurassic World* and propped a pillow under my chest. About twenty minutes in, I heard the ringtone I set for Sari, and her picture popped up, causing the movie to pause. I clicked over.

"Hey, beautiful."

"Hi. I fell asleep. I thought about calling you in the morning, but I wanted to know how everything went with Mr. Ray."

"A lot went on, Sari."

"Spill."

"You know how much I love you, right?"

"Tomie, what's wrong?" I could hear the tremble in her voice.

"Remember when I told you how Lisette wanted me to come to Monroe Creek in the summer to start training?"

"Yes, but you were having second thoughts."

"That was before I ran into Opal's grandmom earlier and Mr. Ray showed me something."

"What? You saw her? Where?"

"At a stoplight, when I was headed to meet him at the gym."

"Please continue."

"She threw a lit cigarette in my car and said something crazy. Mr. Ray explained that she had marked me because of the black ash pattern left on my jeans."

Sari cleared her throat and asked, "She marked you?"

"Yeah, it's when a—"

"I know what that is, Tomie. I've read a few books on the magic arts. So, you're telling me that Opal's grandmom is a witch?"

"Yep. Not just any plain ol' witch… she's a Dark one."

I filled her in about the meeting Verlinda Dawn had with Mr. Fox at the *Pizza Beat*.

"That's really scary. I don't want to be without you this summer, but I think Mr. Ray is right about you going to train with Lisette. So, when do you leave? Next week?"

"Not exactly. He and I are leaving tomorrow morning." All I heard was silence. "Sari, you there? Sari?"

"Yes, I'm still here. I just thought that we would have some time to spend together, that's all," she said with a deep sigh.

"I did, too. Can we meet for breakfast before I hit the road?"

"Definitely want to see you."

Then the silence continued.

"Sari, I'm going to text and call you all the time."

"Tomie, you'll be busy and focused."

"Never too busy for you. You're my girl, remember?"

"Yeah."

"Hey, do you think your parents would let you come down for a weekend?"

"I doubt it, but I could ask."

"Yeah, after you told them about the funeral ordeal, I figured they wouldn't want you hanging out with me."

"Well… I didn't tell them *everything* for that exact reason."

"You don't think they should know?"

"Absolutely not! They would freak, and my dad would probably forbid me to see you."

"Why would he do that after I saved you?"

"Tomie, Dad has been acting really weird since prom

night, when you picked me up and he had a talk with you… and the Pepper incident. He kinda thinks you're somehow connected to her eccentric death."

"What? Are you serious?"

"Yes. I tried to explain to him that you had nothing to do with any of that stuff, and I never gave him any inclination about who you are."

"Thanks for that. Your dad put me in an awkward position when I was at your house, and the warlock part of me reacted."

"No need to explain to me. I understand. I love my dad, but he can be a little too forward sometimes. I'm sorry he made you feel that way."

"Listen, it's getting late, and I need to get up early to pack and meet you for breakfast."

Sari yawned, and it triggered one from me as well.

"Goodnight. I love you, my Tomie Dupuy."

"I love you, too, Sarifena Green."

"Wow, you haven't called me that in a while."

"Yeah, I know. Can we meet at 8:00 at *Café Armadillo*?"

"Sure."

"Night-night, beautiful."

She whispered, "Night."

The call ended, and I navigated to the clock app. I set my alarm for 6:00 a.m. and then resumed watching the movie until I fell asleep.

# CHAPTER
## FOUR

My alarm went off with two snoozes. Lying on my back, I thought about Mr. Ray, Ms. Dawn, Mr. Fox, and leaving Sari for the summer to go to Monroe Creek. I really wanted to talk to Mr. Fox, but I knew it wouldn't be a good idea.

After changing from my pajamas to some black jeans and a Frost High Polar Bears t-shirt, I brushed my teeth and gargled with mouthwash. Rubbing my hands along my face, I felt stubble, so I took out my electric razor and shaved.

Once my bed was made, I pulled a large duffle bag out of my closet and packed my necessities, adding my toiletry bag last. After slipping on some sandals and putting my phone in my pocket, I grabbed my backpack from the chair and put a spiral notebook and the special book inside.

Looking around the room, I made sure that I hadn't forgotten anything. When I noticed a tin of breath mints on my dresser, I slid it into my other pocket. Once I slipped my backpack over my shoulder, I grabbed the duffle bag in my right hand and shut my bedroom door behind me.

Dad walked towards me with a cup of coffee.

"Thought you would be leaving about now."

"Yeah." Nodding, I said, "I'll be back in about an hour, after breakfast with Sari."

"I'll be here."

Grabbing my watch from the living room table, I strapped it around my wrist, and then I went out to my car and headed towards *Café Armadillo*; it was close to 7:50.

# CHAPTER
## FIVE

When I arrived and parked, I saw that several customers were already there. Sari was sitting outside under an umbrella with a glass in front of her. As I approached her, the loose gravel under my feet made crackling sounds. She stood and walked towards me, as her hair shimmered in the sunlight.

She wore blue jean shorts and a black and white polka-dot halter top that showed a peek-a-boo of her firm abs. The outfit hugged her body in all the right places, calling attention to her awesome curves. The black sandals she wore showed off her glittery painted toenails.

Picking up my pace, I rushed towards her and scooped her up, then planted a long kiss on her sweet lips, which tasted like hot cinnamon and grape juice. When I set her down, she wrapped her arms around my waist, and we remained in that position until the waitress walked over and asked us if we were ready to take a seat.

Sari laughed and pulled away, and we both sat down. I ordered a breakfast burrito with the works, chicken fried steak, and a large milk. Sari chose strawberry waffles with chocolate syrup, and then she picked up her large glass of grape juice and took a sip.

I noticed the bracelet she was wearing, which I had bought for her for prom. It fit her wrist perfectly.

"Looks really good on you."

"Love it, Tomie. I just opened it this morning and read your sweet message. Thank you so much."

"Glad you like it. Wish I could have gotten you more."

"Oh, no. This is beautiful and special."

When I smiled, she grabbed my hand and squeezed it, as I stared into her eyes.

"You know I'm really going to miss you, right, Sari?"

"Yeah. I'll miss you so much, too."

I held her hand a little tighter.

The waitress brought out our breakfast and set it in front of us, and I scooted my chair closer to Sari's. We ate as fast as possible, so we'd have more time to talk.

"Tomie, I'm going to try to visit you soon."

"I'd really love that. I know it's a long drive, so maybe you could take the train. I'll pay for your ticket. Just let me know when you can make the trip."

"You don't have to do that."

"I want to take care of it for you. I hope you can spend the weekend with me. I mean, not *with* me, like in the same room."

My face grew warm, and I'm sure it turned a shade of red, so I took a few deep breaths.

"Why, Tomie Dupuy, are you thinking what I think you're thinking?" she asked with a grin and a high-pitched giggle.

"No! Of course not. I mean... I would love to just hold you all night... with no expectations."

"Me, too. My mom might be cool with me visiting you. I told her all about our amazing visit with Lisette. . . minus the witchy parts."

She leaned back in my arms, and we continued to be

entertained by the squirrel circus in a tree a few feet away from us. It was almost 9:30.

"Sari…"

Turning around to face me, she placed her right index finger onto my lips.

"Sshhh. I know. Just five more minutes."

She turned around and laid back against me, and I started to say something else about last night, but I caught myself. That quiet moment I was sharing with her was more priceless than any conversation I could have initiated. Though I wished we had more time to spend together, I knew that beginning my training was vital.

Sari stood and reached for my hand, and I took it. She pulled me up, and then we walked towards our cars. When we stopped, she went to her tiptoes and wrapped her arms around my neck, as I lifted her a few inches off the ground.

"Text me when you can," she whispered in my ear.

I nodded.

My lips found hers without trying, and I set her back down. I opened her door, and she slid into the driver's seat. The window was all the way down, and I bent over and rested my elbows in the opening.

"I'm really going to miss you, Tomie."

"You know I'm going to miss you, too. We'll see each other soon."

She nodded, as I leaned in and kissed her left cheek, while placing my hand on her right.

"Go," she said.

When I stood, I noticed that her eyes were tearing up, so I bent down to be close to her again.

"Hey, I'll stay."

"No, you have to do this, Tomie."

She started the car, and I watched her back out. As she

drove away from me, she beeped her horn, while we both waved. Walking towards my car to head back, I saw that the time was approaching 10:15.

# CHAPTER
## SIX

When I arrived, I saw Mr. Ray and my dad talking in front of his truck, so I parked, stepped out, and waved.

Once I entered the living room, I grabbed my duffle bag and slung it around my body, while tossing the backpack over my right shoulder. Walking into the kitchen, I scooped up some cold bottles of water from the fridge and dropped them into my bag.

Just as I was about to walk out the door, I remembered the fighter jet mobile Dad had hung up for me. I went back to my room, detached it from its hanging anchor, and carried it outside with me.

After opening the door, I placed my bags in the back while looking for a safe spot to stash my mobile. I laid it in an empty plastic crate behind the driver's seat. Then I walked over to Dad and gave him a hug, and he slipped some money into my hand.

"Thanks, Dad."

"Welcome. Now, stay focused at all times and be aware of your surroundings. Mr. Ray, take care of my son."

"Will do, Mr. Dupuy."

We climbed into our seats, and Mr. Ray started the engine and turned the vehicle around. Dad came over and stood on my side.

"I'll see you when you make a run up that way, right?"

"Yeah, won't be too long. Be safe traveling, and call me when y'all get there."

As we slowly pulled away, Mr. Ray blew his horn, and I stuck my head out the door and waved. Dad waved back at me and remained in the street until we got to the stop sign and made a right turn.

My phone beeped; it was a text from Sari.

> S: **Wish I was going with.**
> T: **I wish too.**
> S: **Have y'all left yet?**
> T: **Yep, just left my house and about to get on the highway soon.**
> S: **K… Call me later…**

Three heart emojis followed, and I couldn't help smiling. Before I laid my phone down, it beeped again. I figured that Sari forgot to tell me something, but when I glanced down at the screen, I saw that it wasn't her. The number was unknown.

> U: **Going out of town won't save you…**
> T: **Who's this?**
> U: **Why?**
> T: **How did you get my number?**
> U: **Is that really the issue Tomie Dupuy?**
> T: **You know my name?**
> U: **Think really hard Einstein.**
> T: **Tell me who you are!**
> U: **You're definitely persistent. I like that. We'll meet when it's time. Just**

**remember this: Catawissa**
T: **What?**

The texts ended as quickly as they had started.

Mr. Ray turned to look at me, and he must've noticed the scowl on my face.

"What's wrong?"

"Nothing."

"Whoever it was upset you."

"Nah, I'm good, Mr. Ray."

"I'm just glad that I'm getting you out of Frost for a little while." I placed my phone facedown next to me on the leather seat.

"Whoever it is knows that you're leaving, which can only mean one thing."

"What?" I asked in a quivering tone.

"Someone's been stalking you."

# CHAPTER
## SEVEN

"Did anything strange happen last night when you drove home?" Mr. Ray asked.

"No."

I started replaying everything in my mind from before and after the gym, but I didn't notice anything out of the ordinary. The only weird encounter I had experienced was at the stoplight, when Ms. Dawn flicked her cigarette into my car. At that thought, my stomach felt as if someone had reached way down with both hands and was twisting it like you would wring out a wet towel.

"Tomie, I believe that your enemies will multiply by the time you return to school for your senior year."

"Bet you're right."

"This is confirmation for me that it's a good thing you're spending the summer with Lisette, so she can get you trained."

"Mr. Ray, can I ask you a question?"

"Sure."

"Were you someone else's *Mega* before you became mine?"

"Why do you ask?"

"Curious. Wondering if things turned out okay for him or her."

I swallowed hard and started tapping my right foot on the plastic floor mat.

"Years ago, your mom chose me to be your *Mega* when the time was right, specifically if you completed your transformation."

My body went still, as a tear zipped down my face.

"Wait a minute. You knew my mom?"

"Yes."

"What was she like?"

"Your mom was extremely beautiful and kind. She had the prettiest curly ebony locks, with scarlet tips at the ends, which reminded me of steady flames. All the boys wanted to court her, yet she was smitten with your dad at first sight. She chose to see him in secret for a few years. They married young, had you, and then she chose to perform the forbidden spell. She had her reasons. I begged her not to do it and tried to convince her that we could figure out a way for her, your dad, and you to be together." Turning my head, I stared out the window at all the trees, flowers, and flying birds all around me. "I wish she hadn't used that spell, Tomie."

"Yeah, me, too. There's so much I want to know about her, to share things about me with her, but that'll never happen." I sniffled. "Can I ask you one more question?"

"Ask me anything."

He raised his left hand to stroke his salt-and-pepper beard.

"Does it hurt when you transform?"

"You mean, shapeshift?"

"Oh, yeah. . . that. Well, does it?"

I lifted my shoulders, and they froze for a few seconds,

until he could respond.

"It used to be uncomfortable, when I first started, but it became easier, the more I practiced."

"How long does it take you?"

"Maybe less than a minute now, because I've done it so much."

"Can I shift into anything?"

"Not sure yet. If you can, you'll know soon enough."

Reaching into the backseat, I grabbed the special book and two bottles of water out of my bag. I opened it and flipped through the pages to look for any information about shapeshifting, but I didn't see anything.

As I read through the first few pages, I learned about some interesting witch and warlock history. I marked where I stopped with a highlighter and placed it back in my bag, as Mr. Ray picked up speed to merge onto the highway. It wasn't really busy for that time of the day.

I turned the radio on and found a hip-hop station, but he looked at me and shook his head. He quickly put on some jazz, as I grinned at him.

The sun was partially covered with clusters of milky blue and grey clouds, which I noticed just before I pulled a pair of shades out of my backpack's side pocket and slid them on.

# CHAPTER
## EIGHT

**M**r. Ray had already driven almost an hour from Frost, and as the time passed by, I had been thinking more about the mysterious text. I started to contact Lisette to get her opinion about it, but decided against it.

"Ready for a bathroom break?"

"I'm good." With my knees touching the dashboard because of my slouching, I pressed a button on the side to move the seat back a bit. "Do you need to stop, Mr. Ray?"

"No, I'm good, too. Maybe another hour, and we can get a bite."

My mind drifted back to Sari, and I wondered how she would be without me for most of the summer, what she would do, and if she would be safe from Ms. Dawn and Mr. Fox. I figured the amulet that Lisette gave me would shield her from immediate harm. At least, that's what I hoped.

Picturing Sari in her prom dress, I remembered how I couldn't keep my eyes off of her. Her beauty shone like nothing I'd ever witnessed before. That was when I knew

I never wanted to be without her, not only because she was radiant that night, but because of the way she had always made me feel. Her touch ignited instant peace within me. She made me feel wanted and safe at the same time.

Before I realized it, another hour had passed, and Mr. Ray pulled up to *Jessie's PitStop* and parked.

"That was quick."

"You were busy thinking about your sweetheart." He smiled and removed the keys from the ignition. "Come on, let's get something to eat."

"Mr. Ray, you *glimming* me?"

He smiled, as I grabbed my cell. After hopping out of the truck, I shut the door behind me. He did the same, and then he hit the button on his owl keychain to lock the doors.

Upon entering the restaurant, which was small and packed, we were met with the mixed aromas of country-fried steak, hamburgers, and root beer. The place wasn't quite a hole in the wall, but it was pretty close.

We found a couple of empty seats, and a woman who looked to be in her late 40s, with her auburn hair in a tight bun, approached us. She wore cat-eye glasses with crystals around the outer edges, and they reminded me of Sari's, which she only used when she had to read a lot or study.

The waitress blew a few green bubbles and popped her gum, as she talked with a deep country twang. "So, what can I get you two good-lookin' fellas to start?" she asked, as she handed each of us a menu.

"I'll take a root beer."

"A Big Red for me, please," Mr. Ray said.

"Y'all want those in longnecks or in glasses?"

"Longnecks?" I asked with one raised eyebrow.

She leaned down and whispered in my ear, "Bottles,

cutie pie."

Mr. Ray smiled and lifted his menu.

"Where're y'all headed?"

"Louisiana," Mr. Ray said.

"I used to live there years ago. Loved it, especially Mardi Gras and zydeco dancin'. Boy, I have some great memories of that place..." She coughed. "What part of Louisiana?"

*Zydeco dancing*, I whispered to myself.

"Monroe Creek," Mr. Ray said.

"Now, that's an interestin' little town. My sister used to live there. She told me the strangest stories. Most, I figured she was pullin' my leg, but there was a few that kept me up at night that I always wondered about."

I opened my mouth to blurt out, "What kind of stories?" Mr. Ray gave me the look, so I kept silent.

"Well, I'll give y'all a few minutes and come back."

After looking at the menu, I decided on the fried shrimp basket with golden curly fries and hushpuppies.

She returned in about five minutes and set two ice-cold longnecks on the table in front of us. They had shaved ice skating down all sides. I picked mine up and took a swig or two. It burned my throat when I swallowed, but the sweetness made up for the discomfort, so I gulped down another and another, as Mr. Ray took a couple sips of his.

"Okay, boys, what'll it be for ya?"

"Medium rare hamburger, fully loaded, with golden curly fries," Mr. Ray said.

Then I gave her my order.

"It'll be out in a jiffy for y'all."

As she scurried away, Mr. Ray asked, "So, Tomie, are you getting nervous?"

"Not yet. Honestly, I'm not sure what to expect."

"Someone told me years ago to expect anything,

because you might just walk out with something you never imagined until that very moment. I think that's good advice."

Before I finished my drink, the waitress brought out two more longnecks, and our food followed right after. Mr. Ray said a prayer before we dug in.

Steam swirls rose from my shrimp, fries, hushpuppies, and his hamburger plate. Everything was well seasoned and juicy, but I needed a little more flavor. I spotted ketchup and mustard bottles on an empty table about five feet away from us, so I went over and grabbed them.

A guy was sitting up against the wall nearby, twirling a straw back and forth in his mouth. He was about 5'7", probably late 30s, with a buzz cut, wearing faded blue jeans and a t-shirt that had a few holes around the collar and edges.

"Who gave you permission to take those from there?"

"No one was sitting here. Were you going to use them?" I asked.

He jumped up from his seat and shouted, "You sassing me, boy?"

"Excuse me, what did you say?"

Mr. Ray walked over and got between us.

"We don't want any trouble."

"I bet you don't!"

"Boys, boys! Now, what's all the ruckus about? Gomer, relax. Go back to your favorite spot, and I'll get you a coffee refill," the waitress said, as she shuffled over.

The man looked at us with a fixed, cutting stare. He lifted his hands and headed back to his seat against the wall. He sat back down without taking his eyes off of us.

As we went back to our table, she smiled and said, "Don't pay any attention to Gomer. He's harmless. All bark and no bite, believe me."

I sat with my back to him, but I looked over my shoulder every few minutes and saw his deadly cobra stare on us each time. Mr. Ray kept an eye on him, too, as we finished our lunch.

The waitress returned a while later with two Styrofoam containers, forks wrapped in plastic, and a tin coffee pot on a tray. She filled Gomer's cup and then came to our table. She placed one of the small boxes in front of each of us.

"What's this?" I asked.

"Just coconut double cream pies."

After clearing our table, she pulled the ticket from her apron and set it down, and I glanced at it, as she turned around to go.

"You didn't charge us for the pies, ma'am," I said.

Mr. Ray looked at the ticket and agreed.

Leaning over, she whispered, "On the house. Have a safe trip."

"Thank you, ma'am," he said with a smile.

After pulling out his wallet, he placed a fifty-dollar bill in the center of the table. Then I grabbed our boxes and forks, and we headed out. As we were walking away, I looked back, and Gomer's eyes were still on us.

Mr. Ray unlocked the doors with the touch of one button, and I placed the pies on the floor next to my backpack. We climbed into the truck, and he drove away.

I wondered if someone like Gomer, Mr. Green, or another Pepper Fox would ignite my powers until they were out of control again. That was something I was going to need to work on.

# CHAPTER
## NINE

The GPS showed that we had a little over an hour to go before we reached Monroe Creek, so I texted Sari to give her an update. Then I took my book out of my backpack and continued reading.

There were a few spells in the book, but it was mostly about the history of the craft, much of which I didn't know. Some of the information was overwhelming and sad, specifically how many witches were targeted, hunted down, and murdered in different ways because someone believed he or she was associated with the craft, whether truly guilty or not.

I thought about how it would be in current times. Would those suspected be treated the same as they were back then? I believed so.

Each page I consumed confirmed that it was extremely important for me to be trained by a seasoned witch. My existence was at stake, and I knew a Dupuy Silver Slayer would soon cross my path. My hope was that it would be after my training was complete. Ms. Dawn had marked me, which could make it easier for her, or whoever she wanted, to possess information about me.

Sari's wellbeing was also on my mind. At least for the moment, I figured she was safer in Frost than with me. There was no telling what could've been lurking around to cause her potential harm.

"Tomie. Tomie. You okay?" Mr. Ray asked.

"Yeah, I was just thinking about stuff."

"You want to talk about it?"

"Not right now."

"All right. You can ask me anything. That's part of my role, to help you understand."

"Will you be staying with Lisette, too?"

"No, I have family nearby. If you should ever need me, then I'll sense it."

"Lisette told me that *Megas* are rare, and not all witches or warlocks have them."

"She's correct," he said with a slight nod. "We only appear to the extraordinary in the craft world, and your mom's lineage sealed that for you."

"Did she have a *Mega*?"

"Yes, she did."

"It's weird that Lisette doesn't have one."

"I understand why you would find that strange, but it's not unheard of. There have been cases where a special witch or warlock gets one later."

"So, Lisette could still receive a *Mega*?"

"Maybe."

"You know, if someone had told me what was going to happen last year and what's taking place in my life now, I never would've believed it. Here I am, traveling to Monroe Creek to begin my official training. It's amazing."

"You've been through a lot, Tomie, but it will be to your advantage in the long run."

"I trust you, Mr. Ray. You know, I've been thinking

about how you warned me about Opal Dawn on the bus ride home after school several months ago, and I pretty much blew you off."

"Oh, I know, but it was all destined to unfold the way it did. You had to experience all those events. You needed to truly believe who you were and what you had to do."

"Yeah, I guess you're right. I can't argue there."

"So, are you learning some good information from the book?"

"Yeah."

"Good. You need to become familiar with it, the sooner, the better. There could be something you'll have to recall from it in your immediate future."

As we continued to speed down the road, I read page after page, before realizing we were about fifteen minutes from Lisette's house. I grabbed my backpack and placed the book in a pouch on its side. Then I grouped texted Dad and Sari.

> T: **Hey we're getting closer.**
> S: **Miss you already.**
> T: **Same here. Talk later.**
> D: **You made good time. Be safe and call when you can, son. Don't forget to give Lisette what we talked about.**
> T: **Will do.**

# CHAPTER
TEN

As we drove up the path to Lisette's house, I saw willow trees cascading around her high-roofed wooden home with forest green trimming.

While Mr. Ray parked the truck, Lisette stood near the edge of the porch, her long bronze hair with highlights blowing in the wind. Her purple cat-like eyeliner triggered a twinkle in her emerald eyes. She wore an off-the-shoulder rose sweater, with black cuffed cargo pants. Just as I noticed that her feet were bare, a sable critter shot from her open screen door, straight up her leg, causing me to do a double-take.

Mr. Ray and I stepped out of the truck, as the furry little creature curled itself around Lisette's neck like a choker. I looked at him, and he looked at me.

"Hey, guys! Come on in!"

"Hello, Lisette," Mr. Ray replied.

He motioned for me to go up the stairs first, so I did, and he followed. When Lisette walked up to me and stretched her arms out to hug me, the critter opened its mouth to yawn, and I spotted its fangs. It sniffed the air and then nuzzled its pointed head under Lisette's chin.

Putting my hands up, I asked, "Whoa, what's that?"

"She's a ferret, and her name is Sabra."

"Ferret... like part of the weasel family?"

"Exactly. Sabra won't hurt you. Come on over here."

I moved in closer, and we side-hugged. Unsure of Sabra's intentions, especially with those pearly-white fangs, I knew I needed some time to become familiar with her before I'd feel comfortable around her.

Lisette reached out to shake Mr. Ray's hand, and he returned the gesture.

"Thank you so much for driving Tomie here. Are y'all hungry?"

"I'm good," I replied.

Mr. Ray said, "No, thank you. Tomie, go ahead and get settled in, and I'll see you soon."

"You're more than welcome to stay here with us, Mr. Ray. I have a spare bedroom."

"Appreciate your hospitality, Lisette, but I have family nearby that I haven't seen in a while, and I plan to catch up with them."

Lisette nodded and stroked Sabra's head, as he and I walked back down the steps to get my things. He took my bag out and placed it over his shoulder.

"Don't forget your pie, Tomie."

"Thanks."

I reached in and grabbed the stuff from the back. After placing his pie in my seat, I closed the door, as he walked around to meet me. He gave me a big hug.

"I can carry that, Mr. Ray."

He handed my bag to me, and I hefted it up, so I could cross the strap over my torso and keep my hands free for the rest of my things. Then I tossed my backpack onto my right shoulder, while holding the pie and mobile in my hand.

"See you soon, Tomie."

"Okay."

"Allow your mind to be an open window for all things to float in and out."

"I will, Mr. Ray."

"Lisette, I'll be in touch soon."

She nodded her head.

He got into his truck and drove away, as I rebalanced my bags and walked up the steps. She waited with both hands resting on her slender hips.

"Come on inside and put your bags up. Do what you need to do and meet me in the kitchen."

She walked inside, and I followed her. The screen door shut and latched without her touching it.

"So, is that something you're going to teach me over the summer?"

"Depends."

We went through the living room and stopped in the kitchen, and she pointed to the fridge. I placed the pie on the top rack, and we headed down the hall, where she showed me to my spacious bedroom.

As I laid my bag and backpack on the full-sized bed, I asked, "Lisette, depends on what?"

"If you learn the basics."

"The basics? Seriously?"

She nodded and so did Sabra; my eyes widened. Tiny bells were ringing—they were on Sabra's hot pink collar, which had multi-colored rhinestones on it.

"Hold on, Lisette. Sabra knows what we're talking about?"

"Absolutely. She's very smart."

"Oh, I get it. Sabra's your familiar, like some witches have black cats."

"Sort of. She's my companion."

"That's cool. How old is she, and where did you get her?"

"Not sure how old she is, but I'm guessing she's pretty young. Crow found her in the swamp one night right before dusk. Someone abandoned her, left her floating in a small kennel. He took her home, cleaned her up, fed her, and gave her to me."

"I knew Crow had a big heart, especially for you. How is he?"

I unzipped my bag, took out some shirts, and placed them in one of the dresser drawers.

"Yes. He's good. We'll see him soon. When Crow introduced me to Sabra, we had an instant bond, and that's how she's here with me today. I knew there was something special about her, and it turned out that I was right. She feels natural with me, which means that she was meant to be my companion. I adore her."

"Nice."

"Well, finish unpacking, and I'm going to get started on dinner. We have a lot to catch up on."

"Yeah, we do... Lisette, where's Opal?"

"She's in a very, very special place. I'll show you soon. We're going to focus on your training first."

"Gotcha," I said, putting both thumbs up with a Kevin Hart smile.

"Tomie, I'm serious. You're going to really need to study and pay attention!"

"I got it, and I will. Promise. By the way, Dad and Sari both wanted me to tell you *hello*."

"You're just trying to distract me."

"Of course not. I wouldn't ever do a thing like that."

I winked at her, but she didn't wink back.

"Tell them both *hello*. I thought Sari was coming with

you."

"It's best she's there, and I'm here. She plans to visit one weekend later this summer. I need to focus, right?"

"Yes, you do."

I took an envelope from my backpack and handed it to her.

"What's this?"

"Dad wanted to make sure that I covered your time and my stay here."

"No, sir. I don't require anything like that."

"Lisette, it's for you, though."

"Nope. Keep it. Where was I? Oh, the bathroom is next door to your left."

"I remember."

"Fresh towels, bath rags, and soap—both bar or shower gels—are all on the counter."

"Thanks, Lisette."

"Anytime. See you in a bit."

As I continued to unpack, Lisette turned around and walked out, saying something in a language that I couldn't comprehend. Sabra unwrapped herself from around her neck, crawled down her back and then her left leg, and followed behind her in a bouncing trot, her bells ringing with every movement.

After putting away all my personal belongings, including my toiletries in the bathroom, I placed my bag in the closet with my clothes. Then I hung the fighter jet mobile on a notch I found on the ceiling fan above me.

I took my phone out of my bag and walked backwards, until I got to the edge of the bed, and sat. Scrolling down, I found my dad's number and touched it to call him. He picked up after two rings, sounding like he'd been sleeping.

"Hey, son. Y'all made it in okay?"

"Yeah, Dad. Mr. Ray headed out to stay with his family here, and Lisette is in the kitchen, getting started cooking dinner."

"Tell her *thank you* for me."

"Will do. So, you're back on the road tomorrow?"

"Yes, a two-week stretch in South Texas and part of New Mexico."

"Get some rest. Talk soon."

"All right, son. Learn all you can."

"I will."

"Did you give Lisette the envelope?"

"I tried, but she refused."

"Okay. I'll see you both soon and try to give it to her myself. Love you."

"Love you, too, Dad."

I ended the call and then scrolled to Sari's number and touched it.

"Hi."

"Hey, there, beautiful."

"Y'all got there quick."

"I guess so."

"How's Lisette? Did you tell her *hi* for me?"

"She's great, and I did. She thought you were coming with me."

"I wish," Sari sighed.

"Me, too."

"So, what are you and Lisette up to this evening?"

"I don't know yet. She's making dinner. She asked me to join her in the kitchen, so we can talk once I'm done unpacking. I wanted to call Dad and you before I went in there. No telling how long she'll keep me."

"Understand. I'm sure there'll be a lot to talk about over the next several weeks."

"Right. Sari, what're you going to do tonight?"

"Probably not much. I was looking for some jobs online and fumbling through some completed local college and trade school applications."

"Any good prospects for jobs?"

"I found one at the movie theater and another at the ice cream shop. Plan to apply to both."

"Hey, I didn't know you already applied to some colleges."

"Yeah, my dad kept barking at me to do it a few weeks ago, for early consideration. With everything going on with the Pepper and Opal stuff, I just forgot to mention it to you."

"I thought we were going to apply together in the early fall."

"Well, I know how much you want to go off to the Falcon's Air Academy."

"You know, Sari, I've been thinking about staying closer to home."

"Wait a minute. When? Going there has been all you've talked about over the last few years."

"Well, I want to be closer to you, and Falcon is way out on the East Coast."

"Tomie, I love you, and it means the world to me that you want to be near me, but I'm not going to get in the way of your dreams. You need to soar. I do, too. I plan to apply to Ginger's Fashion Project Academy. I'm not telling my parents just yet, because they want me to attend their alma mater, Harwinton State, to major in business."

"You should definitely apply to the fashion school. You've always had an eye for that kind of thing."

It was so hard for me to tell Sari that. I didn't want her traveling a few states away from me, let alone to the United Kingdom. I knew how much she loved fashion, and she had always told me that was one of the best schools in the world in that field.

"Thank you, Tomie. I'm so glad your dad is finally supporting your dreams. I hope my parents back me on mine one day."

"Me, too," I said, dragging each letter.

"What's the matter?"

"Sari, it's bad enough that I'm away from you this summer, but our senior year is going to fly by so freakin' fast. We'll graduate and spend part of the summer together, and then we'll be going our separate ways."

"I know. We'll talk and visit as much as we can."

"Yeah, I guess. Listen, I better go."

"Tomie Dupuy, you're upset. Let's talk later."

"Sure."

I ended the call. Dropping the phone onto the bed, I stood and walked towards the window, where the curtains were swaying back and forth in the breeze. I stared out and watched the water dance from afar, as the tangerine sun breached the horizon.

As I thought about Sari's dreams, as well as mine, I wondered if our relationship was strong enough to endure the future distances, especially the encounters she would have with guys. Tears rolled down my cheeks, as a flock of black birds flew close to the house and veered up into the sky, each darting in different directions, until they all vanished from my sight.

I turned around and was about to leave the room, when I heard my phone beep and saw it light up. It was a message from Sari.

> S: **Nothing will come between us Tomie Dupuy! I've crushed on you since junior high and I'll always love you! We'll figure it out.**

With a smile on my face, I sent three red hearts.

S: **Text me soon.**

My response was a *thumbs up* sign. Then I placed my phone on the nightstand and headed towards the kitchen.

# CHAPTER
## ELEVEN

Lisette was standing at the counter, with her hair up in a ponytail, wearing a *Wonder Woman* apron over her clothes. Some vegetables rested in a large strainer in the sink alongside a cutting board and a knife.

"Hey," I said with a half-smile. Both of my hands were in my pockets. "Cool apron."

"Thanks. She's always been one of my favorites. Plan to check out the movie soon. I think Crow has already seen it."

Leaning against the counter with my arms crossed around my chest, I said, "Yeah, I heard it was good."

She smiled and shifted her eyes towards the vegetables, which levitated out of the strainer and landed on the cutting board. Then she began to slice the onion.

"Where's Sabra?"

"In her bed in the corner."

I looked over and saw her in a pink and gold plaid bed about the size of a standard pillow. She was on her back, playing with a little toy with her paws.

"Tomie, you want to talk about what's bothering you?"

"Oh, I'm good."

"Nope. I can see it."

"Yeah, I know. You're *glimming* me, aren't you?"

She nodded and said, "Yes. Reading you is quite easy, especially when you're vulnerable. Your emotions are all over the place. We'll need to work on that."

She started chopping tomatoes.

"Lot on my mind, Lisette."

"Sari, being number one, right?"

"Yeah. I just thought we were going to be together after graduation."

"You don't see it now, but later on, you'll know how much she loves you."

"I guess so, Lisette. Enough about that. What're you making?"

"Something tasty."

"What's in it?"

"Tomatoes, onions, lettuce, shredded cheese, Frito chips, and some chili beans with cayenne seasoning that I made a few nights ago."

"Sounds yummy." I took out the pie I'd put in the fridge earlier and walked back to stand closer to Lisette. Leaning against the counter, I opened the container as a fork floated over to me and hovered at eye level, causing me to laugh. "Thanks."

"Anytime."

After plucking the fork from the air, I took a bite of the pie. It was sweet, with a tinge of tanginess.

"You want some?"

"No, thank you. Enjoy. A nice little snack before dinner."

When I finished eating it, I asked, "So, is Crow joining us?"

"Nope, just you and me. Tomie, I want you to imagine

the trashcan opening up, that Styrofoam box floating into it, and the top closing." I did as she asked. "Do it with your eyes shut." After another attempt, still nothing. "Try again, really focusing on the tasks."

"I am."

Closing my eyes tighter, I pictured those things happening. When I opened them, I saw that the container was rising from the counter.

"Now, concentrate on lifting the trashcan lid." That time, the top moved up with a slight creaking sound, and the box floated in midair, hovered over the open trashcan, and then dropped into it. "Close it."

I did.

Jumping, I shouted, "Man, did you just see that?"

"Sure did."

"I really didn't think I would be able to do it."

"Why not?"

"This is still all new for me, ya know."

"Yeah, I understand what you're saying. Once you accept who you truly are and believe, your magic is going to be so much easier for you to perform. Since you were born from a natural witch, you won't be hard to train."

"Lisette, I want you to know how much I appreciate you taking the time to train me. I'm sorry I was so resistant to you when I first found out."

"Don't worry about it. It's normal for denial to be the first reaction to the kind of news that I shared with you."

She finished preparing the dish, while I set the table. Then she brought over a large pitcher of peach tea, and we fixed our plates, as Sabra sniffed all the spicy aromas in the air.

As Lisette poured my glass full, she asked, "Tomie, did Mr. Ray show you one of his active visions about Ms. Dawn and Mr. Fox?"

After taking a sip, I set it down next to my plate.

"Yeah. I wanted to contact Mr. Fox and make him believe the truth, rather than the lies Ms. Dawn was feeding him, but Mr. Ray said it would be best to leave it alone and come here to start my training with you instead."

"He did the right thing. Your attempt to meet with Mr. Fox wouldn't have been in your best interest."

"I sort of figured that out once Mr. Ray explained it to me."

"Ms. Dawn marked you with something?"

"Yeah, she threw a lit cigarette into my car, which landed on my jeans and left a stain on them."

I picked up my fork and dug into the pile of vegetables with chili beans stacked on top, as melted cheese flowed down like hot lava.

"Did you bring them?"

"Think so."

"I need for you to check, Tomie."

"Right now?"

She nodded, as she took a bite.

After pushing my chair back a bit, I went to my temporary bedroom. Unable to recall what I had done with them, I rummaged through the clothes I had hung in the closet. Since I didn't see them, I figured that I must not have brought them.

When I got back to the kitchen, I said, "Lisette, I must've left them at home."

I sat down in my chair and scooted back up to the table.

"Okay, where would they be in your room?"

"Bathroom hamper, maybe."

After taking another bite, I swallowed and then drank several huge sips of my tea, because my lips felt like they were melting.

"Dang, Lisette, how much cayenne is in this?"

Since I was guzzling my drink, I needed a refill. Lisette lifted her fork and pointed it at the pitcher. It rose up, floated towards my glass, and filled it without spilling a drop. Then it returned to its original position.

"Okay, describe the jeans."

"Light colored, with a few rips on the legs."

She closed her eyes, and before I could take another bite, she was holding my jeans up.

"Are these the ones?"

"Yeah!"

When I spotted the dark stained symbol near the knee, I blinked a few times to be sure of what I was seeing, as Lisette dropped them onto the floor. She stood up from the table and walked over to her cabinet at the far end of the kitchen, and it unlocked and opened. As I continued to devour the spicy meal, with frequent tea-drinking breaks, I watched her every move.

A six-inch-tall red bottle with a cork stopper floated from the top shelf and landed on her palm. One wave of her hand triggered the cabinet to close and lock. As I swallowed my last bite and finished my tea, she returned to the jeans and kneeled in front of them.

"What're you going to do?"

"Remove her mark."

After scooting out of my chair, I wiped my mouth with a napkin, walked over to Lisette, and sat on the floor to study her.

She set the bottle down next to her, folded the pants, and laid them out in front of her. When she pulled the stopper out, a copper-colored smoke swirled around and paused until she whispered a few words in an incomprehensible language. Then it floated down to the dark spot and sucked it up into the bottle. In that very instant, the mark disappeared.

Lisette quickly replaced the stopper. She stood and went out onto the back porch and got a slender wooden container about the size of a shoebox with a lid, and then she brought it inside.

"What's that for?"

"The bottle and your jeans."

"You're getting rid of my jeans?" She nodded. "Lisette, those are my favorites. They've been with me all junior year."

With a smile, she said, "They've got to go, just in case I missed some of her marking with the first step."

"If they could talk, then you wouldn't toss them out!"

"Sorry, Tomie. They have to go."

I sighed deeply, and she rolled them up tightly. She then placed them and the bottle inside and put the top on it.

"Tomie, please hand me that toolbox on the shelf near Sabra."

Sabra stood up in her bed, watching and sniffing my leg, as I grabbed it. Then I carried it over to Lisette and set it down next to her.

"Okay, Tomie, take out three nails, place them a few inches apart, and hammer each one in."

"Is this a spell?"

"Absolutely. The kind of spell she put on you can act like a GPS tracking system. Only the target can trap his or her particular mark with nails that will sprout out a permanently sealed metal coating. You must then place the box in water, where it will sink to the bottom and out of sight. Then Verlinda Dawn will be unable to locate you and know what you're doing."

"Seriously?"

"Yes, now, get busy!"

I did as she instructed, and as soon as I got the third one in and removed my hands from it, the container began to rock back and forth. The nailheads melted and transformed into several branches, which sprouted out and encircled the box until it was completely covered in a metal cage.

"Pick it up and follow me outside."

As I carried it a few hundred yards, walking with her towards the lake, it felt like it weighed almost twenty pounds. A slight breeze was blowing, and a few fireflies were floating around our heads and ended up resting on swaying tree branches.

When we reached the edge of the water, Lisette said, "Repeat these words out loud: *This mark no longer belongs to me.*" I followed her instructions. "Now, toss it out as far as you can into the lake."

When it hit the water, it floated for a few seconds, and then it was as if something pulled it down, and it was out of our sight.

"So, that's it?"

"Yep, you did it. Now, she can't track you anymore."

"What if she tries to mark me again when I go back to Frost?"

"I doubt she will. She'll figure out pretty soon that you completed this spell, so it wouldn't do her any good."

We walked back to the house and cleaned up the kitchen. Lisette washed, and I dried. She fed Sabra, as I was stacking the last few dishes on the kitchen counter for her to put away.

"Thank you for helping, Tomie."

"No problem. Thanks for doing that spell. Hey, what was the smoky stuff in that red bottle?"

"*Lasiurus cinerus breath.*"

"Wait, you're telling me that was breath from a hoary

bat?" I yelled.

"Yep."

"You're kidding, right?"

"No! They drink blood, and the mark she used had traces of hers in it."

"How did you know that?"

"I could smell it. We'll talk more in the morning and start our first lesson."

"What will that be?"

"You'll just have to wait and see. Good night."

When I got to my room, I grabbed my pajama bottoms, swung them over my left shoulder, and went to the bathroom. After I showered and washed my hair, I picked it out, added moisturizer, and let it dry naturally. Then I brushed my teeth, rolled on some deodorant, and returned to my room, where I slid a t-shirt on and crawled into bed. My thoughts went straight to Sari, and I wanted to text her, but it was almost midnight. I figured that I would do it in the morning, before my first lesson with Lisette.

My eyes closed, and dreamland welcomed me.

# CHAPTER

TWELVE

The next morning, the sunlight woke me, because I forgot to close the curtains the night before. When I sat up and rested my feet on the floor, I thought about a dream I had. In it, someone in a dark hooded cloak with a covered face chased me. The mystery figure whispered an incomprehensible, repetitive chant. There was no way out, so I found an unlocked door and hid in the back. It found me and held something in front of me; its nails possessed different glowing symbols on each one.

I reached for my phone and texted Sari.

T: **Morning**.
S: **Good morning. You still upset?**
T: **Nah I'm good.**
S: **Sure?**
T: **Yeah. What are you up to today?**
S: **Taking those two applications back later and hanging out with Mom.**
T: **Sounds good.**
S: **How are things going there?**
T: **Ok so far. We worked a spell last night.**

**Not sure what she has planned for today.**
**S: Wow! I know Lisette's going to teach**
**you some amazing things.**
T: **I believe so.**
S: **Well get ready for your day and text**
**me when you can.**
T: **Will do.**

Several hearts followed.

I lay back down on the bed, and after thinking about my dream for a few minutes, I rolled over, got up, and put on my forest green basketball shorts, a sleeveless grey Frost t-shirt, and black tennis shoes. When I finished making the bed, I went to the bathroom and picked my curly hair out. Then I pulled it back and wrapped a rubber band around it to form a fluffy ponytail.

After putting *Blue Mountain* body spray on my arms and chest, I placed my hands on the counter and leaned in closer to the mirror to see if I wanted to shave. Rubbing my right hand across my jawline, I decided to let it grow out a little, at least for the summer.

As I approached the kitchen, I smelled fresh vanilla coffee. When I walked in, I saw two cereal boxes, a bowl, a spoon, and a glass of orange juice sitting on the table. A large cup of coffee was in Lisette's spot, but she wasn't there, and neither was Sabra.

I took the milk out of the fridge and sat down. Granola was my choice, and I poured my bowl full and added the milk. Just as I scooped up a spoonful and stuffed it into my mouth, Lisette and Sabra came in from the back door.

Sabra was wearing a purple leopard harness with a matching leash, and Lisette wore black leggings, a t-shirt that read *Real Witches Rock & Fly* in large red glittery letters, and tennis shoes.

"Good morning," Lisette said.

"Morning."

Lisette closed the door behind her, unhooked Sabra's leash, and took off her harness. Standing up on her hind legs, Sabra looked right at me, and then she walked past me to her water and food bowl next to her bed.

"Hope the cereal is okay."

"Yeah, thanks. Love the t-shirt."

"Thank you. Sabra and I went on a walk around the lake. I'm going to freshen up, and then we'll get started. Sound good?"

Since I had a mouthful of cereal, I lifted my left thumb and nodded. Lisette then walked out of the kitchen.

After I emptied my bowl, I poured another one and continued to eat, while Sabra scarfed down her breakfast. When she was done, she ran over towards me. She stood up on my leg and stretched, and her mini claws felt like sharp stickers burrowing down into my skin. I didn't move, because she yawned, and I saw her fangs. As I took some deep breaths, I hoped she would get down, and she did. She curled herself under my chair and closed her eyes. When I looked at her, she was already falling asleep.

I drank my juice, and then I read some news stories on my phone until Lisette returned. After about twenty minutes or so, she came in and noticed Sabra lying underneath me.

"Think she likes you."

Lisette smiled, pulling her hair back into a messy ponytail. Then she poured herself a cup of coffee and added some cream. After stirring it, she sat in the chair next to me.

Looking down at Sabra, she commanded, "Go to your bed."

Without any hesitation, Sabra lifted her head and scurried over to her fluffy bed. She walked in circles a few times, before she finally lay down and rested her head on the edge, watching Lisette.

"Wow, she really minds you."

With both hands, she lifted her cup and sipped from it.

"Yeah, she's a good girl."

"I bet she keeps you a lot of company."

She set her coffee on the table and tapped her left hand against the cup, making a clicking sound.

"Especially when Crow is away for several days, working."

"Hold up, Lisette! What's that?"

A three-carat princess-cut diamond ring was on her third finger, with a spiral row of marcasite baguettes wrapped along the sterling silver band.

"What?" she asked, as she lifted her hand up in the air and rotated it back and forth with a giggle.

"You know exactly what!"

"Oh, this."

"Yep, that."

"Crow proposed to me for the sixth or seventh time, and I finally accepted."

"What the…? I don't know how I missed it before. Why didn't you tell me?"

"I just put it back on this morning. I took it off the day before you arrived, because I was doing some landscaping, and there's been a lot going on."

"Yeah, yeah, I know, but this is major for you! I thought you would never want to walk down that aisle, but when I met Crow, I could see you doing that with him."

"How?"

"Just the way he treated you and was so attentive. He's seems like a really cool dude."

"Oh, he is and more," she said with soft laughter.

"What do you mean?"

"Oh, nothing. Don't mind me."

"I'm happy for y'all. Can't wait to tell Sari. She'll be happy, too. So, when's the big day?"

"We haven't decided yet. Maybe next summer, right after you graduate, but before you head off to the academy."

"If I'm accepted."

"Whatever. You will be, and they'll be so lucky to have you."

"Thanks."

"I would love for you and Sari to be there."

"We wouldn't miss it!"

"I have a humongous favor to ask of you."

"Go for it."

"Would you give me away, Tomie?"

Shocked, I was silent for a few seconds, as I thought about the fact that Lisette never had a relationship with her biological dad, who left her and her mom when she was young.

She watched me with her shimmering emerald eyes, looking like she wanted to cry, but she fought those teardrops off, probably with magic.

"I would love to, and I'd be honored, Lisette. When you set the date, let me know."

"Okay. It'll probably be early June."

"Sounds good," I said, as I reached out to hug her.

"Thank you. I've known Crow since we were teenagers, and I finally figured out that I wouldn't be happy with anyone but him. I've dated here and there, yet no one measures up to my Crow."

"I understand. I've had a few dates with other girls, but for me, it's always been Sari... since I realized my true feelings for her a few months ago."

We sat there until she finished her coffee. I helped her clean up the kitchen, and then we went outside and down to the lake.

Lisette had a special little carrier for Sabra—a slender pouch that attached to her leg by two sturdy Velcro straps. She poked her head out of it and made a few high-pitched chirping sounds, as we walked along the dirt path.

"Is she talking to you, Lisette?"

"Yeah, I need to slow down a bit."

When she did, Sabra's chirping ceased, and she dropped down inside the pouch.

We found a shaded area with a bench and sat down. Lisette unwrapped the straps from her thigh and placed the carrier on the bench next to her. Sabra poked her head out but remained inside.

"Lisette, there are so many things I want to discuss with you."

"I know."

"Don't know where I should start."

"Just start anywhere. It's okay. We have the whole summer and then some. My main goal while you're here is to prepare you with the basic training skills, just in case you come face-to-face with trouble."

"Ms. Dawn has convinced Mr. Fox that you, Sari, and I were the only ones behind Pepper Fox's death at our junior-senior prom."

"Yes, she has."

"What am I supposed to do, with Mr. Fox now thinking that I'm part of the reason why his only daughter is dead, instead of the one who actually manipulated the spell you gave us into something way more sinister?"

"Tomie, you're going to be strong and be ready if and when the time comes."

"For what?"

"To take your stand and fight."

"All right. What's the first lesson?"

"Have you been reading the book I gave you?"

"Yeah. I read a few chapters on my drive up here with Mr. Ray."

She nodded and stood up, as she asked, "So, you're becoming familiar with your history?"

"Yes, some of the stories are pretty heartbreaking. Those trials, tortures, and killings many centuries ago were horrible. Some of them weren't even true witches, but that didn't stop them from being accused."

"Our kind has faced so much hate that many went into hiding or terminated their powers for a long time. Even today, you'd think people being more modernized would make them accept us, but that's far from the truth."

"Sad."

"Then there're the witch hunters who are sometimes in disguise, just waiting to catch and kill us. I have to be careful when I use my powers, which is where I want to start with you."

Beads of sweat broke out along my skin, and it wasn't very warm that day. The temperature was about seventy-five degrees, according to my watch.

"Do you mean when to and when not to use my *warlock-witchy* powers?"

She laughed and said, "Absolutely. Tomie, as I've told you before, you come from a very powerful witch line. Our lineage goes back to Marie Laveau. For that reason, it won't take much to teach you these skills. You just need someone to reveal them to you."

I reflected on what went down at the café where Mr. Ray and I stopped for lunch on our way to Lisette's house. My temper wasn't on fire, or anything like that, when the stranger attempted to pull my trigger, but what if it had been? I mean, he could've initiated a fight or continued to say things to upset me, and I wasn't sure what I would've done. I didn't want to repeat what happened at Sari's house right before the prom, when her dad touched me.

Back then, I could at least say that I wasn't truly aware of my powers and how to control them. Ever since that incident with Mr. Green, I've felt that he's perceived me differently, and he's avoided me, as well.

"Lisette, I was thinking…"

"Go on."

"Do I only use my powers when absolutely necessary?"

"If you can avoid using them in front of non-witches, that's best. However, you're going to find yourself in situations when you have to use them."

"So, then, what?"

"Try to wait until there aren't so many people around who could identify you. Always be as discreet as possible."

"You really think we could be hunted down like back during the Salem times?"

"Possibly. How much do you know about the Dupuy Silver Slayers?"

"Dad told me a little, and I read some about them in the book. They sound pretty ruthless."

"Yes, they are. They, as well as the non-slayers who are simply fearful of witches, are the ones that we have to be most concerned about."

"Wow."

"I want you to remember this, Tomie: Never use your powers to show off or to prove who you are. Sometimes it's best to walk away, which is not always the easiest thing to do. It could be in that very instant that a slayer or *slayer sleeper* sees what you do and could identify you. They usually have an agenda to wipe out the witch on their assignment, sometimes including loved ones."

"Are you serious? You really think they might come to Frost or Monroe Creek?"

Lisette walked closer to me and nodded.

"I do because of the attention that Opal brought to Frost. They sit and wait for news like this."

"How do you know so much about them?"

"My family told me stories about them. Your dad's parents moved away from here after your mom's unfortunate situation. They knew a slayer could find out about your lineage."

"Wow. I never expected things would be so different when Sari and I devised a revenge plan with Opal. My life won't ever be the same again, will it?"

"Afraid not. Your life was never meant to be normal because of who your parents are."

I stood up and stretched, reaching my arms over my head, turning to my right and left, while Sabra continued to sleep.

"Can you sense when a slayer is close?"

"Sometimes. It depends on how strong he or she is. Some can prevent witches from penetrating their minds, while others are a little careless. However, you have an advantage over me."

"How?"

"If there are no special spells being cast beforehand, your *Mega* will give you an advance vision to warn you of a slayer's arrival."

"Really?" She nodded. "Okay, well, as soon as I receive my vision, I can warn you."

"Very thoughtful. Thank you." She walked away from me, then turned around and whispered, "It may be enough time."

"What do you mean by that?"

"To prepare. The slayer will most likely come for me

first and then you."

"Why would they come for you first?"

"To knock out your closest and strongest allies. The more of them he or she has out of the way, the less he or she has to contend with."

"In other words, you're a prime target because of me?"

"Yes." I squatted near the water's edge and closed my eyes, but her next words made them pop open again. "Tomie, I believe one of the biggest fears in being part of this world is feeling alone."

"Yeah, I felt that way, but knowing I have you makes it easier."

I stood up and turned around to face her.

"You have no idea what that means to me, but I also want you to be prepared if something should ever happen to me."

"Wait, don't talk like that!" I shouted.

She took both of my hands and squeezed them, looking deeply into my eyes.

"I hope I'm here for you for a long time, but in case I'm not, I want you to know that you aren't alone. There are others who'll be able to help you if you need it."

I let go of her hands and stepped back.

"You mean, there're other teen warlocks like me?"

"Yes. There are other *supras,* which you may not have ever heard about. All will be revealed in its own time, I promise."

I had wondered if there were others, especially after Opal's transformation.

Lisette blinked her bright eyes, which seemed to glow for a few seconds before fading.

"Let's refocus on training for today," she said, as she stretched.

"Okay, let's do this!"

# CHAPTER
## THIRTEEN

Clasping my hands together until my knuckles popped, I looked back when I heard a few chirping sounds. Sabra was waking up. She stretched out her furry arms, and her claws appeared to glisten, as she flicked her tongue out against her ivory fangs and crawled out of her pouch. As she started to climb down, Lisette said a few words that I couldn't comprehend, and Sabra backed up and remained on the bench, watching us.

"What are you teaching me today?"

Before I could turn around, with the flip of her wrist, Lisette slammed me down to the ground hard on my back, dust and grass flying up into the air upon my impact. It felt like someone had thrown a bag of bricks at my chest.

"Dang, woman! I didn't expect that!" I wailed, coughing.

"Get up!" she snapped. I tried to follow her order, but she pressed her foot down on my chest. "No, I want you to close your eyes and raise yourself up with your mind."

"Really, like levitate?"

She pressed harder on my chest and said, "Yes. Tomie,

you're very strong. Now, concentrate and imagine your body being weightless, as if you were floating in a pool."

I closed my eyes and tried to picture myself in a pool, but that wasn't the only thing in my vision. Sari, in a leopard bikini with red tassels around her waist, was swimming towards me. When she reached me, I pulled her underwater and kissed her. I was grinning and reaching up in the air with both hands.

Her giggles and something wet dragging across my cheek brought me out of my fantasy. When I opened my eyes, I saw that Sabra was licking me.

"Lisette!"

Sabra jumped and ran up Lisette's leg, wrapping herself around her neck when she reached her shoulder.

"Okay, you really need to concentrate and stop daydreaming about making out with Sari."

"You saw that?"

"Of course."

"You *glimmed* me again." I raised my hand and wiped my cheek off. "Will you teach me how to *glim*, too?"

"You already possess that ability, among many others. I just need to help you unleash them. We'll practice that soon. Okay, let's try this again. You know what to do."

She lifted her foot off my chest and stepped back, and I closed my eyes and tried to focus on being weightless in a pool, rather than on Sari. It felt like I stayed that way for over an hour, when my body began to levitate several inches off the ground. I raised one lid and could only see Lisette's knees, with pebbles, leaves, and sand particles floating in a speedy circular pattern around my body.

"Shut it, mister!"

I obeyed her command, and I felt myself rising up and moving into a vertical position.

"Now, open your eyes," she said in a low tone.

When I did, I couldn't see her at all anymore.

"How do I get down?"

"Open your hands and allow them to guide you, while still concentrating on your landing spot below." Following her instructions, I drifted down to stand right in front of her. "Practice levitating from here to the bench," she ordered. With my eyes shut once again, I focused, as my feet left the ground, and I floated to where she had indicated. "Now, go to the tree."

In a matter of seconds, I reached out to touch the leaves, as the sun's rays hit my face.

"What now?"

"Go sit on my roof. Remember to concentrate and visualize what you want to do." Focusing on my intended destination, I levitated over a hundred feet away from Lisette and Sabra. I almost made it, but my left foot landed wrong, and I fell backwards and started sliding down. "Tomie, stop yourself before you hit the ground!" she yelled in the distance.

I was concentrating, but it did nothing to slow my descent.

"I can't stop!" I shouted, as I tried to grab the rough shingles, but I missed and scraped my hands up instead.

# CHAPTER

FOURTEEN

Before I reached the edge of the roof, I was floating away from it, towards Lisette. Both of her hands were out, guiding me in like an aircraft ground marshal with two orange batons, and finally, I was safe.

"Whew! Thanks!"

"No problem. I sensed that you were in trouble and couldn't refocus in time. We'll practice more later."

"Cool. I'm starving."

I didn't know if levitation burned calories, but my stomach was growling. Looking down at my hands, I saw that they were both scratched and bleeding, throbbing with a burning sensation.

"They'll be as good as new before we get back to the house."

"Lisette, I've healed pretty fast before from an incident at Sari's. Will I always have that ability?"

"You will. It emerged after your transformation started."

"Do all warlocks and witches have that gift?"

"No, only special ones."

"You're probably referring to bloodlines, right? I read some things about that in my book."

"Yes, so glad that you're taking this seriously."

"Me, too."

When I glanced back down at my hands, they looked like they had never been injured.

"Come on. I'll whip up some lunch, and then we can go and see Crow."

"Okay."

Lisette fixed two sub sandwiches with jalapeno-cheddar kettle cooked chips, a sliced dill pickle on the side, and a tall glass of lemonade. She duplicated my lunch and poured some of the drink into a thermos. Then she placed the items in a lunch bag, which I figured was for Crow.

My small feast was gone in no time, while Lisette still worked on her half-sub. After she finished eating, she fed Sabra and changed her water bowl, while I cleaned out her litter box. Sabra watched us for a bit and fell asleep.

"Tomie, give me a few minutes to freshen up, and then we'll be on our way."

I went to my room and put on clean clothes. When I checked my messages, I saw that I had one from Sari, so I texted her back and told her that I would talk to her soon.

After throwing my dirty clothes into the hamper in the bathroom, I joined Lisette in the kitchen. She had changed, too. She had on charcoal sandals with a short heel, white capris with hot pink ruffles below her knee, and a matching off-the-shoulder blouse with ruffles around the waist. Her black eyeliner made her eyes pop, and her pink lipstick glistened.

"Looking nice. I can only imagine why," I said with a chuckle, nudging her with my elbow when I walked past her; a light orchid mixed with jasmine scent followed.

She smiled back, picked up her purse, and grabbed her keys.

"Come on, let's go."

"Sabra okay to leave alone?"

"Yes, she'll sleep and be just fine until we return."

Lisette shut the door and locked it behind her. As we walked down the steps towards her Jeep, my phone buzzed.

We both climbed in and fastened our seatbelts. Then she put her key into the ignition, and we were off. When I looked at the screen, I saw it was Mr. Ray.

> R: **How's training going so far?**
> T: **Good. Learning to levitate.**
> R: **Nice. Will let you focus and check in on you soon.**
> T: **Talk more later.**

By then, we had traveled down her gravel driveway and onto the main road.

I'd never heard anything like the music playing on Lisette's stereo. It was bluesy, but I could hear diverse instruments playing, such as an accordion, a fiddle, a guitar, and a washboard. It possessed a feel-good Cajun and country sound with catchy lyrics that told an interesting story, and it made me tap my feet and want to dance.

"Lisette, what are we listening to?"

"Zydeco."

"Oh, the waitress at the diner that we stopped at on the way here mentioned that."

"It's a combo of Louisiana French accordion and Afro-Caribbean beats. In the earlier days, it served as an escape for the unfortunate to express their struggles of life through music and dance."

"Can I download songs like this?"

"Yep. I can share some of my favorite artists for you to check out. I'm glad you like it. I fell in love with it when I was about your age."

"I can see why. I'm going to tell Sari about it, too."

"Oh, you know, the annual *Deep Bayou Festival* is coming up in a few weeks. It's a fun time, with amazing Cajun food, games, dancing, cooking contests, plenty of zydeco bands, a talent show, costumes, and cosplayers. I bet Sari would really enjoy it. You should invite her to come here for that weekend. We'll be halfway through your training by then."

"Sounds fun. I'll see if she's interested. I bet she will be."

"It's a pretty big event for Monroe Creek. People come from all over Louisiana to be a part of it. I think we had over 25,000 guests last year."

"That's a lot of people."

"Yeah, it just keeps growing."

We arrived at *Crow's Airboat Tours* about twenty-five minutes later, and Lisette rolled the windows down. I saw him, packing a bundle of tree branches. He took them from his boat to a shed, holding them with one hand and waving at us with the other.

He yelled, "Y'all, come on over! I'll be back once I put this away!"

Crow was talking to someone else, but I didn't see anyone at first.

Lisette parked the car and grabbed the lunch bag, and we headed for his office.

Before we could reach the door, I heard footsteps running from the dock towards us, and a high-pitched voice with a heavy Southern accent screamed, "Miss Lisette!"

When I turned around, I saw a girl with blonde and

orange highlights and two braids, waving in the air. She rushed over to Lisette and almost knocked me down in the process. While still grasping the lunch bag, Lisette reached out to her. The girl wrapped her arms around Lisette's neck, and they hugged.

"So good to see you, Lisette!" Moving back a few steps, she said, "I've missed hanging out with you and Uncle Crow. Just a lot of stuff going on back home."

"Understand. How's your mom doing?"

"She has her good and bad days."

"Let me know if you need anything."

"Thank you."

"Your beauty continues to glow, Caya."

"Aaww, thanks, Lisette."

"Oh, where are my manners? Tomie, this is Caya."

She turned around and held out her hand, and I paused for a few seconds. Her eyes seemed to glow a shimmering violet with golden specks, which then faded to a light mocha. Her eyelashes were long and thick. She wore blue-jean overalls with a cut-off lime t-shirt underneath.

"I don't bite." She grabbed my limp right hand and shook it, and I responded with a firmer grip. "Nice to meet you, Tomie… what?"

"Tomie Dupuy. Good to meet you, too."

She jerked away and took a few steps back, stumbling into Lisette.

"Caya, it's okay. He's one of the good ones. No need for you to be concerned."

"Oh, I didn't know."

"Didn't know what?" I asked.

"Let's all go inside and talk," Lisette said.

# CHAPTER
## FIFTEEN

Crow was still sorting stuff out in the shed when Lisette, Caya, and I walked into the small office area that had two ceiling fans that looked like they were resurrected from an ancient fan graveyard. There was a cash register to my left and a round table with a few plastic chairs. A small TV was mounted on the wall, along with black and white pictures of alligators, fish, and trees.

Lisette walked over, put the lunch bag down, and asked, "Are you hungry, Caya?"

"Not really. Thanks, though."

"So, can we talk now?" I asked in a low tone.

"Tomie, you're curious about what Caya said, aren't you?" Lisette asked.

"Yeah."

"Caya, do you want to tell him?" She remained silent. "I take it, you're pleading the fifth?" She nodded with wide eyes. "Tomie, Caya thought you were a slayer."

"Because of my last name?"

"Yes," Lisette said.

Just then, Crow walked in. His sleeveless plaid shirt was stretched across his bulging muscles that made me examine mine. I slouched down a little in my seat.

"What're y'all chatting about?"

He went to Lisette, leaned over, and kissed her on her cheek. Smiling, she reached up and ran her hand along the side of his bearded face.

"Oh, not much. Caya thought Tomie was a *you know what*."

Crow looked at Caya and then me, before he walked next to her and squatted down.

"Hey, you all right?"

"Yeah, just thought he was…" Caya uttered, while staring up at me.

I said, "Lisette, I saw something strange with her."

"What did you see?" she asked without blinking.

"Her eyes changed from a violet to a mocha tint."

Caya said, "No, you didn't. Only a witch could see that. Wait a minute… you're a warlock, but how? You're a Dupuy!"

"Tomie's mom is from the Laveau bloodline," Lisette replied. "He walks the path of *crafters*, not hunters."

Caya stood and then curtsied in front of me.

"What the heck are you doing?" I asked.

"You're witch royalty because of your mother's line," she said with a wink.

"Come on. Lisette, she's exaggerating, right?"

"Well, not really."

"So, you're telling me that I'm a *Warlock Rockstar*?"

I laughed out loud, and Crow stood with a deep chuckle.

"Yeah, you could put it that way," he said in his gruff voice.

Lisette asked, "Tomie, do you know what you did

when you saw Caya's eyes change colors?"

"No, what?"

"That was your first *glim*. She attempted to conceal that from you, but you were able to see her truth for a short time."

"Hold on. I don't even know how to *glim* yet."

"Like I told you, there will be some magical abilities that will come to you without any assistance from me, and that's because of our powerful bloodline."

"Okay, I can accept that, but I have a question for Caya."

"What?" she asked, her cheek resting in the palm of her right hand.

"Are you a witch?"

Lisette and Crow looked at each other.

# CHAPTER
## SIXTEEN

S omething like that," Caya said.

"What do you mean?"

"Well, I possess some witch abilities. I can't teleport or *glim*, but I can move things and make some cool potions."

As her eyes locked on mine, her right and left braids twirled without her touching them.

"Okay, so if you're a half-witch, that means you're half something else, right?"

"Impressive. Lisette, why don't you tell him?"

"You sure?" She nodded in a slow motion, giving her consent. "Caya is also half-rougarou."

"Rouga-what?"

"A rougarou is known to be a shapeshifter in Cajun country, with the werewolf being the dominant supernatural creature."

I sat down to take in what Lisette just shared with me.

After taking a few deep breaths, I asked, "So, you're telling me that not only do witches and slayers exist, but there're rougarous, too?"

"Yes," Lisette replied.

"Feel like I'm in a *paranormal never-ending* story."

"Tomie, I know it's a lot to swallow, but the world as you knew it is not the only reality. The supernatural world is extremely complex, with many diverse layers."

I remained silent, as I stared at Caya.

Then I asked, "So, what else is out there, Lisette?"

"A lot. We'll deal with it as needed. It's too much to explain to you without making you feel overwhelmed."

"Wait a minute. So, if Caya is a hybrid, what does that make Crow, since they're related?"

"Good question. I believe Crow can tell you himself."

He walked over, picked up a chair and turned it around, then sat in it with its back facing his wide chest.

"*Glim* me," he commanded.

"You want me to *glim* you?"

"Yes."

I stared into his eyes for several minutes and saw him transform from his human form into a massive hairy beast, with turquoise piercing eyes, glistening fangs, and long razor-sharp claws. Goosebumps popped up on my arms, as sweat slid down my sideburns. My legs trembled, and I began tapping my feet.

As I scooted a few inches away from him, Crow asked, "Do I scare you?"

"Of course not!" I squealed, like I had just hit puberty again.

Lisette said, "Tomie, a lot of awful stories about rougarous have been passed down. Just like anything else in our world, there's good and bad. Crow's a good one, and he would never hurt anyone or anything out of malice. The only way he would do something like that is if he was defending himself or being protective."

"I just never would've pegged you for a shifter, Crow.

However, you definitely possess the body for it."

He let out a deep laugh, which sounded like a muffled roar.

"So, do you experience the transformation every full moon?"

"I can change *at will*. I could show you right now if you like," he offered, as he began to stand up from the chair.

"Crow," Lisette said, "you know, right now is probably not the best time. We just dumped a lot on him."

Caya added, "Yeah, I agree. Why don't you two spend some time outside? I'll let Tomie pick my brain for a bit."

"Are you sure you don't want to witness my shifting? I could do a partial to keep from freaking you out."

"You know what, Crow? I'm good. Why don't y'all take Caya's suggestion? We got all summer. Cool?"

"Yeah, it's cool."

He stood up and slapped my back, which almost knocked me off my chair and left me feeling like a dozen yellow jackets had stung me.

"All right, then. Lisette and I'll be outside."

I nodded, as my eyes watered at the pain, but I held the tears back.

Lisette said, "Tomie, I wanted you and Caya to meet today, because she's going to be part of your training."

Crow picked up the lunch bag that Lisette had fixed for him, and they went outside to talk, while Caya and I remained in the office.

"Tomie, you okay?"

"Just keep getting surprises since I discovered my abilities."

"It's overwhelming at first, I know."

"Can we talk about something else?"

"Sure."

"So, what year are you, Caya?"

"I'll be a senior in a few weeks."

"Yeah, me, too. Where do you go to school?"

"South Bayou High, home of the mighty Green Gators football team, maybe an hour away from here. You?"

"Texas... Frost High, Polar Bears."

"That's a weird mascot for Texas."

"Yeah, some people have tried to change it, but it always gets shot down. Hey, when did you first discover that you were a hybrid?"

"I knew when I turned eleven. A boy from my class blew out my birthday candles, and I started crying. I focused on them, and when I wished them to be all lit again, one by one, the little flames reappeared. Rolling my tongue around my mouth, I felt that my teeth were like needles, and a few drops of blood fell onto my baby blue birthday dress."

"Did anyone notice?"

"Nope. My mom took me into the bathroom to clean me up. She later had *the talk* with me about my ancestry and abilities. She showed me what she knew, and Crow and Lisette have been teaching me other helpful stuff over the last few years."

"That's cool."

"Yeah. What have you learned so far?"

"Levitation."

"Looks like you're getting the *glim* thing down."

"That was a shocker. I didn't know I could do that, but I still need to practice."

"You'll get it with no problem."

"Glad you think so."

"Tomie, you have no idea how powerful you are, do you?"

"No."

"You will."

"How do you know?"

"Your history. Read more about it when you get a chance or ask Lisette."

"Will do. When I find out, I'll make sure to let you know."

"Are you here for the rest of the summer?"

"Yeah. So, what do you do around here for fun?"

"Hmm. Well, there's airboat tours, hiking, gator feedings, and swimming—don't do the last two things together!" We laughed.

"Tough to figure out which one to dive into first. What do you suggest?"

"Depends on whether you're a risk-taker or not."

"What do you mean by that?"

"There're two kinds of gator feedings around here—the safe ones, where you pay and staff are around to make sure nothing goes wrong… and the risky ones out in the swamp at night."

"People really feed the gators?"

"Yeppers. They use just about anything that bleeds for bait, including fresh roadkill."

"That doesn't sound tempting to me."

"Have you ever tried it, Tomie?"

"No."

"Then, how do you know if you'd like it or not?"

I shrugged my shoulders and stood up, stretching my arms, and then I turned to the right and left.

"So, you want to go on a little night adventure soon?"

"Are you serious? That's the worst time to do something like that, because there's no sunlight. Gators possess the *bright carpet*."

"What's that?"

"When light reflects back into a gator's photoreceptor

cells, which can improve its vision in the dark. If you see red eyes staring back at you, there's probably a gator in close proximity... which translates as, *You're in trouble, and you better move like the Flash!*"

"Wow, I never thought when I woke up this morning that I would encounter not only a warlock from one of the most powerful witch bloodlines, but also *Mr. Wildlife*," she said, laughing.

"Whatever. I love learning stuff that intrigues me."

"Just kidding. So, you up for it?"

"Maybe."

Looking out the window, I saw that Lisette and Crow were still talking, while he was putting up some tools in his shed.

"I have some friends who go all the time. We could hang out with them."

As I stared into the distance, my mind drifted to Sari. I wondered what she was doing at that moment and if she was thinking of me.

*Would Sari go out at night with someone she just met and hang out with some strangers?*

I figured that maybe I was just overthinking it instead of enjoying my last summer of high school.

# CHAPTER
## SEVENTEEN

I turned around to face Caya to give her my answer, but before I could, she walked up to me and demanded, "Phone, please."

"Why?"

"To add my number. So, when I text you about it, you can tell me if you're game or not. If you are, I'll tell you where to meet us."

After yanking my phone out of my hand, she added her contact info.

"There you go." She held it out, but when I reached for it, she snatched it away and put it behind her back. "If you decide to go, don't mention a word about this to Lisette or my Uncle Crow."

I grimaced and asked, "What's the big deal?"

"They'd tell us not to go."

"Imagine that. Now, my phone, please," I said, reaching my hand out.

"You really want it?"

"Caya, enough already."

"Okay, come and get it."

"Really?"

I focused on my phone. Raising my hand, I guided it up from behind her back and brought it towards me, until it landed in my right palm.

"Good job," she said, as she high-fived me.

Lisette and Crow entered his office, his arm around her shoulders and hers around his waist.

She said, "Glad you two are getting to know each other."

"So, what now?" I asked.

"Crow needs to wrap up his last tour for the day," Lisette said. "What about a movie in town tonight?"

"Sounds good," I replied.

Lisette asked, "Caya, do you have any plans?"

"Not really."

"Would you like to join us?"

"If you're sure it's okay."

"Of course, it is. You're practically family. Plus, you and Tomie can learn more about each other. What would you two like to see?"

"Doesn't really matter to me, Lisette," I said. "Just about anything."

"Me, too," Caya added.

"Well, there's this little theater that shows only classics. I usually go there every couple of weeks or so, with or without Crow."

"What's showing tonight?" I asked.

She pulled her phone from her bag to find the schedule, while Caya started texting on hers. As Lisette was searching, I decided to call Sari, just in case it ended up being too late to contact her after the movie.

"I'm going to step out to make a call."

Lisette waved at me to go ahead.

I scrolled down to Sari's name, touched the button,

and waited for her to answer.

"Hello, Tomie."

"Hey, beautiful. How are you?"

"Fine," she said, her voice trembling.

"Something wrong?" She didn't respond. "Sari?" Still nothing. "Sari, you there?"

After another few seconds, she said, "I'm all right. How's your training going?"

"It's okay, but that's not important right now. You are."

"Tomie, I'm fine. Just…"

"Just what?"

"I'd rather not talk about it."

"Why not?"

"Let's talk about something else, please!"

"No! I want to know what's up with you."

With a long sigh, Sari said, "I'll tell you about it later. I'd rather hear more about what you've been up to."

"Just training with Lisette, but I'm wondering what's wrong with you now."

"Tomie, seriously, I'm all right. Give me some time, and I'll discuss it with you when I'm ready, okay?"

"Fine, I'll drop it, then."

"So, what are you doing for fun?"

"Lisette was talking about going to a movie tonight… not sure if I'm up for it anymore."

"Why not?"

"Sari, you're really going to ask me that question? Really?"

"You don't have to say it like that!" she snapped.

"How am I supposed to react? Obviously, there's something bothering you, and you won't share it with me." I paced up and down the walkway and then leaned against the building. "I just thought we were closer than this. Thought you could tell me anything… and vice versa."

"We *are* close, and I *can* tell you anything, but not right now."

"Whatever!"

She sighed and said, "You're mad."

"I'm not."

"Yes, you are."

"Just frustrated. You're there, and I'm here. I can't touch or hold you, and it's driving me crazy. You know, I could just come home."

"No, you need to stay there and finish up with Lisette." I huffed, and then I heard someone talking to her in the background. "Okay, I'll be right there," she said. "Tomie, can we talk later?"

"Yeah. Who was that?"

"My dad. Going to help with dinner, okay?"

As soon as she mentioned her dad, I knew what she was probably bumming about. I had a good idea that their conversation had something to do with me dating her and what happened at her house on prom night.

Honestly, I didn't mean to freak him out, but he must have triggered something inside me when he was trying to intimidate me about taking Sari out—he pressed hard on my shoulder. I had no intention of burning his hand, but my subconscious powers took over.

When I ended the call, I wondered what still might be bouncing around in Sari's mind, and I wanted to see her. Lisette didn't believe I was ready to learn about teleportation yet, but I was thinking that I might have to figure it out on my own, because I couldn't wait much longer to see Sari.

I had to know if I was on the right track about her dad, and I needed to find out soon… really soon.

# CHAPTER
## EIGHTEEN

When I walked back into the office, Lisette and Caya were both sitting at the table, talking to each other.

"Everything okay with Sari?" Lisette asked.

"Yeah."

I shifted my eyes to the ground.

"So, I found out that there are three movies showing tonight... *Casablanca*, *To Kill a Mockingbird*, and *Psycho*."

Caya said, "I've read both *To Kill a Mockingbird* and *Psycho*. Enjoyed both, but I haven't seen any of them. Whatever y'all pick is fine with me."

"I'm thinking I'll take a raincheck on this one. Y'all go and have fun."

"Tomie, we want you to come with us," Lisette whined.

"Hey, it's all right. I'm just not feeling a movie tonight. Another time, cool?"

Lisette looked into my eyes, and I knew she was *glimming* me. I sucked at blocking out my emotions, so I was sure she picked up on every one of them.

"We can always go another time."

"No, y'all go tonight. I'll do some reading and probably turn in early."

"You sure?" Lisette asked.

"Yeah."

Lisette stood, walked over to me, leaned in to my ear, and whispered, "We'll talk later."

She gave my arm a quick rub to comfort me. I nodded, and we all walked out the door, and then Lisette closed it behind her.

When she saw Crow at the end of the dock, she said, "You two, go ahead to the car. I need to update Crow on the plans. Tomie, here are the keys."

After taking them from her, I turned, and Caya and I walked towards the car. I pressed the green button on the keyring, and the doors unlocked.

"Want up front or back, Caya?"

"Doesn't really matter."

"You take the front."

I opened the door for her and shut it once she was in, and then I slid into the backseat.

As I reached up to place the key in the ignition in order to turn on the radio and let the windows down, Caya asked, "Does your girlfriend know how lucky she is?"

Stunned, I tried to figure out where that came from. We had just met, and she didn't know much about me aside from my bloodline and that Lisette was my cousin. All of those things didn't really matter. What mattered was my response.

Looking into Caya's eyes, I said, "I'm the one who's lucky. Sari could've been with anyone, but she chose me. I was clueless for a long time. I had no idea about her feelings for me. Then one day, I realized how I felt about her, and that was it. She's inside my heart, and she'll always be a part of me."

Caya's mouth dropped open.

"Are you okay?"

She nodded.

"You really do love her, don't you?"

"Yes, and no one could ever take my love from her. No one."

"I respect that. You're definitely one of the good guys, Tomie. I'm glad we met."

"Thanks."

Lisette came over, jumped into the car, and fastened her seatbelt.

"Sorry, guys. That took longer than expected. Hope you didn't get too warm."

"No, it wasn't that long. Right, Caya?"

"Nope."

"You two getting to know each other a little?"

"Yeah, we are," Caya said. She looked at me, and I nodded, so she turned back around. "So, the movie's still a go?"

"Sure is. Crow will be getting off in about an hour. He'll go home to clean up and meet us at the theater around 7:30."

I looked at the car clock, and it was about 5:15.

"We'll head back to my place, and I'll feed Sabra dinner and let her exercise a bit. Then we can head out. Sound good?"

Caya nodded, as Lisette glanced at her and then into her rearview mirror at me. On the way back to her house, I saw a field splattered with yellow and red wildflowers. When we came to a stop, I took a picture and sent it to Sari with a message.

T: **Thinking of you.**

She didn't respond.

Caya said, "Lisette, Crow was telling me about Sabra."

"I bet. You'll meet her soon."

"Lisette, can we practice teleportation tomorrow?"

"Not yet, Tomie. You still need to master levitation, because if you can't do that properly, you can end up hurting yourself or someone else in the teleporting process."

"When do you think we'll start that lesson?"

"Maybe in another week or so."

That was too long to go without seeing Sari. I knew what I had to do.

# CHAPTER
## NINETEEN

In no time, we arrived at Lisette's house, and she parked and turned off the engine. When we were all out of the car, she locked it. Her front door opened with one nod.

As we walked inside, Sabra popped her head up and started sniffing the air. She knew that someone else was with us. Lisette went over to her, kneeled, and picked her up.

"Come here, Caya."

She stepped over with her hand stretched out, ready to pet Sabra.

"Wait. She needs to get used to your scent. I'll hold her up, so she can smell you."

"Sure."

Sabra sniffed all around and then licked her a few times.

"Her tongue feels like sandpaper," Caya whispered.

"I know. She licks my hands all the time." Lisette grabbed Sabra's harness and put it on her and then attached the leash. "Let's go out for a little walk by the lake."

"Catch up with y'all in a few minutes," I said.

When I got to my room, I grabbed my book, sat on the bed, and flipped through the pages, looking for instructions for teleportation. I searched through the table of contents and found a small section about it, but it wasn't enough to give me the tools to attempt it.

Frowning, I stared at my bag hanging on the chair and then recalled Lisette's big spell book that she kept down in the basement. If I was going to find directions on how to do it anywhere, it'd be inside that gigantic thing.

When I reached the concealed basement door, I tossed the throw rug back with my foot, lifted the round metal handle up, and pulled it all the way open. As I went down the first few steps, I noticed a light switch to the side and flipped it on, which lit up the entire space. Before I got all the way into the stairs, I saw the book resting in the middle of a table. Once I approached, it began to produce a slight amethyst glow.

When I stepped back, the front cover flipped open, and the pages waved in the air, each one turning after the other in a speedy fashion... until it stopped. There in front of me were the instructions to complete the teleportation process. I read the page twice to make sure I understood what I needed to do.

Just as I was about to close my eyes and imagine where I wanted to go, I noticed pink light projecting at me from a crystal ball about the size of a small goldfish bowl. It was inside a locked cabinet—not the one Lisette kept all the lifelike miniature dolls in.

This one appeared to be antique, with glass in the doors and intricate golden trimmings around the top and sides. It was equipped with special locks that reminded me of the Renaissance period. As I walked closer to it, I saw something I didn't expect. At least, not right then, because all I wanted to do was teleport to see Sari and return before Lisette figured out what I was doing.

Once I peered inside, I saw a three-inch doll that looked like Opal. It had her face, eyes, and hair. The eyes blinked, and I jumped. It wasn't a doll—it was really Opal… downsized!

She held her mini fists up and slammed them as hard as she could against the inside of the ball. She glared up at me as if she was shooting countless arrows at me—dabbed with toxic secretions—while mouthing something I couldn't make out. She then began to point towards Lisette's spell book.

I raised my eyebrows and gestured to it, believing that Opal was attempting to get me to help her out of the awful mess she had created all on her own. Apparently, she actually thought I would consider doing that, after everything she had done prom night and since then, specifically setting Pepper Fox on fire in the middle of the dancefloor and then attempting to kill Sari during Pepper's funeral.

Walking closer to her, she kept her malicious yet pathetic cold eyes locked on mine, and I slowly mouthed, "*No way!*"

She stood from her sitting position and started pacing around in her small space. After some time, she approached the front of the dome and slammed her tiny fist against the glass over and over again.

"I'm right here. I can see and hear you with no problem."

Opal slid her index finger from her left ear, under her chin, all the way to her right. She then spat on the glass. Her saliva ran down like thick venom, and I knew exactly what her nasty little gesture meant. I winked at her and waved.

When I reached the table, I read the teleportation instructions one more time. Focusing on the book, I made it close.

Glancing back at the cabinet, I saw that Opal was still pacing, her arms crossed tight over her chest, as she sent more daggers in my direction from her evil eyes.

After going up the stairs, I closed the attic door with my mind. Focusing my powers once more, I lifted the rug a few inches up into the air, and it landed over the closed door. It was a bit crooked, so I used my foot to straighten it out to look as it did before I entered.

# CHAPTER
## TWENTY

**W**hen I returned to my room, I shut the door and stood in the middle of the floor with my eyes closed. Then I focused on the exact location where I wanted to teleport to, which was outside Sari's bedroom window.

At first, as I began to levitate, I felt my feet rising off the floor. Colorful swirls spun around me, as I rotated in different directions. My heart was beating fast, like someone was banging a drum against the inside of my chest, and my breathing sped up, too. As my eyes scanned the room at a rapid rate of speed, I began to feel nauseated.

With my eyes closed, I heard a voice call out my name. Someone pulled me down. After about thirty minutes, I woke up and found myself in my bed. Mr. Ray stood over me, holding something out to me.

"Here, eat this now." I reached up to grab it, but I couldn't locate it, so he lifted my head and placed the mysterious item inside my mouth. "Chew it." It tasted like bitter chocolate and warm Pepto-Bismol. I swallowed it down, and then he handed me a bottle of water. "Drink."

After taking a few sips, I sat up and leaned my back against the headboard.

"Hey, I'm glad you're here."

"I bet."

"What made you come?" I asked.

"To save you!" he shouted.

I'd never seen him upset, not even when the most belligerent and noisy kids were on his bus route. He always possessed an inner calmness, but not at that moment.

"Thanks, Mr. Ray."

I took a few more sips of water and placed it on the nightstand.

"Tomie, do you know that you could've died?"

"What? No!"

He brought the chair from the desk over, positioned it a few inches from the bed, and sat down.

"Teleportation is nothing to play around with. If you don't have the proper training, you could get disastrous results, as you almost accomplished."

"Lisette said that I come from a very special bloodline, and some things will come naturally to me, so I wanted to try it. I could feel it working."

"Yes, she's right. Sure, you did some of it correctly, but it was getting out of control. I could feel that something was wrong, which is why I'm here right now."

"I would've been fine."

"Were you feeling fine before I arrived, and you woke up in your bed?"

"No, sir."

"Well, that should teach you not to pursue something that you don't know much about. Understand?" I nodded in agreement. "You have to wait for Lisette to train you. Teleportation can cause instant death! It speeds everything up about a hundred times, possibly more. You must learn to control your breathing and your heartbeat."

"Didn't know that."

"Where were you trying to go, anyway?"

"Sari's house."

"My goodness, young love… I can relate. I probably would've done the same thing if I was in your shoes, with the exception of having proper training first. So, you and Sari having problems?"

"I don't think so, but I know someone is really weighing heavy on her mind, and I have a pretty good idea who it may be."

"Hope you two work it out soon. No more teleporting, young man, okay?"

"Absolutely not. I'll wait until Lisette trains me."

"I'll be watching you, Tomie."

"I know you will."

Mr. Ray stood up from the chair and placed it back in its original position.

"If you start feeling nauseated again, eat another piece of the bar I left in the bag on your table."

"What is that stuff?"

"Oh, it's a remedy from the old days that knocks out nausea brought on from teleportation imbalances."

"It's pretty bitter."

"Yet, fast-acting, right?"

"Yeah."

"Well, Tomie, I'm going to go."

Before he walked out of the bedroom, I called out, "Mr. Ray?"

He turned around and put his left hand on the doorframe.

"Yes."

"Can we keep this between you and me?"

"Oh, you mean you don't want me to tell Lisette about

your irresponsible behavior?"

"Right."

"I won't say a word, but I believe you'll share it with her sooner rather than later. By the way, there's nothing like receiving an old-fashioned love letter out of the blue from the one you love. Add a spritz of the cologne she likes, and I can almost guarantee that things will at least move in a good direction for you two, minus the outside noise."

He winked, closed my door halfway, and vanished as if he had never been there.

The back door opened, and I heard voices.

# CHAPTER
## TWENTY-ONE

**W**hen I felt something pulling at the blanket, I looked down and saw that it was Sabra. As I picked her up, she made some cute chirping sounds. After I set her on the bed, she walked in circles a few times, before she found her special spot and curled into a little ball next to my feet.

Lisette knocked on my door and asked, "You decent?"

"Yeah, come on in."

"I assumed Sabra was with you. As soon as I unhooked her leash and took off her harness, she shot in your direction. She's getting used to you."

"It looks that way."

"We missed you on our walk. It was a nice one, too. We took a trail on the opposite side of the lake. Figured you needed some alone time. I think everybody does."

She sat on the edge of my bed.

"Thanks, Lisette. You're right."

"You and Sari okay?"

"Yeah, we will be, but we have to work through whatever's bothering her."

"Well, if you want to talk about it, you know I'm here for you anytime."

"I appreciate that. So, where's Caya?"

"In the living room, flipping through the channels and eating a snack before we go to the movies. You sure you don't want to join us? It might take your mind off some things."

"I'm sure, but thanks."

She stood up and asked, "Anything exciting happen while we were out?"

"Ya know, when you get back, we can talk about that."

"Everything okay?" she asked, twitching her mouth to the side.

"All good here. Go and enjoy the movie."

"Okay. You do know that I'm already aware, right?"

"You *glimmed* me again? Dang it, Lisette." She covered her mouth with her hand and laughed. "So, why even ask me if something happened if you already know?"

"Integrity is part of your training, too. To be a good witch, it's important to demonstrate it, especially within your circle." As she walked away from my room, she yelled, "I'll leave some stationary and stamps on the kitchen table for you!"

I smiled and leaned my head back. Sabra crawled up my leg, and when she curled up on my chest, I could hear her tiny heart beating. Then I shut my eyes and dozed off like she did.

When I woke up, she was in the same position. An hour had passed, and my body still felt a little heavy, though my nausea was gone. The teleportation experience wiped me out like I hadn't anticipated.

After placing Sabra in the middle of the bed, where she wouldn't roll off, I sat up and put my feet on the floor. My head remained down for a few minutes, and then I stood up. My balance was shaky at first, but I quickly regained it and reached my arms out to stretch.

Walking into the kitchen with my water bottle in my hand, I opened the fridge's freezer door, scanned the shelves, and found an orange plastic container. As I lifted the lid, I saw that frozen pasta with Andouille, corn, carrots, and lima beans filled it. So, I set it into the microwave to defrost and cooked it for a few minutes.

My mind focused on the door, and it opened. I mentally guided the warm container, floating in the air, until it landed on the table. After grabbing my water off the counter, I sat down to eat.

The box of stationary that Lisette left was positioned near me. I laid a few sheets of the paper in front of me and then grabbed a pen. While thinking about what I wanted to write, I stirred up the casserole to allow it to cool.

With the pen near my temple, I tapped it a few times, as if that would make the words fall out onto the paper and arrange themselves into a perfect line, but nothing was happening. It had to be positive, with no negative vibes at all.

I considered telling her about Caya, Lisette and Crow's recent engagement, everything I had been learning, or, of course, Sabra, but I decided to wait until I could see her face-to-face to share all of that. Then it hit me that I should write her a poem. My handwriting was terrible, so I printed it painstakingly, so she would be able to read it.

Sari, I wanted you to know how much you mean to me, so I came up with this. I know that you have something heavy weighing on your heart, and I have an idea what it is.

Until you're ready to tell me about it,
I wanted to share this with you. I hope
to talk to you soon and see you, as well.
I know that I'm not a poet, but these
are my feelings for you in the best way
I could express them to you.

Where do I begin?

My fingers tracing your soft brown
eyes, high cheekbones, and rosy lips...

My hands fall to my waist to reach
outward to find your hands.

They meet mine with no difficulty.

My arms slide in to engulf your
existence, until the midnight sky meets
dawn.

My eyes cast a spell over you to always
know that my heart belongs to just one,

and that one is you, my love.

Know I'm here for you whenever you
need me, whether you wish to sing your

words to me or allow them to be silent.

Your wellbeing is my priority, and I want to make sure that I do my best to fulfill it.

I hope that I never disappoint you, but I'm aware that I could sometimes be the culprit, causing your tearful waterfalls.

If I should ever make you unhappy, please promise you'll let me know, so I won't repeat my crime.

I would rather spend infinite days in a dungeon without sunlight in Gotham than to have you vanish from my world.

You, and you alone, triggered a wakefulness inside me that I never knew.

I thank you for giving and showing me true love, when I was so clueless.

Instead of accepting it, I rejected you.

You waited and never forced me to fall in love with you.

I did that all on my own...

I picked up my letter, read it aloud about five times to make sure that my words sounded okay, and then walked back to my bedroom and found some body spray that I knew Sari liked—it smelled like vanilla, leather, and faint cinnamon. After I sprayed it on the fanned-out sheets, I checked on Sabra and saw that she was still asleep.

After scooping her up, I held her against my chest and then went back into the kitchen and laid her in her bed. She opened her eyes and stretched out her hind legs. Then she curled up into a ball, closed her eyes, and fell back to sleep.

Turning on the faucet, I washed my hands and returned to the table. After placing my gift in an envelope, I sealed it, addressed it, added a forever heart stamp, and went outside. I set it inside the mailbox and lifted the flag, so it would be picked up the next day.

When I returned inside, I walked into the kitchen and put away the stationary, while Sabra continued to sleep.

Once I finished with my shower and brushing my teeth, I went into the living room to watch some TV and found a cool sci-fi movie just starting. My lids began to droop.

A while later, I felt someone tapping my shoulder, and I opened my eyes to find the end credits of the movie rolling. Lisette was standing over me.

"Time for bed. It's almost midnight."

Stretching, I said, "I must've dozed off. How was the movie?"

"It was good, as always."

"Lisette, I want to talk with you about what happened earlier."

"We'll do that tomorrow morning before training. Right now, you need to get some rest. Sweet dreams."

I stood up from the couch, walked into my room, peeled the covers back, and crawled into bed. After turning off the lamp with a nod, I fell asleep.

The next morning, I found Lisette outside. She was sitting on the ground on a mat with her legs crossed, her eyes closed, and her hands resting next to her sides. Another mat was spread out a few inches from her.

"Come and sit with me," she whispered without lifting her lids. I walked over and took a seat next to her. "Now, shut your eyes, Tomie."

"Why?"

She opened one and raised a brow, so I followed her order.

"Relax and breathe in at a slow pace."

"I am."

"No, you're not. Your heartbeat is still too loud and fast. Count backwards, starting at 100, and think of something that calms you."

As I followed her directions, I thought about Sari sleeping on my chest, with my arms wrapped around her, and my pulse slowed down almost immediately.

"Good. Continue to focus."

"Can I open my eyes?"

"Not yet."

Lisette touched my hand, and it felt as if hers fused with mine, as my body began to move, and the ground started vibrating.

"You can open them now."

When I did, we were both standing in the living room, and I realized that she had just teleported me in from outside.

"Lisette, that was awesome! I feel a little lightheaded, but nothing like last night."

"Good. It's not simple. Tomie, why did you attempt to

do something that you had no knowledge about?"

"After everything you've told me about the strength of my bloodline, I just figured it would come naturally to me. Plus, the spell didn't appear to be that complicated. However, the book left out one major detail—**WARNING**: First-timers may experience a sudden illness!"

"I'm glad that Mr. Ray sensed it and came to help you."

"Could I have really died last night, trying to teleport to see Sari?"

"Yes! Mr. Ray wasn't exaggerating that part at all." When I looked into her eyes, I knew that she was being completely honest with me. "Tomie, I want you to promise me something."

"I have a pretty good idea," I said, as I placed my right hand on her shoulder. "What?"

"Not to practice serious magic unsupervised until I've given you the okay for it." Nodding, she asked, "Well?"

"Promise."

"Come on and let's get some breakfast before we continue."

As we were cleaning up the dishes, Lisette turned around from the sink and leaned up against it.

"Did you find anything else interesting in my basement?" she asked, while keeping her shimmering eyes fixed on mine.

"Yes. I saw where you're keeping Opal." She batted her long lashes. "Are you going to keep her there forever?"

"I hope to. Opal would do more harm if she were free. I put a containment spell on her to prevent her from hurting anyone else. Teaching a lesson is one thing, but she practiced dark magic with evil intentions, murdering a mortal, which is forbidden, especially if your life is not in danger."

"She was a doll before, but now she's like a living super-mini Opal. How?"

"A human transformed into a doll can only remain in that vessel for a short time."

"Okay, so, does she get hungry or need to go to the bathroom?"

"No, the spell causes her body to cease those functions."

"Do you think her grandmom knows where she is?"

"Yes, but she's barred from entering this house. I placed a special lock-out spell around my home years ago."

"Can she reverse the containment spell?"

"Opal broke a major witch rule, and because she did something as horrible as that, no one can reverse a containment spell on her, unless…"

"Unless what?"

Lisette lifted herself up from the counter and spoke her words slowly, as if she were contemplating their magnitude. "If Verlinda Dawn seeks assistance from a *Sorciere Des Ombres Noires. . .*"

"A who?"

"A Dark Shadow Witch."

I squinted and said, "I don't follow. Ms. Dawn is a Dark Witch. Are you saying that Dark Shadow Witches are way more powerful and evil?"

"Tomie, there are different levels in our hierarchy, and she would fall under the moderate category."

"How do you know so much about all these things?"

"I read my spell books, study, and when I was your age, I listened to the stories from my elders… and I continue to."

"I have a lot more to learn, don't I?"

"Oh, yes! Learning is ongoing, and it's a personal

choice, what you want to master."

"Can we practice more teleportation?"

She nodded.

We went back outside, and Lisette told me to face her. When I did, she asked me to count backwards, again starting from a hundred.

Midway, she said, "Focus on your breathing and heartrate." I took in deep breaths. "Imagine yourself sitting in the passenger seat of my car. Picture it."

I closed my eyes and did as she asked. A few minutes later, I felt my knees wobble and found that I was right where I had seen myself in my mind. She appeared in the driver's seat in seconds.

"Good job!" She raised her hand up towards me, and I lifted mine to slap hers, but she pulled back and said, "Too slow!" She laughed, and I grinned at her. "Okay, you need to build up some endurance, Tomie. I want you to run a few laps around the perimeter of the house."

Without asking any questions, I followed her order, knowing she was preparing me to become the best warlock that I could be. When I was finished, I went inside and showered, then put on clean jeans and a t-shirt.

Walking out of my room into the kitchen, I didn't see Lisette, and Sabra wasn't in her bed. When I entered the living room, no one was there, so I looked down the hall and saw a light reflecting off the wall, and I knew exactly where she was.

"Lisette, you down there?"

I approached the basement door and noticed it was propped open.

"Yes! Come on down."

When I got down to the bottom of the steps, Lisette was sitting at the table with the spell book in front of her and Sabra curled around her neck, her favorite spot. The pages were flipping one by one without her physically touching them.

"What are you up to?"

"Thought we could practice a spell."

I clapped and did a forward moonwalk towards her with a half turn.

"I like your enthusiasm, but we're going to start off small."

"Hey, that's cool."

"Great. Let's see what you got. All of the ingredients are located on the wall there."

She pointed towards a cabinet at the far end of the space.

"What am I cooking up?"

"You're going to complete a transformation spell."

# CHAPTER
## TWENTY-TWO

L et's do it!"
"Grab the white candle, the matchbox next to it, and the blue bottle to the left."

I gathered the objects and placed them on the table.

"Now, read the spell on the page."

As my eyes scanned it, I could see the words floating up in front of my eyes, and then each one vanished like smoke.

"Light the candle, sprinkle some dust from the bottle, and repeat these words three times, while concentrating on changing an object of your desire—*Little candle of mine, shine bright and transform this in front of my sight.*"

Taking a match from the box, I dragged it across the strip on the outside and lit the wick. After I unscrewed the bottle and shook a few silver dust sprinkles over the flame, I stared down at Lisette's nails and began to repeat the spell.

When I was through, the scarlet-colored polish peeled off each one and vanished into her nailbeds. Glossy burnt orange with a white longhorn symbol in the middle appeared instead, and I had to take a second look to be sure I was seeing what was right in front of me. With a smile, Lisette lifted her hands to gaze at them.

"Wow, Tomie, you definitely pulled it off with no hiccups at all! I'm impressed. Not only did you change the color, but you threw in a fancy little design."

"Thanks. I thought you might like that," I said with a wink.

"You know, it takes someone with a gift to complete a simple spell with creativity."

"Really?" She nodded. "It was nothing. I just gave your nails what I was thinking. So, how long will it last?"

"Maybe a day or so. It'll then fade back to my original color, but I'm digging this design, so I may extend it myself."

We both laughed.

"What's next?"

"Have you finished the book I gave you?"

"Almost. A few more pages left."

She walked over to a cabinet, and with the swipe of her hand, the doors flew open. A thick golden book with a lock on the side of it floated off the shelf and landed in her hands. When she came back over, she set it down in front of me.

"What's this?"

"It's yours."

"You already gave me one."

"Yes, but you've graduated to the next level. This is a tome of spells and more with special meaning. Take care of it."

"Why is it so special?"

She picked up my hand and set it on top of it near the lock, and it opened. Surprised, I pulled back a bit.

"Don't be afraid, Tomie. It knows you, because it was

passed down to your mom."

I thumbed through the pages, wondering which spells my mom practiced. A few of my tears dripped onto a page, and it began to glow, projecting a bright beam of silver light into my eyes. The contents of the book were absorbed into my mind. Then the shining stopped, and the book was no longer on the table in front of me.

Looking all around, I asked, "Lisette, where did it go?"

"It's inside you."

She tapped my chest with her hand, and I frowned.

"Wait. You mean it…?"

"You now possess all its spells. It's safe."

"No way."

"Yes," she whispered with a wink.

"So, my training is completed?"

"Oh, no. You just have a lot of the tools now. We still have to practice."

"Did my mom leave this for me?"

"Yes. She wanted you to have something very personal of hers."

"Would it be okay if we start again tomorrow?"

"Of course."

She must've known I needed some alone time and where I was headed.

As I started up the stairs, she said, "Take my car. Where you're going is too far to walk."

"How did you…? Never mind."

"Tomie, I think you'll find what you're looking for there."

Lisette wrote the address down on a sheet of paper and handed it to me.

I whispered, "I got a good feeling I will, too. Thanks, Lisette."

After going to my room, I grabbed my phone and Lisette's keys off the table. When I got to the car, I slid into the driver's seat and programmed the GPS with the lake address.

Driving for almost an hour, I saw that the paved road turned into a dirt one, with houses positioned farther back from the water. Lake Beaudin was just ahead, and it looked inviting, but I had only one agenda—having a conversation with my mom.

# CHAPTER
## TWENTY-THREE

I parked the car and sat there, gazing out at the water, listening to the tiny waves roll in and out. A few people were sunbathing, and an older man fishing on the other side of the lake caught my attention.

The first question that crossed my mind was where my mom committed her forbidden act, and I wondered what she could've been thinking.

After I opened the door, I stepped out of the car and locked it. Unsure of which direction to go, I closed my eyes, and all of a sudden, I felt driven to travel towards the West. I approached the shoreline and squatted down to toss some rocks across the water. They skimmed the surface in an angle, seeming to pause for a moment before they vanished underneath.

Then I stood up and found a large rock and sat on it, leaning back with my hands behind me, my legs dangling beneath me. No one was near, so I figured I could talk aloud, but not too loud.

What was I supposed to ask? Would she even respond, or *could* she respond? Did I really want to hear her voice?

So many things were popping into my mind.

Dad had told me stories and memories of my mom whenever I'd asked him about her. Judging by the sound of his voice and his body language, there were times when it was hard for him. When that happened, I switched to a different topic, and he stared at me and shook his head in what seemed like gratitude for not forcing that door open.

My phone vibrated, so I pulled it out and saw that it was a message from Dad.

> D: **Hey there son. I have a short break in between jobs. I'll be in town by the end of the week. Okay with you?**
> T: **Sure. I'll let Lisette know. See you soon.**
> D: **How are things going so far?**
> T: **Pretty good**.
> D: **What you up to?**

I thought about his question for a minute before I responded.

> T: **Just hanging out at the lake.**
> D: **With Lisette?**
> T: **No. She's doing some stuff at the house. Just me.**
> D: **Okay. Hey son I gotta go. A business call coming thru. See you soon.**
> T: **Cool. Be safe**. **Love you.**
> D: **Love you too.**

When I sent my last message, I turned off the ringer and slid it back into my pocket. Stepping off the rock, I walked closer to the edge of the lake and kneeled. I placed my hand on top of the cool rolling water. Closing my eyes, I searched my mind for something special in my mom's book, and I was led to the awakening spell.

After reading it, I looked around to confirm that no

one was near me. When I didn't see anyone, I shut my eyes again and began to chant.

*Mom, please hear me. I call upon you to awaken and tell me the things I need to know. Awaken, Awaken, Awaken...*

As my lids rose, the water remained rolling on top of my hand, but nothing else happened. After reviewing the spell again in my mind to ensure that I followed it correctly, I attempted it once more.

Still nothing.

I slammed my hand against the water and whispered to myself, "This is stupid. Who am I kidding?"

Just as I was about to stand, a shimmering seven-foot wave rose in front of me. I stumbled backwards and fell to the ground. Raising my head, I reached my right hand back to massage above my hip.

When I sat up, I witnessed the wave transforming into a watery female figure.

# CHAPTER
## TWENTY-FOUR

The woman floated from the lake and stepped onto the sand, and she appeared to absorb it as soon as her feet touched it. Her features became more apparent, and her body began to resemble the mocha-colored granules. I knew it was my mom, from the pictures I had seen of her over the years.

Unable to produce any words or sound, she moved closer to me and placed her gritty hands on my face. Her aqua blue eyes glowed, and her long curly locks floated upwards from her shoulders. Large white magnolia flowers covered her body with a glistening purple one positioned on the right side above her ear.

She continued to stroke and hold my face, while staring deeply into my eyes, and I knew that she was *glimming* me. Tears began to roll down my cheeks, as I attempted to touch her hands, but mine went right through hers. Within a few seconds, they had reformed.

Looking at the rock behind me, she motioned towards it. I walked over to it and sat down, and she took a seat beside me. Her sandy body then absorbed the solid rock, and when I reached out to touch her, she felt just like the warm stone, but that time, her hands didn't lose form.

When my lips became unparalyzed, I asked, "Mom, it's really you, right?"

I continued to focus on her glowing eyes.

Nodding, she answered, "Yes, Tomie," as she scooted closer to me.

"I have so many things I want to ask you."

"Start anywhere."

She continued to smile, looking at me from head to toe.

"Why? I mean, Dad told me why you did what you did, but I want to hear it from you."

She bowed her head and said, "Tomie, I want you to know that I loved you the moment I knew you were part of me and your dad."

Tears streamed down my face.

"Why did you do it, then?"

"You're so young. I don't expect you to understand."

"Maybe I will."

She took some deep breaths and then lifted her head to look into my eyes.

"My family would've never allowed your dad and me to be together. Once they found out, we ran off to get married, and not too long after that, I became pregnant with you. They punished me by taking you away from me and forbidding me from ever seeing you or your dad again. I couldn't accept that, ever. So, I retreated into a very dark place, and I made a permanent decision that I so regret, even now. There's so much I dreamed of teaching you."

Tears rolled down her face, dropped into the sand, and then quickly vanished.

"Mom, if you had a chance to make things different,

would you?"

"You don't even have to ask. Of course, I would. I terminated my time with your dad and you, when I should've thought more about the consequences of my decisions, but I didn't. I made a choice in haste."

"Why did your family hate me so much?"

"Oh, Tomie, it's not that they hated you. They were extremely upset that I fell in love with a descendant from the Dupuy Silver Slayers—witch hunters. So many of my ancestors have been slaughtered or tortured by them over the centuries."

"But Dad wasn't a slayer."

"You're right, but in my family's eyes, he was one of them, which is why our marriage was forbidden. I decided to get back at them by my fatal and final act. Instead of punishing them… I lost the two loves of my life."

She looked away from me.

"Mom, thank you for telling me."

"Tomie, I'm so, so sorry. If I could change it, I would."

"I know."

"Listen, I have to go soon, but I want you to be aware of some things."

"Like what, Mom?"

"You can only work this awakening spell two more times to call upon me."

"Why is that?"

"Some spells are just limited. Some can only be used once, while others have no restrictions."

"That's not fair! I can only see you two more times? That sucks!"

"I know, but there are other ways you can communicate with me. Mr. Ray and Lisette will share that with you when they think you're ready."

"She's doing a good job with my training, Mom."

"I always knew she was different from my other family members. My older sister, her mother, stopped bringing her around me once she found out that I was dating your dad."

"That wasn't right."

"No, but when you make a choice to go against your coven, they'll go against you and shun you. I'm so glad that she reached out to you and is training you."

"How do you know? Oh, never mind," I said with a smile. "Where's Lisette's mom? She never talks about her."

"She has her reasons."

"Did she go against the coven by reaching out to me?"

"Yes."

"Lisette is putting a lot on the line to help me, huh?"

"She is, Tomie. Appreciate and respect her. She truly loves you."

"I do, and I will."

"Don't rush your powers. Just allow them to come to you when it's time. Lisette was right when she told you that your magic is much stronger than you realize."

"How's that?"

"My bloodline dominates your dad's. It goes back to one of the most powerful witches in Louisiana, Marie Laveau."

"I've read stories about her."

"When you have time, learn more about her and her teacher."

"I will."

"Tomie, I have to go back to where I came from." She placed her hands on the sides of my face. "I want you to know that I love you, and I never stopped."

"Love you, too, Mom. One more question."

"Okay."

"Do I have to be here to call on you?"

"Yes. This is where I completed the forbidden spell, so part of my eternal punishment is to remain here."

"You can never visit me wherever I am?"

"More will be explained or shown to you soon enough. I must go now. Don't ever forget how much I love you. Please tell your dad that I miss and love him. . . and to be patient."

I nodded and said, "I will."

When she stood, her body of rock transformed back into sand. As she walked towards the lake, she turned around and waved. I ran to her, and as soon as my arms wrapped around her, she crumbled into a pile of sand, which vanished when the water touched it.

My tears returned, as I stared out over the lake. As the tiny waves continued to roll back and forth on the shoreline, I wiped my face.

Mom didn't return.

Placing my hands in my back pockets, I took a few steps backwards. Walking towards the car, I pulled out my phone, turned my ringer back on, and texted Lisette.

T: **Hey Lisette.**

L: **How did it go?**

T: **Will tell you when I see you.**

L: **Okay. What's up?**

T: **Dad texted me. He'll be in town by the end of next week for a short visit. Is that okay?**

L: **Yes. That's fine. I'll cook him a nice meal. I bet he wants to hear what you've learned so far.**

T: **I guess. I think he's just checking in and probably a little lonely.**

L: **Probably. See you in a bit?**

T: **Yep. Going to get something to eat. Want anything?**
L: **Chicken sandwich, fries, and orange soda.**
T: **Okay. See you in a bit. Lisette thanks.**
L: **For what?**
T: **Just thank you.**

Taking one last look at the lake, I noticed a spray of water shoot up. I smiled, opened the door, and hopped into the car. Then I backed up, turned around, and headed back to town.

# CHAPTER
## TWENTY-FIVE

O n my way, I spotted *Big Green Al's Drive-In*, a local burger joint. I pulled into an empty spot and placed my order—large Cajun curly fries, two burgers with everything, and a root beer for me, and then I told them what Lisette wanted. While I waited, I checked my messages and saw one from Caya.

> C: **Hey Tomie.**
> T: **What's up Caya?**

She responded a few seconds later.

> C: **You busy?**
> T: **Nope.**
> C: **Plans tonight?**
> T: **Not really. What do you have in mind?**
> C: **What I talked about before.**

I laughed and leaned the seat back a little.

> T: **Enlighten me.**
> C: **Seriously?**
> T: **Yep.**
> C: **You up for some dangerous fun?**
> T: **Like what?**

C: **Some gator nite feeding.**
T: **I thought you were just kidding.**
C: **No. This is really a thing around here.**
T: **Oh.**

A waitress who looked to be in her late teens rolled up next to the car, carrying a large bag and a drink holder. She had two auburn ponytails with red bows, and she was wearing a red and white checkered blouse tied above her waist, with denim shorts that had ruffles on them. Her skates were white with crimson wheels.

She spoke in a high tone. "Hey, there, hottie. I got your order all ready. Two large Cajun curly fries, two burgers with everything, large root beer, chicken sandwich, and a medium orange drink. Right?"

"Yeah, that's it. How much do I owe you?"

She looked at the ticket stapled to the paper sack, and then she batted her long blue painted eyelashes at me and said, "That'll be twenty-four dollars even."

Lifting my rear up, I dug my wallet out of my back pocket, pulled out some bills, and handed her twenty-eight bucks. She gave me my order, and I placed the bag in the passenger's seat and the drinks in the cupholders. Then I turned the ignition and started the car.

"Hold on. You gave me too much."

"I know. Consider it your tip."

Before I started backing out, she rolled up closer to my window.

"You're not from around here, because I know just about everyone in Monroe Creek," she said with a wink.

"No, I'm not. Just visiting my cousin for the summer. I'm from Texas."

"I knew it. Who's your cousin?"

"Why you want to know?"

"Just asking. No offense."

"None taken."

"Can I at least get your name?"

"Tomie Dupuy."

"I know that name from somewhere."

She squinted her eyes and rubbed her heavily freckled nose.

"What's your name?"

"Ranae... Ranae LeBlanc. No tricky pronunciations."

"Maybe I'll see you around."

"Got a real good feeling that you just might, Tomie Dupuy. Bye for now."

She winked again and stood there, waving at me, as she rolled backwards.

After throwing my hand up to her, I headed towards Lisette's house. I turned on the radio and found some sweet zydeco music. As I listened to it, I thought about my visit with my mom and how I would never be able to spend the entire day with her and tell her about my Sari or how my day went. I figured that Lisette and Mr. Ray probably knew something about how to extend my contact with her, and I planned on exploring that with them at the right time.

# CHAPTER
## TWENTY-SIX

As I took a sip of my root beer, I heard my phone buzz. When I stopped for a red light, I checked it and saw that it was a text from Caya. Knowing that it was dangerous to do it while driving, I decided I would respond to her once I was back at Lisette's.

When I arrived, I parked and grabbed the bag and drinks. After stepping out of the car, I locked it and walked up the front porch steps. Focusing on the door, I willed it to open.

Lisette was sitting on the couch with Sabra in her lap. Her little head popped up, and her nose was bobbing up and down to sniff the food.

"I see that you're getting used to your powers."

"Yeah, the things you've been teaching me are growing on me."

"Good. I wasn't sure if I would ever hear those words from your mouth, especially not a few months ago."

"Wouldn't have thought so, either."

"Think I know where all of this is coming from." As I placed the food on the coffee table with the drinks, I looked up at her. "How was it? Seeing her."

"Really good, Lisette. I didn't know how I would respond to her at first. In fact, I wasn't convinced that it was even going to work."

"You mean, the awakening spell?"

"Yeah. How did you know I was going to choose the right one?"

While Sabra stayed on the blanket on the couch, Lisette stood and walked over to me. She placed her right hand on my chest.

"Tomie, you just have to believe who you are. Once you master that, everything else will fall into place."

We went into the kitchen to wash our hands and returned to the living room. I sat on the floor, and Lisette sat on the couch. She opened the bag, pulled out the food, and placed it on the table.

"Thank you," she said.

"I figured you were hungry."

She took a bite of her chicken sandwich and chomped on a few fries. Then she picked up a napkin and wiped her hands and mouth, while Sabra watched every move we made.

"She looks hungry."

I took a large bite of my burger and gulped a fourth of my root beer down.

"She ate right before you got here. She just wants human food. Not today." When Lisette turned around and looked at Sabra, she put her little head down onto the blanket and partially shut her eyes. "So…?"

"What?"

"You know what."

"Want me to spill it about my experience, right?" She nodded with her cheeks full. "I finally saw my mom for the first time."

"Tomie, I can only imagine what it was like for you."

"I was nervous, scared, and excited all at once. I didn't know what to say at first."

"Yet it all worked out, right?"

"Yeah."

"Were you comfortable with the awakening spell?"

"I think so. Is it a more advanced one?"

"Yes."

I finished off the rest of my burger and fries.

"What did you think of your mom when you saw her?"

"She wasn't in human form. She absorbed the elements around her. Why was that?"

"It has something to do with her terminating her life. That's part of her punishment."

"Will I ever get to see her in the flesh?"

"Tomie, I wish I could answer that for you, but I can't, because she worked a forbidden spell, and consequences are always extreme."

"Oh, she did tell me that it was limited, but that you would teach me a way to communicate with her when the spell could no longer be performed."

"Yes, I know what she's referring to, but that's only when Mr. Ray or I believe it's time."

"Time for what?"

"Don't worry. We'll know when, and so will you."

I threw my trash in the bag and asked, "You done?"

"Almost. You upset?

"Nope. Just not a fan of the riddles."

Lisette scooted over next to me and nudged me with her elbow.

"Yes, you are."

"Nope," I said, as I picked up my drink to finish it.

"Be patient. You'll know everything sooner than you think. Hey, I need to get a few things downtown. Want to join me?"

"Sure. I'll meet you outside in about thirty minutes or so."

"All right. I'll clean this up and let Sabra get some exercise out back."

"Take her with us."

"Okay. I'm sure she'll love that."

I walked to my bedroom and sat on the edge of the bed. After scrolling through my messages, I saw that there was nothing from my Sari, and I wondered if she had received my letter and what she thought about it. I sent her a quick text and then went to the one from Caya.

> C: **You there?**
> T: **Sorry. Got busy.**
> C: **So you wanna go tonight or not?**
> T: **You do this a lot?**
> C: **Yeah why?**
> T: **Just wondering.**
> C: **Are you scared?**
> T: **Nope.**

My foot started tapping.

> C: **So you in?**
> T: **Sure.**
> C: **Meet me at Crow's place right after 10:00. I got keys to his airboat.**
> T: **Does he know that?**
> C: **Of course. I negotiated the contract with him this morning. Just kidding!! He would kill me! Especially if something happened to Baby Girl—his boat!**

Lisette yelled, "Tomie, let's go!"

"I'm coming!"

> T: **Gotta go. See ya then.**
> C: **K**

She signed off with a GIF of an alligator winking with long eyelashes and a pink bowtie around her thick neck. I smiled and went to the bathroom, and then I ran my fingers through my curls, sprayed some cologne over my upper body, and brushed my teeth.

When I walked out the back door, I saw Lisette sitting in the driver seat and Sabra's little paws perched over the open window on the passenger side. An orange ribbon was tied in a bow around her neck. When I opened the door, she slid down and backed up, and after I was settled in, she found her spot on my lap.

As I fastened my seatbelt, I asked, "Hey, Lisette, can I borrow the car later tonight?"

"Sure. Big plans?"

"Just hanging out with Caya and, I think, a few of her friends."

"Where are y'all going?"

"She said it was a surprise."

"Okay. Make sure it's nothing dangerous."

She shot me a stern look, and I gave her a half-smile.

# CHAPTER
## TWENTY-SEVEN

L isette started the car and backed it up, and we headed downtown.

When we arrived, she parked next to a store that had a large wooden sign with plum letters and golden accents hanging in front of the door. It read, *Daphne's Wands & Potions*.

"Is this what I think it is?"

"Yep," she said with a grin.

"So, some witches need wands?"

"Absolutely. They aren't all as gifted as we are. Some still use special broomsticks for transportation."

Sabra crawled up and wrapped herself around Lisette's neck, resting her head on her right shoulder. We stepped out of the car, and she locked it with a wink. She led the way to the red door with a bell above it, which opened without a touch from either of us.

The shop was bigger than it looked on the outside. Purple, gold, and forest green candles appeared to float above the high shelves. Rows of books lined the walls, and odd-shaped bottles were planted in special cubbyholes all over the shop. Two antique plush plum couches were positioned in the back with a geometric-shaped table between them. The scent of cooking bay leaves, lavender, and strawberry licorice saturated the air. Sabra tilted her nose up to breathe in the rich aromas.

The glass counter contained a diverse array of jewelry, wands, and other items I wasn't familiar with.

Pointing at one of the crystal balls, I mumbled, "Do they really work?"

Lisette leaned next to my ear and said, "Yes, and why are you whispering?"

I shrugged my shoulders. Honestly, I wasn't sure why. Maybe because it reminded me of a library, or I didn't want Lisette to think that I was a half-baked warlock— *Oh, wait. She already knew I was, since she was teaching me.*

This was definitely a shop where witches, warlocks, and possibly other *supras* spent some quality time.

A bright yellow hanging bell sat on the counter. Lisette and I looked at each other, and she motioned for me to ring it. Shaking my head, I pointed at it, signaling for her to do it. After all, that place was more of her familiar stomping grounds, not mine.

Sabra watched us both, and then she climbed down from Lisette's shoulder, stretched out her tiny paw, and tapped the bell twice.

"Did you see what she just did?" I asked. Lisette nodded. "Did you teach her to do that?"

"No, it's all her."

Sabra climbed back up to Lisette's shoulder and curled her body around her neck, as I heard footsteps approaching from the back of the store. When the person came into sight, I knew she looked familiar, especially when she spoke.

"Hey, there, two burgers with everything and Cajun curly fries," she said while popping her gum and blowing tennis-ball-sized bubbles.

It was Ranae LeBlanc from the burger restaurant. She had abandoned her roller skates and exchanged them for red sneakers with candy-striped shoelaces, jeans, and a black t-shirt with the shop's name written in twisty fuchsia letters. There was a glass bottle logo on it with lime-colored smoke twirling from the top. The shirt was tied up in knots on both sides, with a few inches of her belly exposed.

"You two have met before?"

"Yeah. Met her earlier today."

"Oh."

"Hey, you work at both places?"

"Sometimes. My mom is Daphne, the owner. She needed some extra help this evening, so when I left *Big Green Al's*, I came over here. Hi, Miss Lisette and Sabra."

Ranae reached up and stroked Sabra's back, and she purred and nudged her head up against Lisette's chin a few times.

"Tomie, Daphne and I went to high school together," Lisette said.

"Hope I'm not coming off too forward, but... Ranae, are you...?"

"A witch, you mean?"

"Yes."

"Oh, no. I'm a *Lecteur*."

"Like a fortuneteller?"

"Yeah... and a little more. I can read your thoughts by touching any part of your body, especially your hands, eyes, and heart. Would you like a reading?" she asked, staring down at my hands.

"No, thank you," I said, tucking them into my pockets.

"There's so much going on in this town, I'm almost afraid to ask about your mom."

Lisette said, "Tomie, don't be. I want you to become familiar with this world."

"Mom's practically normal," Ranae said with a giggle, as she adjusted her ponytails tied with fuchsia ribbons, while leaning on the counter.

I tuned in more and asked, "What do you mean by *practically*?"

"Nothing, really."

Lisette scanned the glass cabinet of goodies, looking up at Ranae and then back at me from time to time.

"So, you're gonna just leave me hanging, Ranae?"

She started flipping through a book.

"Why are you so curious?"

"You're the one who brought it up."

I turned and walked towards a shelf full of books. They were in alphabetical order by author. Some appeared to be new because of their jackets, while other covers looked worn and dated.

Running my index finger down the rows, I came across an interesting title, *Supernatural Secrets of New Orleans*. I pulled it out of its tight space, flipped to the table of contents, and found a section about Marie Laveau, as well as other interesting topics. It was in good condition; I turned it over to check the price. It was only eight bucks, so I tucked it under my arm.

When I felt a tapping on my shoulder, I turned around and saw that it was Ranae, swinging a wire basket behind her back.

"You may find some other interesting things in here."

She handed it to me, and I placed the book inside.

"Thanks."

As I walked towards the back of the store, she followed

me and asked, "Ya wanna tour?"

"I think I can find where stuff is located."

"Okay. If you're not sure about something, let me know. I'll be up front."

A metal cage covered with buttons, bumper magnets, earrings, leather bracelets, and necklaces hung on the back wall. I couldn't resist the *Warlocks Rock* red leather bracelet with black lettering, the *Brake for Flying Brooms*—in a wavy font—sterling-silver dangling earrings with a broom underneath for Lisette, and the *Boom, Witches!* hot pink necklace for Sari. Everything was 40% off.

After grabbing them up, I tossed them all inside my basket. I found a t-shirt to place on top of the items just in case Lisette's eyes wandered over. Then I walked around the store for several more minutes, before I met up with Lisette at the same spot where I had left her. She had a few hand-sized beige satchels, white and yellow candles, and a sheet of geometric silver stickers in various sizes. I placed my basket on the counter next to me.

Ranae said, "Lisette, I see you found some pretty cool items."

"I sure did." Lisette looked at my things. "I see you did, too."

"Just a book and stuff."

"Oh, which one?"

"*Supernatural Secrets of New Orleans.*"

"That's a good one. Let me know your thoughts when you read it."

"I will. What's up with the stickers?" I asked.

"They're for the festival. I'm going as a fortuneteller."

"You're going to need a new crystal ball, because your current one is definitely out of commission, probably indefinitely," I said.

Lisette winked at me and slid a new one in front of her.

Ranae wrapped the ball in a few sheets of tissue paper with the stand, placed it in a box, and taped it down. She pulled out a bag with handles and set the box inside at the bottom, while stacking Lisette's other items around it. Then she took her payment.

"Tomie, I'm going to visit with Daphne for a bit, but feel free to walk around town if you like. I'll call you when I'm done if I don't see you."

"Okay."

Lisette walked towards the back of the store with her bag in hand, and then she disappeared behind the shiny midnight blue curtains.

After ringing up my purchases, Ranae placed my items in a bag.

"Cool gifts."

"Thanks."

"That'll be sixty-five twenty-eight."

I pulled three twenties and six one-dollar bills out of my wallet and handed them to her.

"Here you go." When she held out the change, I said, "No." I pushed it back to her. "Donate it to the runaway teens charity."

She dropped the coins into a plastic container, and I took out a five-dollar bill and put it in, as well. After sliding my wallet into my back pocket, I picked up my bag off the counter.

"Oh, here's your receipt, Tomie. Do you want it in the bag?"

"Yeah, please. Thank you."

As I was about to leave the store, she asked, "So, you doing anything fun tonight?"

"Just hanging out with a new friend."

"You have a girlfriend, right?"

"Yes, but I never told you that."

"Your gifts gave you away. Not too many single guys will buy a female friend a gift. Also, Lisette confirmed with me when you were shopping earlier."

Smiling, feeling pretty flattered, I said, "Ya know, you're the second girl who's mentioned something about me having a girlfriend."

"Really? Who was the first?"

"Oh, you probably don't know her."

"Try me."

"Caya."

"I do know her. You're hanging out with her tonight?"

"Yeah, why?"

"She's just…"

"Just what?" I placed my bag on the counter. "Come on, tell me. You like starting a conversation, but not finishing one, like when I asked about your mom."

"It's no big deal."

"Then, what is it? And what were you going to say earlier?"

"Okay. My mom volunteers at a special underground place that provides counseling for witches and warlocks who've been banished from their covens."

"Wow, that's pretty cool. Why didn't you just tell me that?"

"Don't know."

"I would imagine a lot of them really benefit from her help."

Ranae nodded and said, "Yeah, I guess so."

I held out my fist, and she bumped hers to mine.

"So, what about Caya?"

"Don't get me wrong… Caya's cool and sweet. It's just her mini squad she hangs out with."

"What do you mean?"

"Garth Turnidge and Sleazy Samuel Oliver. She and Garth are boyfriend and girlfriend, on again, off again, every time you blink. He doesn't treat her right, either. At least, that's my opinion. By the way, Samuel is oblivious to personal boundaries, and he and Garth are best friends. . . when Garth feels like it."

"Hmm."

"It won't take you long to see them for who they truly are, so be careful. They don't always play nice."

"Gotcha, but I think I can take care of myself."

"I like your confidence, Tomie, but you don't know those two like I do. Just be on your guard when you're around them."

"Okay. Thanks, Ranae. Why don't you hang out with us tonight?"

"No, thanks. I'd rather clean up my room twice and work a double shift. Where're y'all going, anyway?"

"Caya mentioned something about night gator feeding. At first, I wasn't sure, but then I thought it might be fun."

"Tomie, just watch out, especially if they're tagging along, which they usually do. Don't trust them."

"Thanks for the info, but I'm going to let it play out and decide how I feel about everything, ya know?"

"Sure. See ya."

"Later."

I grabbed my bag off the counter and headed towards the front door of the shop. As I was walking out, I turned around and waved. She threw her hand up with a fretful look on her face.

# CHAPTER
## TWENTY-EIGHT

An ice cream shop was a few blocks away, so I decided to check it out. Upon arrival, I ordered a double chocolate milkshake with shavings and raspberry cream on top. A shaded area with a bench was nearby. After setting my bag down, I sat and leaned back with my arms stretched out.

The conversation I had with Ranae about Caya's friends played over in my mind, while I sipped on the jumbo green straw of my cup. If those guys showed up, I wanted to give them a chance without prejudging, but what if she was right? She lived in Monroe Creek and knew more than I ever would about it and the people in it.

As I considered all the things that could go wrong on a trip like that, I thought about cancelling, but what would be a good excuse? Maybe I could say that I was expecting a call from Sari… or Lisette had plans I totally forgot about. After weighing a few lies, I figured they were all pretty lame.

I knew what I needed to do, which was to tell Caya the truth—that I wasn't feeling her gator night feeding adventure. Not because I was afraid or anything like that. Well, maybe a little. Okay… okay, maybe a lot. After watching all those specials on *Animals & Natural Hunters Channel*, I wasn't exactly a fan of gators or crocs.

Finishing up my shake, I even debated with myself about talking to Lisette about it, but I knew that she would figure out Caya's plans to take Crow's boat. So, I erased that thought and decided to go for it. The way I saw it, I was no ordinary warlock, so what did I have to fear?

*Nothing.*

The gator adventure was back on.

I then received a text from Lisette, telling me that she was ready to go home, so I headed back towards the car. She looked up and waved me over. After putting our bags in the back, we hopped in.

"So, did you have a nice visit with Ranae?"

"Yeah, it was interesting."

"In what way?"

"I didn't know she knew Caya and some of her friends."

"It's a small town, and there isn't much that people don't know about one another, especially those who are more *show and tell it all*. Ranae was right about Caya being a sweetheart. However, like she said, Caya's friends are sour as spoiled milk… that's been expired for two weeks… brewing in the hot sun all day. I'm glad she warned you about them. I hope you make the right decision tonight, Tomie."

Lisette obviously knew about those guys, but I wasn't sure what else. I had a funny feeling that she knew more than she was sharing with me at the moment for her own reasons.

We drove to the grocery store a few miles out. She wanted to pick up a few extra items because of Dad coming into town. She placed Sabra in a small carrier, as she told me that the owner knew her and Sabra.

While we were at the checkout, I was typing a text to Caya to let her know that I decided not to go with them and that we could hang out and do some magic whenever it was good for her.

Before I hit the *send* button, I got a message from her.

> C: **Excited for tonight. Hope you don't chicken out!**

She followed it with laughing emojis. My pride kicked in, so I deleted what I had written and sent this instead:

> T: **See you at the dock at 10:00 sharp.**
> C: **Thought you were going to cancel on me.**
> T: **No way!**

Closing my eyes, I thought about how I just blew my chance to tell her the truth.

After the cashier put Lisette's groceries in one reusable bag, we went back to the car, and Lisette drove home with Sabra resting beside her on the seat.

"So, did you decide what you're going to do tonight?"

"Yeah, I'm going to hang out with Caya for a bit and then come on back."

"Remember what we talked about—only use your powers when you absolutely have to. No need to be showing off for those who have no appreciation for the craft."

I didn't know how many times Lisette was going to remind me of that, but I was sure that wouldn't be the last.

When we arrived at her home, she placed Sabra on the ground, so she could run around for a bit before going inside.

After gathering up the bags, I walked onto the porch. Lisette waved her hand from where she was in the grass, and the door opened. I went into the kitchen and placed the groceries and Lisette's things on the counter.

I entered my room and took my new leather bracelet and book out of the bag. After setting the book on my nightstand, I wrapped the bracelet around my wrist and clicked the three black snaps together, securing it in place. It was tight enough to not turn side to side when I moved my wrist back and forth.

As I sat on the bed, I looked at my phone and saw that I still had no texts from Sari. I wanted to teleport over to see her, but I knew I needed more practice with Lisette before I could pull that off smoothly. Plus, I made the *promise*. Then I thought about Facetiming her just to see her, but I tossed that idea out because Sari despised video conversations. The *Deep Bayou* shindig was only a few weeks away, and I hoped to see her then.

Time was dragging by for me. It felt like I'd been away from her for years. I sent her a short message and hoped she would respond. After staring at my screen without blinking for a few seconds, my eyes started to water. Just as I was about to lay my phone down on my bedside table, it beeped. When I flipped it over, I saw Sari's name.

> S: **Hi Tomie.**
> T: **Hey I miss you so much! Did you get my letter?**

The screen remained blank.

> T: **Sari you there?**
> S: **I'm here but this isn't Sari.**

# CHAPTER

TWENTY-NINE

My eyes grew to almost twice their normal size, and I could feel sweat breaking out on my face, chest, and the midsection of my back. Lifting my shirt, I wiped my forehead, as I stared down at my phone. I knew exactly who it was—Sari's dad.

He was never going to forget what I did to him when I was waiting for Sari to finish getting dressed for our prom. She told me that he went to the emergency room later that night to get his hand checked out, but he didn't tell the doctor the truth about how he received the burn. My special warlock senses must've picked up on his plans to inflict harm on me, and they reacted.

Then another message appeared on the screen.

S: **You know who this is?**
T: **Yes. Mr. Green. Where's Sari?**
S: **Occupied.**
T: **She always keeps her phone close.**
S: **Sari is on a date and forgot it.**
T: **Whatever!**

I huffed.

S: **She really is.**

I could practically hear him laughing. He sounded like a sickly weasel coughing up a string of hairballs.

T: **I know Sari and you can't psych me out.**

S: **Okay. Listen up Tomie Dupuy.**

T: **What Mr. Green?**

S: **Stay away from my daughter! I found out about you and your wicked family. Now you have Sari involved in your mess.**

T: **What exactly do you think you know?**

S: **Don't you worry about it. Mr. Fox shared more than enough with me!**

Shaking my head, I wondered how he knew Mr. Fox. Trying to explain myself to someone who didn't care what I had to say… I knew that I wouldn't get anywhere, so I decided to let it go.

T: **Okay.**

S: **Just stay away from her and there'll be no trouble.**

T: **Trouble?**

S: **I don't think I need to repeat myself son.**

T: **Please don't call me SON because I'm far from that thank you!**

S: **If I find out that you're still trying to contact my daughter, you'll get just one warning…**

After throwing my phone onto the bed, I lay back with my arms behind my head, thinking about what he said. The one thing that stuck in my mind the most was about her going on a date. I didn't want to believe that she would do that. Her dad had to have been just saying that to upset me and get me mad at Sari.

What if she did actually go out with some guy? We'd been apart for a little while, but not months or anything like that. She was lonely, of course, but I still couldn't see her doing it. Her dad could have cooked up anything to convince her to go out on a date.

I was trying to figure out what I could do to see Sari face to face and talk to her, since there was no way her dad was going to allow her to travel to Louisiana to spend some time with me, especially after that conversation.

When I grabbed my phone, I saw that it was getting close to 9:30. After considering canceling once more, I decided to go ahead and meet Caya at the dock.

After taking a grey Frost High hoodie from the closet, I tied it around my waist and then went to the bathroom to freshen up. I wrapped a heavy-duty beige rubber band around my hair, making a ponytail. When I walked into the living room, I found Lisette and Crow curled up on the couch with some treats, watching TV. She lifted her head off his chest, and he stood up to greet me.

"Hey, Tomie. How are you doing tonight?"

I thought I was tall, but Crow had me beat by several inches, not to mention his Thor-like physique. My abs were tight, with a great-looking six pack, and I worked out, but he was bulky and really strong. When he hugged me, it felt like someone had me in a vice for several seconds, before he let me go; then I took in some deep breaths.

"I'm all right," I said, glancing more at the ground than at him.

"Everything okay with Sari?" Lisette asked.

"I really don't know."

"You want to talk about it?"

"No, maybe later. I got to go. Meeting Caya in a little bit."

She stared at me and squinted, and I didn't try to block my emotions or experiences from her.

"Tomie, you sure?"

"Yeah."

"Why don't you just call Caya and ask her to come over and watch movies with us?" Lisette asked.

"I don't think she can break her plans."

I bent over and scooped up the car keys off the coffee table.

"So, what kind of plans do y'all have tonight?" Crow asked, while grabbing his bottle of root beer off the table.

Lisette laid her head back on Crow's immense chest, as I tossed the keys back and forth in my open hands.

"Something Caya cooked up."

Crow nodded and drank the full bottle of soda in less than ten seconds.

"All right. Y'all be careful, and don't be doing anything foolish," Crow said in a firm tone.

With a half-smile, I said, "Have a nice night. Don't wait up."

When I opened the door, two bright lights lit my path, and I walked down the steps to the car. After pushing the button to unlock it, I jumped in and buckled up, and then I headed out to Crow's place.

As I drove, I kept replaying the conversation with Sari's dad over in my mind, wondering where she was. Before I knew it, I saw the dock ahead. It was lit with some swinging bulb lights that hung high on poles.

After parking the car, I unbuckled my seatbelt, stepped out, and locked it. As I walked towards the dock, I saw Crow's airboat and Caya waving me towards her with both hands.

She had on white jeans cuffed near her ankles, a white and blue glittered *The Last Unicorn* t-shirt, and black tennis shoes, and her hair was pulled up in a high ponytail.

The wind started swinging those lights even more, and the temperature felt like it had dropped a few degrees, so I untied the hoodie from my waist and put it on.

I noticed an owl watching me in the swaying tree above. It hooted seven times, and then it bolted off the branch and flew around me. I knew exactly who it was—Mr. Ray. He made some strange sounds, and then he appeared right in front of me, wearing blue jeans, a New York Yankees t-shirt, and grey sneakers. He gave me a long stern look without one blink.

"Tomie, what do you think you're doing?" he asked with a frown.

"Hanging out."

"You understand that not everyone will have your best interests at heart." I remained silent, and he continued. "Why are you hanging with people you don't know?"

"We're just going to have some fun."

"On a boat in the middle of the night with strangers, probably doing something you shouldn't be doing? Is that what you consider fun?"

"Maybe." I shrugged my shoulders. "Mr. Ray, don't worry. I'll be fine."

"It's my job to worry about you, because you're my responsibility. My duty is to watch out for you and protect you at all costs, Tomie."

"Maybe I don't need your protection tonight!"

"I know you're worried about something, which is why you're acting like this. Let's talk about it."

I looked into his eyes and then lowered mine.

"Maybe another time. Sorry about what I said. I just want to hang out, that's all."

I needed a distraction, even if it was just temporary.

He transformed back into an owl and zipped out of

sight, before I could blink twice.

I turned around and walked over to meet Caya. After I climbed down the wobbly wooden stairs, I stepped one foot into the boat and then the other, as it rocked slightly.

"What was that all about?" she asked.

"Nothing. Ready to go?"

"Sure."

"You know how to operate this thing?"

"Umm, yeah, I think I can manage. Crow taught me how to drive Baby Girl almost a year ago." She grinned. "Have a seat and buckle up."

She sat down and pointed her finger at the ignition, and the motor revved up for a few seconds. Then the airboat shot off and glided on the water like a skater on ice. Caya looked comfortable in the driver's seat, waving her hands in a circular fashion to guide our path.

"Where are your friends?"

A light spray hit my face whenever she turned in a certain direction.

"We're meeting them closer to the feeding grounds."

"This Garth dude... he's your boyfriend?"

Caya glanced at me and said, "Lisette must've told you, because I didn't."

"Yeah, she mentioned him and his friend."

"Garth and I have dated and broken up a few times, but as of tonight, we're off. Not sure if we'll be getting back together."

"Okay. So, how many times have you two actually broken up?"

"Too many to count."

A box of cigarettes floated out of her pocket in front of her. One of them squiggled itself free and drifted up towards her mouth.

"You do know what you're putting into your body

with that thing, right?"

"Nope. Yeah, I know, but why do you care? It's not your body, Tomie."

"You should do some research on it, especially the effects of secondhand smoke on non-smokers."

"Your nagging reminds me of Crow."

The cigarette found itself between her shiny pink lips, and she snapped her fingers to light it. When it did, I blew towards it, and the flame ceased—and I wasn't even close. She tried again, and I did the same. She turned around with a pronounced scowl painted on her face.

"You better stop it, or…"

"Or what?"

"I'll push you into the water! The gators'll find you and chomp on you until they're done."

"Whatever. You're premeditating my death, while I'm trying to save your life. Really cool, Caya. Go ahead and *puff, puff* away." I imitated her with my fingers held to my mouth, pursing my lips to take a drag and then blowing out nonexistent smoke a few times. "Suck down the entire pack! Like you said, who cares?"

Leaning back in the cushioned swivel chair, I used my legs to turn away from her. My mind continued to drift to Sari and everything her dad had texted to me. I needed to contact her, but how?

Figuring he could access her phone whenever he wanted, I thought about calling their landline, but that probably wouldn't end well for me, unless he had left for work. Unfortunately, I didn't know his schedule.

Teleporting myself to Sari was the perfect answer, but I knew I was reaching with that one. I decided to talk it all over with Lisette before I attempted to solve my problem.

Looking up at the ebony sky covered with twinkling stars, I saw that the moon was full, too. Then I noticed that I didn't smell any smoke in the air.

"Hey, you didn't light up."

She turned around to face me, while the wheel rotated when it needed to without her touching it.

"Yeah, I thought about what you said, and you're right. Crow's been on me about it for a while. I need to stop."

"What made you start in the first place?"

"You really want to know?"

I leaned forward and rested my arms on my knees.

"Yeah."

"Garth. He's been smoking since he was thirteen years old. One night and three months after we started dating, almost a year ago, he asked me to just try it and swore I'd love it. At first, I pushed it away. I didn't like the smell. Garth kept begging and telling me I was too afraid to do something new. He wasn't sure if he wanted to hang out with someone like me."

"You tried it that night, didn't you?" She stared down at the floor of the boat. "Wow, Caya. I wouldn't ever pressure Sari to do something she wasn't comfortable with. That's just *not* cool. Everyone should be allowed to say *no*, right?"

"I guess so."

"Absolutely. You have that right, just like I do and everyone else does."

"Tomie, it's easier for guys."

"What do you mean?"

"I always feel like Garth expects something from me, and if I don't give in, he'll ignore me, make fun of me, or break up with me like he's done so many times."

"Why do you keep going back and hanging out with this dude?" She remained silent and stared at me with huge teardrops waiting to fall from her eyes. "Can you stop the boat?"

She waved her hand behind her to slow it down, and it eventually came to a halt. I unbuckled my seatbelt, stood up, and walked over to her, and then I kneeled beside her, as her tears fell to the floor. She held up her hands to cover her face.

Patting her on her shoulder, I said, "Man, I haven't even met this dude, but I can already tell you, I don't like him. You want me to turn him into something, so you can keep him in a miniature jar or a cage?" She lifted her head and grinned a little. "See, I knew I could get a smile out of you." After a pause, I added, "You know you don't have to see him tonight… or any night… if you don't want to. Right?"

She nodded.

"I hope I get a chance to meet Sari one day."

I stood up and said, "I'm not so sure that'll happen."

"Why not?"

"Oh, Caya, it's a long story."

"Give me the short version, then."

I walked to the end of the boat and turned around.

"Her dad believes lies someone told him about me. He knows what I am, and he doesn't want her hanging around me anymore. He's trying to keep us apart."

Caya placed her hands over her heart and swayed back and forth as she said, "Oh, a supernatural modern-day *Romeo and Juliet*!"

"Seriously?" I asked, glaring at her.

"Yes. Anything I can do, Tomie, let me know."

"Sure, hope I can figure it out."

"How did her dad find out about you?"

"A powerful guy in town told him, and that man's late daughter was the one who was tormenting us since junior high. So, we decided to place a simple spell on her which became tainted with an eviler one by someone we thought was a friend."

"Wait a minute. You're talking about that Pepper Fox and Opal Dawn incident?"

"Right. Lisette must've told you about it."

"She did. Opal Dawn and her family are truly evil. It's a good thing that Lisette has her where she is."

I nodded in agreement.

"Enough about this. So, Caya, do you still want to meet Garth, or not?"

"The gators are spectacular beasts up close... but not too close!"

"If he tries anything, I'm ready to transform him into whatever crosses my mind first."

She laughed and said, "Thanks, Tomie."

"For what?"

"Just being someone genuine to talk to... with no expectations."

"You're welcome."

I walked back to my seat, and we both buckled up. She waved her hands, and we were off again. A question kept coming to my mind, so I blurted it out without thinking about how it sounded.

"Caya, do you shift when the moon is full?"

"I was wondering when you were going to ask me that. I can actually shift *at will* like Crow does. The full moon has magical properties that amplify my abilities, though."

"That's cool. Care to elaborate?"

Two guys paced on a dock up ahead, and I already knew.

"My senses are heightened. I can track something in half the time when the moon is full," she said, her voice cracking a little more with each word.

Her hands began to tremble, as we approached the dock.

"Caya, you okay?" She didn't respond at first... so I asked, "Are Garth and his friend *supras*?"

# CHAPTER
THIRTY

As she parked the boat and shut off the engine, she nodded in slow motion.

I *glimmed* her, as I thought, *Rougarou*.

Caya knew I had read her mind, because she nodded again and turned around to stare into my eyes. She waved her finger over the ignition and turned the boat off.

As I stood in front of the wooden stairs, I motioned for her to go first. She stepped back, indicating that she wanted me to go instead.

I mouthed, *"You sure?"*

She nodded, so I climbed the few steps and pulled myself up to the dock, where they stood almost fifteen feet away. I was pretty sure I knew which one was Garth. He was close to my height, with shiny bronze skin. His hair was styled in a fohawk—taper fade on both sides, with a long colorful mane on top and a seven-inch braid curled around his neck. His eyes were piercing daggers of grey, and he had a slim mustache trying to break out. He wore black jeans, with a sleeveless denim shirt that allowed his wannabe muscular arms to show.

Samuel, his friend, was thin, with a shaved head. A dime-sized pimple on the right side of his mouth, with stubby hairs sprouting in all directions, appeared to pulsate every few seconds. He gave a half-smile, and his teeth reminded me of butter. When Garth looked back at him, he elbowed him in the chest, and Samuel's grin vanished.

I walked towards Garth and held out my hand, but he just stared at it with a nefarious smile. Samuel attempted to reach his out to me, but Garth made a strange grunting sound, and Samuel withdrew his offer.

As Caya climbed up the stairs, she was struggling to pull herself up onto the dock. I glanced at Garth, assuming he was going to help her.

Instead, he yelled, "Come on, already! You're always late!"

He and Samuel walked away, and I ran over and pulled her up.

"Thanks, Tomie."

"Yeah, no problem. Stay close to me tonight."

She nodded.

We walked towards those two, and as we neared the end of the dock, I saw a white cooler. As I got closer, I noticed what looked like dry blood on the top and sides of it.

"What's in there?" I asked.

"Master Warlock, shouldn't you already know?"

Garth belched and then laughed. I thought he was going to beat his chest with both of his fists.

Caya said, "Garth, he was just asking."

He walked up to her and pointed his finger in her face.

"You, shut up and don't speak until you're spoken to."

Jerking himself around, Garth stooped down to the cooler and started to open it up. When Samuel attempted to help him, he gave him that look. Samuel moved back and stood there with his hands in his pockets, staring down at his dirty and torn tennis shoes.

I said, "Garth, I know we just met, but there's no need for you to talk to Caya like that."

She touched my arm, and he saw it. His eyes traveled over me, from head to toe, as if he was staring right through me. He then jumped up from crouching and stood with his face a few inches from mine.

"Oh, I see. You two a thing now?" he asked, followed by low grunts.

"It's not like that, Garth!" Caya cried out, as she stepped closer to him.

"What *is* it like, then?"

I said, "Listen, let's face it. You're an insecure kind of dude."

He stepped closer to me, sniffed the air like a wild dog waiting to pounce on its weak prey, and asked, "What did you just say?"

"You heard me the first time, and I'm not going to repeat myself."

Samuel took a few steps backwards and grabbed Caya by the hand, trying to pull her away from us.

Garth's whole face turned a dark cranberry tone, as deep brown hairs started sprouting up all over his face and on his arms in rows. His grey eyes switched to an iridescent yellowish green, and his fingernails slid off and were replaced by seven-inch milky-looking claws. His lips opened, and his teeth became fangs, with saliva dripping down onto his puffed-out chest.

"Please, Garth! He didn't mean it!" Caya screamed, touching him.

Then he pushed her towards the edge of the dock, and I ran over and caught her arms, preventing her from falling into the water.

"Caya, go and wait for me on the boat!"

"Come with me! He'll hurt you, Tomie!"

I smiled and said, "I'll be okay. Go."

She turned and ran, and Samuel was right behind her.

As Garth continued his transformation, his shirt split open and fell away, showing his thick hairy chest. His jeans split up both sides and dropped onto the dock. His upper fangs protruded even more, as his fiery eyes stayed fixed on me without a blink.

I knew I could stop him in his tracks with a special spell of my own, but I wanted him to do what he thought he could. Noticing an owl resting high in a tree that had swinging Spanish moss hanging from it, I winked up at Mr. Ray.

Chances were good that he was going to swoop down and save me, but I didn't want him to. I wanted to do it all on my own. He must've sensed that, because he remained in a stationary position, with his large glistening topaz-colored eyes watching me.

Once Garth stood in his full rougarou armor, I closed my eyes and levitated. He jumped several feet up into the air, swinging his arms out towards me, the sharp claws on the ends of his fingers fully extended. He slammed down onto the dock, and the claws on his feet buried into the wood, leaving him stuck for a few seconds. I floated above him in a circular fashion with my arms crossed.

He yanked them free, and a few claws tore from his toes and bled a bit before new ones replaced them. Standing over seven feet tall, he growled up at me, and his breath smelled like sewage and rotten cabbage.

Covering my nose, I hovered a bit higher. He kept jumping up, trying to pull me down with his razor-sharp claws as I moved around, avoiding his attempts to grab onto me. He howled a few times and soon started panting. Garth crouched, looking up at me as his breathing slowed, and he began to transform back into a human. His fur, fangs, and claws all receded, and his eyes turned back to grey.

After returning to the dock, I picked up his shredded shirt and jeans and threw them at him. He wrapped and tied the ragged bits of cloth in a few knots around his waist to cover the most important parts.

Garth didn't say a word to me; he only glared at Caya and his friend. They walked up behind me.

Samuel asked, "We still going to feed the gators?"

"Might as well," Caya said.

Samuel, Caya, and I went down to the lower dock area, where the cooler was, and he lifted the top. It was full of raw bloody meat. After taking some gloves out of his back pocket, he slid them onto his hands, and then he picked up a few chunks and tossed them into the water. Caya grabbed a flashlight that was lying on the dock next to the cooler and pointed it out there. The gator bait floated at first, and then it sank, so Samuel tossed out a few more pieces, as Caya kept the bright beam on them.

Garth walked up, but he kept his distance from us. He grabbed a chunk from the cooler and ran his sharp index fingernail across it. Holding it over his mouth, he slurped up the blood that oozed out. He looked at me and threw it, but before it could hit the water, a huge alligator with glowing red eyes appeared with its mouth open and caught it in midair, chomping down on it. A few others joined the first, as Garth and Samuel tossed in more of the tasty treats, but they were all eaten within a minute.

After Samuel closed the lid, Caya handed him the flashlight, and he secured it on the side of the cooler with a Velcro strap. He then carried it towards the upper deck, where a black 1990 Mazda B-Series pickup was parked.

Garth attempted to talk to Caya, but she jerked out of his grip every time he tried to pull her towards him. I watched from a few feet away, ready to toss him into the water, but as it turned out, I didn't need to do that. She left him standing there.

I climbed down into the boat, and Caya followed me, as I took her hand and helped her.

He walked over, kneeled, and said, *"Mr. Save the Day Pretty Boy*. You think you're funny, but just wait. We're not finished!"

"Garth, fix your skirt!"

While I laughed, with my right hand covering my mouth, he looked down, saw that it was fine, and stood up fast, holding the threads around his waist.

"I promise, I'm going to get you back!"

"Okay… I'll be waiting for you."

Garth picked up his pace and walked towards his truck, as his shredded blue jean skirt swished around his thighs.

He yelled at Samuel, who was lifting the cooler into the back, "Hurry up, stupid! Let's get out of here!"

Caya and I sat down and buckled ourselves in.

"Tomie, no one has ever said stuff like that to Garth. If anyone dared, then they would've suffered the consequences."

She turned the engine on with a swipe of her finger, and as she moved her hands, we were off.

"Really?"

"Yes."

"Caya, does he talk to you like that all the time?"

She lowered her head and turned around to face me as she said, "Yes."

"You don't have to put up with that." She remained

silent. "Has he ever hurt you... physically?"

With her eyes on the water, she didn't say a word, so I *glimmed* her. I could see that there had been times when he'd shoved her down, threatened to push her out of a moving boat, and made her do awful things that she never wanted to do.

"Does your mom know?"

"No," Caya said with her eyes staring at the ground.

"I could talk to Lisette about it. . . if you want me to."

"Please don't. I wouldn't want her to know."

"I bet she already does, Caya."

"Maybe, but she hasn't mentioned it to me."

"There're people you can talk to, you know."

"I know. I'd just rather not. At least, not now."

"Being a hybrid—witch and rougarou—you're stronger than Garth. You know that, right?"

"Maybe," she mumbled.

"Caya, you are."

"Can we talk about something else?"

"Yeah, sure."

"What about practicing some magic tomorrow afternoon?"

"Sounds good."

When we arrived at Crow's place, Caya parked the airboat right where it was earlier. We climbed the stairs, her first, and then I walked her to her 2015 midnight blue Volkswagen Beetle. I opened the door for her, and she slid in.

"It was nice, learning a little more about you, Caya, but not so much about the big bad wolf, Garth."

I looked up to the sky and howled, and she smiled.

"No more hanging out with Garth and his sidekick for me."

"Understand. I'm really sorry, Tomie. I didn't think he

would show you his true colors so soon."

"Guys like him never hold back when they have an opportunity to show off. Think about that, okay?"

"See you tomorrow."

After I shut the door, she started the engine with a swipe of her finger and drove off.

I walked over to Lisette's car, and with a wave of my hand, I unlocked it and opened the door. When I got inside, I checked my messages and saw that there were none from Sari or her dad.

As I was about to drive off, my phone started buzzing. I put my foot on the break and looked at it. An unknown number popped up on the screen. After parking, I turned the music down, and at almost midnight, I hit the answer button.

"Hello?"

"Tomie, it's Sari. I'm calling from a friend's phone."

# CHAPTER
## THIRTY-ONE

"Sari, I've been so worried about you! I'm so glad you called."

"I miss you so much. I'm aware that my dad texted you."

"He told me you were on a date and forgot your phone."

"What? Are you serious?"

"Yeah. So… you're not dating anyone else?" I asked, as my right foot started tapping the floor mat.

"Tomie Dupuy, you actually believed what he told you?"

"Not really, but he made it sound believable. All the stuff he knows about me, us, and the whole Pepper Fox thing…"

"First of all, I love you, and I wouldn't date anyone else."

"For real?" I asked with a smile.

"You already know that."

"Listen, I was thinking about coming back home before school starts."

"Don't you dare. Just stay there and continue your training with Lisette. Wow, there's so much I want to ask you."

"There's a lot I want to tell you, Sari. It's been your dad making you feel down lately?"

"Yeah. He wants me to break up with you, because he thinks you'll be the *death* of me."

Pausing, I took a few seconds to really process Sari's words.

I was a warlock from a line of powerful witches who were, and continued to be, targets of the Dupuy Silver Slayers and other warlock assassins. As much as I hated it, I couldn't disagree with what Sari's dad told her. It held some truth. Her life almost ended a few months ago, when Opal Dawn attempted to throw her in front of oncoming traffic to kill her. With that in mind, I realized that I could one day be the cause of Sari's life being in extreme danger… or worse.

"Tomie, you there?"

"Yeah. I was just thinking about everything you said. It's just so good to hear your voice."

"What were you thinking?"

"Nothing. Are you really okay?"

"I am. You?"

"Of course. Especially now, talking to you."

"I want to see you," she said.

"You will soon."

"No, I want to come there."

"You think that's a good idea, with all that's going on with your dad?"

"We won't be together if we don't make it happen."

"You're right. There's a festival coming up in a few weeks. Do you think you can be here for that?"

"I'm sure I can."

"How are you going to get here without your dad knowing?"

"Don't worry. I'll figure that out. I'll call again when I can… soon."

"Okay. I really miss you."

"I miss you, too. Talk soon."

"Love you, Sari Green."

I blew her a kiss through the phone.

"Love you, Tomie Dupuy. Bye for now."

"Wait, did you get my letter?"

"You wrote me a letter? Wow, that's so romantic!"

"More like a poem… at least, sort of."

"I don't have it yet, but I'll look for it and let you know when we talk again."

"K."

"Bye, Tomie."

"Bye."

The call seemed to end just as it started. I stared at the screen until it faded to black. I wanted to dial the number back but didn't. If it was okay, Sari would have told me during our conversation; she didn't.

I turned the music up, fastened my seatbelt, and drove off towards Lisette's house with a smile painted on my face, though Sari's future with me was weighing heavy on my mind.

Will Sari and I be together after senior year or beyond?

# CHAPTER
## THIRTY-TWO

Just before 2:30 a.m., I arrived at Lisette's. Crow's truck was gone, and the living room light was on. I wondered whether Lisette left it on for me or if she was waiting up for me.

After parking the car, I locked it and walked up the steps. When I waved my hand over the door, it unlocked and opened. I walked in and flipped my hand backwards to close it without slamming it, and then I saw that Lisette was sitting on the couch, sewing something.

"I see you're becoming more and more comfortable with your powers."

Shiny and colorful sequins lined up and floated in the air, awaiting her command to land where she wanted them.

"Yeah, you can say that. What're you working on?"

"My costume."

"What is that?"

"A blinged-out bustier, with a three-layered candy corn-colored tulle skirt, with tattered candy corn wings with purple jewels outlining them."

"Nice. You have a hat to match?"

"Absolutely."

When she waved her hand over the edge of the couch, a black velvet textured witch hat rose into the air. It had candy corn-colored tulle in a layered fashion wrapped around its brim, and the base had a thin strip of iridescent purple tulle on it. It floated near the ceiling and then landed on the center of the coffee table.

"You're going to rock that."

She smiled and said, "I hope so. I also have facial crystals and sparkly purple and black-striped tights and six-inch lace-up leather black boots."

"The star of the *Deep Bayou*, Lisette Laveau."

"Whatever. What're you going to dress up as?"

"Not sure yet. I'll have to think about that one."

"I have a chest of costumes in the basement that you might want to rummage through."

"Okay."

"So, how was your night, Tomie?"

She continued sewing one sequin after another onto her bustier.

"It was different."

"In what way?"

"I learned more about Caya, and I met Garth and his sidekick Samuel."

"So, what did you think of Garth?"

I walked over and sat down on the edge of the couch to face her and then placed the keys on the corner of the coffee table.

"Honestly, I didn't think much about him at all except that he's a real jerk."

"I'm not surprised. He can be pretty aggressive and wants to run things his way."

"How do you know so much about him?"

"I went to school with one of his brothers. Mind you, his brother Ash was a senior when I was a sophomore. However, based on the stories I heard about him and the things he did for fun, like torturing innocent animals and controlling everyone in his circle, I knew that apple was rotten to the core… and spoiled the other ones, too. Did Garth do something tonight?"

"Yeah. I'm sure you already know."

She smiled and looked up at me, as the needle continued to sew.

"You did well, Tomie. I'm proud of you. Crow and I watched everything."

"How?"

"Mr. Ray allowed us to see through his eyes."

"Okay. I knew he was there, but I thought he was just watching out for me."

"Oh, he was, but he allowed us to have front-row seats to a live *glim* play."

"Will I be able to do a live *glim*?"

"Yes, in time. That's a more advanced technique, but you may pick up on it faster than I expect."

"Awesome. Lisette, I want to talk more about Caya. Did you catch the way Garth was treating her?"

"No, just the interaction you had with him."

"Do you know about Caya and Garth?"

I yawned against my will and covered my mouth with my right hand.

"I do, but let's talk more in a few hours. You need to go to bed."

"Okay." I stood up from the couch and started walking towards my bedroom. "Hey, did you and Crow have a good time?"

"Yeah. We watched a movie, and I shared some wedding plans with him."

"Cool. I want to talk more about Crow and his *supra* abilities soon, okay?"

"You can ask him anything, or me. Probably best coming from him."

I peeped in on Sabra and saw that she was sleeping in a tight furry ball.

When I got to my room after a quick shower, I sat on the bed and flipped through the book that I purchased at Daphne's shop. I saw a small chapter about rougarou legends in Louisiana, and it crossed my mind that the tales weren't just legends. Especially after what I saw earlier, not to mention what I knew about Caya and Crow, I was sure they were real.

After reading a few pages, I placed the book on the desk, and soon, I was out for the next eight hours or so.

# CHAPTER
## THIRTY-THREE

When I woke up, I checked the time on my phone. It was around noon. I laid it back down and told myself that I would sleep another fifteen minutes and then get up.

Thoughts of Sari filled my mind, and I was hoping she'd sneak another call that day. I was tempted to text her cell, but I already knew that her dad most likely had it, so I didn't risk it.

After rolling out of bed, I pulled out some navy-blue cargo shorts and a classic comic *Aqua Man* t-shirt from a drawer. To my surprise, they weren't wrinkled at all. I rolled on some deodorant and sprayed on some knockoff *Sean John* cologne.

When I got the shorts and t-shirt on, I folded my pajamas, placed them in a drawer, and put on some socks and my tennis shoes. My bathroom morning routine was completed in less than a half hour.

As I walked towards the kitchen, I heard voices. Lisette, Caya, and Crow were sitting at the table, and it looked like they were about to eat lunch. A platter of deli meats, cheeses, pickles, olives, onions, and chips were laid out. Mustard and mayo sat near the sub sandwich bread, as well as knives, plastic plates, cups, and a large glass pitcher of strawberry lemonade.

Lisette turned around and said, "Come on, Tomie. Fix your plate."

I sat next to Crow and across from Caya.

"Hey, guys," I said.

They all responded, and I began to make my sub, as Lisette filled a cup with crushed ice from a bowl next to her and handed it to Crow. He grabbed the pitcher, poured lemonade into it, and set it next to me.

"Thank you."

They all continued to eat their sandwiches.

"You slept well?" Caya asked. I nodded, since my mouth was full. "So, Tomie was saying last night that we could practice some magic together today."

"That sounds like a good plan," Lisette said. "Let's finish lunch, and then we'll get started."

Sabra galloped under the table with her bells jingling, hoping to find a surprise or two. I pulled out a thin strip of turkey and held it down for her. She found it and ran back to her bed to enjoy her little treat.

When we were finished eating, Lisette motioned us into the living room. Crow sat at the end of the couch, while Lisette, Caya, and I sat on the floor around the coffee table, looking at a baby blue canvas bag that was lying on it.

I elbowed Caya and whispered, "Do you know what's in there?"

Lisette responded before she could.

"No, Caya doesn't know what's inside. We'll get started soon enough."

She waved her hand towards a shelf that was behind

Crow. A pocket-sized burgundy book flew above his head and positioned itself right in front of Lisette's face. She turned the pages with a nod, and they stopped as soon as she raised her right index finger. The bag opened, and a ceramic bowl and strips of paper floated out and landed on the table in front of us.

"Caya, have you ever created fire or ice?" Lisette asked.

"No, I haven't. Are we going to do that today?"

Lisette nodded.

With wide eyes, I said, "Man, this warlock thing gets more awesome every day!"

I clapped then rubbed my hands together for a few seconds.

"Caya, Tomie, place a few strips of paper inside the bowl… with your fingers. No levitating for this one. You're both going to work on a fire spell." We followed her directions. "Now, close your eyes and think of something hot and say these words: *Fire, fire, burn so bright, show me the light.*"

After repeating the phrases, our lids rose. No spark or flame. We looked at each other, probably thinking the same thing: *Why didn't it work, especially with both of us?*

"It's my fault. I wasn't concentrating," Caya sighed.

Lisette said, "It's okay."

"You all right?" I asked.

"Yeah, let's try it again."

We attempted it once more, and the strips of paper lit into about a twelve-inch flame.

"Now, bring it down halfway," Lisette instructed.

It remained high and continued to climb. Sensing it was Caya's emotions, I held up my hand and lowered it. The fire followed at first, but then it zipped back up.

Lisette stared at it and extinguished it.

"Tomie, do it again."

While Caya watched, I lit the paper and put it out several times, gaining more control. I was wondering if Garth had said something to Caya that might've been distracting her, so after practicing for almost thirty minutes, I asked Lisette if we could take a break.

"Sure. When you're done, you and I are going to practice some teleportation," she said with a wink.

I gave her a *thumbs up* and a wink back, as Caya and I walked out the back door.

We took a short walk away from the house, and I picked up a branch from the ground and moved it between my fingers, as the sun played peek-a-boo behind the clouds.

"So, what's going on with you?"

"Nothing, Tomie. I'm fine." Her voice sounded a little shaky.

"Really? You sound funny. Want me to *glim* you?"

"Go ahead. Whatever you want to do."

I stopped and shouted, "No! You have a choice. You always have a choice. Don't let anyone make you believe you don't!"

"I guess."

Her head was lowered towards the ground.

"So, you want me to *glim* you, or not?"

I stomped my right foot on the ground, dirt kicking up in a small cloud around my shoe.

She gave me a half-smile and said, "Not really. I'd rather tell you."

"Okay, good. Let's talk, then."

Glancing around, I spotted a log. I checked it for creepy crawlies, because I was not a fan of surprises, especially by little creatures that were difficult to see with the naked eye. It was safe, at least for the moment, so she sat down, and I took a seat a few inches away from her.

We turned towards each other, as she said, "Tomie, I'm sorry about Garth's behavior last night."

"Hey, you shouldn't apologize for him. You didn't do anything wrong. Besides, the gator feeding was pretty cool."

"Garth called me this morning and said he was sorry."

"Did you accept?"

"I didn't give him an answer."

"His apology threw you off focusing on your witch game?"

"Not exactly."

"What, then?"

"I thought about what you said last night."

"I said a lot, so you'll have to be more specific."

I continued to twirl the branch between my fingers.

"The part when you asked if Garth made me do anything I didn't want to do."

"Okay… I take it, he did."

Nodding, she said, "Yeah. Lots of stuff. I did something, and I've been feeling really bad about it."

"What?"

"About a month ago, he told me he needed money for his brother, who was in some kind of trouble. He knew I could open Crow's safe without leaving any fingerprints."

"You didn't."

"I did. I unlocked it and removed $250," she said, as she started tearing up.

"Crow never figured out?"

"Nope. He blamed it on being so busy that he must've misplaced or lost it."

"Wow, that's really not cool."

"I know." Her tears fell in a steady stream. "I started

thinking about it, because Garth asked if I could help him out again."

"Are you serious?"

"Yeah."

"You're not going to do it, right?"

"No, I can't. Crow's done so much for me."

"The guilt's getting to you." She nodded. "Well, there're only two things you can do. Tell Crow and repay him the money you stole or forget it and never mention it again."

"What do you think I should do, Tomie?"

"I think you know, but you need to make the best choice for you, Caya. As long as you hide this, it'll continue to haunt you, believe me."

"Thanks for listening."

"Sure. You ready to get back?"

"Yeah."

We stood up and headed towards the house.

"Caya, are you going to hook up with Garth again?"

"Don't want to, but he always knows how to slither his way back inside my heart."

"When we get done, why don't you talk to Lisette? I bet she can connect you with someone who can help."

"Maybe."

As we approached, we saw Lisette and Crow waiting for us on the porch.

"Okay, ready to practice some teleportation, Tomie?" Lisette asked.

"Yeah!" I replied, as I glanced up—an owl was resting in a tree.

"I want you to concentrate on the living room."

Closing my eyes, I thought about it.

"Imagine yourself sitting on the couch, recognizing different items in there. Listen to the beats of your heart and slow it down. Starting at twenty, count backwards and envision yourself rising a few inches off the ground."

After I did everything that Lisette told me to do, my feet began to move up, and it felt like my body was being stretched like a rubber band. When I opened my eyes, I was in the living room.

I ran my hands down my face and chest and screamed, "I did it!"

Lisette appeared right next to me and high-fived me, and then Caya and Crow ran in to see. They both looked a little pale.

Caya said, "Wow, Tomie! I've heard of witches doing that, but I never witnessed it until today."

She walked up to me and gave me a fist bump.

Lisette had me practicing all over the house for a while. I teleported outside twice, to the living room three more times, the basement, my room, the car, and the lake. She showed up right behind me at every location to see that all my experiences with it were positive. After each one, she took my pulse and blood pressure to make sure my vitals were okay and that I was in good shape.

"Okay, Tomie, I want you to pop over to the grocery store we shopped at last and buy a small item."

I closed my eyes and concentrated, finding myself there within seconds. After browsing the checkout display, I picked up five candy bars and paid the cashier. Then I went to a secluded place where I could hide and focus, so I could return to Lisette's. She told me that I had to always be discreet. I couldn't just appear or disappear in front of someone—I needed to be out of sight.

Seconds later, when I showed up in the living room, I had the candy bars in my hand, and I tossed them over, keeping two for myself.

"Outstanding, Tomie!" Lisette shouted, clapping her

hands. "Do you know how long it usually takes to master teleportation?"

"No, how long?"

Sitting down next to Caya, I ripped open the wrapper.

"About a year. Sometimes longer."

"I guess I'm one of your prodigies."

I winked and munched on the candy bar.

"You definitely are."

"Lisette, how long did it take you to learn it?"

"Oh, I think, maybe three or four months."

"Well, there you go. You were a fast learner, too. So, will I be able to teleport living objects, like another human?"

"Yep."

"When can we work on that?"

"Soon, but not now. You've accomplished quite a bit today. Now, I want you and Caya to continue the fire spell and then work on this one," she said, pointing at a page in a small book.

Before Caya and I started to practice, she told me she wanted to talk to Lisette and Crow, and I nodded.

As they walked into the kitchen, I read the freezing spell in the book, and then I went down to the basement and gathered a few materials that we needed. When I started to head up the stairs, I heard banging, and I knew Opal was at it again. I almost didn't walk over to hear her nonsense, but my curiosity won over good judgment.

After I peered into the enclosure, she glared at me as if she had daggers hidden behind her back, ready and waiting to swing them at me. It was difficult to comprehend what she was trying to tell me because of her rapid speech. I told her to slow down, but she wouldn't, so I turned around. She banged even harder and began to use her fingernails to etch something into the glass.

Tapping my foot, I waited for her to finish. She must have cut herself somehow, because blood ran down over the crooked etched letters, but I was still able to make out what it read:

*Soon...*

"What? You're locked inside there. Your powers have been stripped."

She pointed out each letter, backed away, and sat down, flashing an eerie smile that made me shiver. I shot up the stairs, and then I closed the basement door, locked it, and threw the rug on it with a glance of my eyes.

My heart pounded, as I silently repeated what I told Opal. Even though she had no powers, I knew her grandmom had it in for me, and her lies were already spilling over into Frost with Mr. Fox and Sari's dad. I figured she must have found a way to communicate with her, but how? Even if she had, she couldn't break Lisette's containment spell.

At least, that was what I was hoping for.

Lisette was still at the table with Caya and Crow, so I went back into the living room to practice, but I couldn't focus. Opal's etched word and everything related to her kept running through my mind, so I turned on the TV and flipped through most of the channels.

Remembering my mom's spell book stored inside me, I scanned through it and came across directions on how to communicate with someone by using telepathy.

I shared my immediate thoughts with Lisette, and it worked.

*Tomie, you can communicate telepathically?*
*We really need to talk as soon as possible.*

Within a few minutes, she walked into the living room and sat on the couch next to me.

"Wow. I was going to have you practice that technique,

but there's no need now. You got it."

"Where're Caya and Crow?"

"I told them we needed to talk in private. We're going to meet up with them later tonight for dinner."

"Okay. I'm sorry. I know that Caya was sharing some important stuff with you both."

"We were pretty much done before you tapped into my mind."

"Is Caya okay?"

"She will be. She and Crow are going to talk more and work out a plan for her to repay the money. I gave her the number to an adolescent therapist in town that deals with *supra* teen issues, including dating violence."

"Whoa! You just never know when someone is in a really bad situation. I'm glad she talked to y'all."

"You inspired her, Tomie," she said, as she patted me on my right shoulder.

"Really?"

"Yeah. It's hard when you lose yourself because of someone chipping away at you day-in and day-out. Eventually, your self-confidence diminishes, and you're game for anything. I mean, *anything*."

"I hope she makes an appointment with the therapist."

"I'm pretty sure she will. She has a bit of healing to do."

"Lisette, did you know about her being off and on with Garth and how he treats her?"

"I've always known. I've tried to talk to her more than once, but she wasn't ready to hear what I had to say. You helped her. I'm not sure if you understand how much you've done for her in such a short period of time."

"I didn't think much about it. I just sensed that she was troubled. She deserves so much better than Garth."

"I agree. I hope she'll eventually realize that. I think

she's starting to, especially by taking the big step of sharing what she did with you and reaching out for help."

"Yeah, I'm proud of her."

"Me, too. You're a good friend for her. I'm so proud of *you*. Your dad has raised you well."

"Thank you. Ya know, he'll be here tomorrow."

"That's right. I've been so busy. What does your dad like to eat? I want to cook something he'll enjoy."

"Pretty much anything, but he loves beef lasagna and cherry pie."

"That's easy. I think I have all the ingredients on hand. I might make the pie early tomorrow morning. Now, before we discuss anything else, tell me more about Opal's message."

"It's better if I show you."

"Okay, let's go," Lisette whispered.

# CHAPTER
## THIRTY-FOUR

**W**hen we got down to the basement, Opal remained in her sitting position, with her legs crossed and her arms hugging her chest. I walked over to her glass house and searched for her creepy etching, but it had vanished. I turned the glass dome around. Nothing.

She fell to her side and stomped her feet on her floor, as Lisette came up and stood beside me.

"I swear, she wrote a message right here."

As I ran my left index finger across the rounded glass, she stuck her tongue out like a spoiled five-year-old kid and turned her entire body around, so she faced away from us.

"I believe you. Either she erased it, or someone else did it for her. I bet you can guess who that could've been."

Opal's head tilted to one side, and I knew she could hear everything we were saying. Lisette tapped on the glass a few times with two fingers. Opal didn't move, so Lisette did it again and still got no response from her. Then she waved her hand, and Opal's little house rose and floated in front of us, bobbing up and down. Opal stood and walked closer to us, bracing herself against the glass.

"Opal, listen up. You sent a message to Tomie?" She gave a sinister smile along with her creepy glare. "Now, you can cooperate, or not. If you don't, you and your house may shatter into itsy bitsy pieces on the floor. Don't think you'll survive such a fall."

When Lisette rotated her finger in a circle, Opal's enclosure spun around several times, rising higher in the air and then back to our eye level.

"I'm going to ask you one more time." Opal immediately nodded. "Good. What's your grandmother up to?" She shrugged her shoulders and sat back down with her legs crossed. "Remember what I told you about crashing?"

Opal's eyes grew wide, and she started writing another message.

*Danger coming 4 u 2*

"Are you referring to your grandmother?"

Opal nodded and then scratched something else under her previous message:

*5*

As Lisette continued to interrogate her, I thought about what she was attempting to say.

"*Five*? What do you mean by *five*?" I asked.

Opal rolled her eyes and laughed, and then the etching began again.

*Soon 5 will come…*

A few seconds later, it all disappeared, and Lisette looked over at me. She telepathically told me that we would continue the conversation in private, away from Opal's spying ears.

Her house floated back to its original spot, and she stood and started banging on the glass with her fists.

Lisette and I headed up the stairs, and I looked back and saw Opal pointing her finger at me. I closed the door, locked it, and placed the rug back just by staring at it.

Lisette walked into the kitchen, and I followed. She paced the floor a few times before she leaned on the counter, while I waited. After our encounter with Opal, I was sure she had something heavy to say.

"Tomie, I really believe that Verlinda, Opal's grandmother, is planning something awful for you, me, and whoever else gets in her way."

"What do you think she'll do and when?"

"That's just it. I don't know, and I have no idea who the five are that Opal was referring to. I'm just so glad you decided to spend this summer with me to train, so you'll be prepared. Not just for what's coming soon, but also for what may happen later."

"You think others might try to attack me after Opal's grandmom and the so-called five?"

"Maybe."

"Why me? What did I do to become such a target?"

"Tomie, it's not you. You haven't done anything wrong. You have a beautiful heart, but you'll stand your ground when tested. The feud between the Dawn Coven and Laveau Coven has been going on for a long time. Verlinda Dawn is full of dark twisted magic and feeds off revenge, chaos, and pain. She craves destruction and will do just about anything. You can say that she replanted seeds of animosity within both covens, when peace was finally being restored after many years of division."

"What started the feud?"

"There was a time when their coven was considered equal to ours and others that strived to practice good magic and concealed powers from mortals."

I ran my fingers through my hair.

"I have an idea where you're going with this."

"You may be surprised."

"Please, go ahead."

"My grandmother shared this story with me when I was young, Tomie. She told me that when Verlinda was sixteen years old, she put a spell on Tatiana Laveau, the head of our coven back then, which caused her to fall extremely ill, to the point that she became bedridden."

"That's low, but I'm not surprised."

Lisette nodded and continued. "Verlinda swooped in to 'take care of' Tatiana, but she was secretly using poisoning spells on her in the drinks and foods she consumed. Her primary focus was to place a love spell on Sebastian Jackson, Tatiana's handsome fiancé, who belonged to the Jackson Coven, the highest of all for warlocks."

"Did Tatiana die, and Verlinda ended up with that Sebastian dude?"

"Not quite."

Lisette paused for a minute and went to the kitchen to get a bottle of cold water from the fridge. She slowly unscrewed the top with her magic and then tilted it back to take a few swigs.

"Come on, are you going to make me beg? What happened next?"

"You really want to know?" she said with a smile.

"Of course, I do. Tell me."

She set the bottle next to her and said, "Tatiana used the little energy she had left to perform a reflection spell, which allowed her to see what Verlinda had been doing to her and why. Tatiana stopped drinking or eating anything that Verlinda had prepared."

"What about the love spell on Sebastian?"

"When Tatiana became stronger, she broke it, and he

didn't recall the days leading up to her breaking the spell."

"What happened to Verlinda?"

"She was banished from the Laveau compound forever."

"So, Tatiana and Sebastian got married and lived happily ever after, then?"

"Yes, and Tatiana sent a message to the head witch of the Dawn Coven. They sent word back to let her know that they also planned to exile Verlinda and didn't want to have anything to do with her."

"Wow, they were serious about kicking her out. Did Verlinda find out?"

"Yes, she overheard some of the Laveau witches whispering about the Dawn Coven's plans the morning before she was escorted from Laveau compound. Verlinda was furious, seething with vengeance. The night of her return to her coven to gather her personal belongings, she did something unspeakable."

"What'd she do?"

"She killed all her sisters that night," Lisette said in a low tone.

"Wow, what a straight-up twisted savage! I'm sure they sensed that she was crazy mad at them, so why would they trust her in any way?"

"They didn't. She secretly poisoned all thirteen, one by one, with what they craved the most."

"What do you mean?"

"Two of them loved to read before they fell asleep, so she used the pages of their favorite books to do away with them. One sister loved sitting on the porch, breathing in the fresh air."

"She poisoned the air?"

"Yeah. She used the deadly spell, which of course, is forbidden, especially on members of your own coven."

"What kind of spell is that?"

"Really dark magic that calls for three drops of venom from each of: a black widow, a rattlesnake, and a box jellyfish, along with two tablespoons of fresh ground-up corpse flesh."

"Oh, that's nasty. Did Tatiana find out what she had done?"

"Yes. She demanded that Verlinda's powers be stripped from her, but the *Upper Witch Counsel* disagreed and decided to place a hit on her by leaking her contact information to a Dupuy Silver Slayer."

"I take it, he or she was unsuccessful, because she's still alive, although older now."

"You're right, Tomie. She completed a transformation-switch spell, which allowed her to change into someone else's body and turned that stranger into her. She was undetected by the slayer, who murdered the wrong Verlinda many years ago."

"She's pretty powerful, isn't she?"

My hands began to quiver, and my feet began to tap.

"Yes, she is."

"I have a lot to be worried about, don't I, Lisette?"

"I believe that she's become much eviler than before. That's why I've been training you."

"Can a Light Witch defeat a Dark Witch?"

Lisette remained silent for a few seconds before responding.

"With the right training and support, yes."

"Would a Dark Witch have more power over darkness?"

"Tomie, what are you asking me, exactly?"

"Should I choose Dark over Light? We know Verlinda isn't going to play fair, so why should I?"

"Tomie, there are risks when you cross into that realm. You might not ever return. I've been there, and I promise you, that's not what you want."

"That's a risk I'm willing to take to protect my dad, Sari, you, Crow, and whoever else she goes after."

"You really need to think this through," Lisette pleaded, staring into my eyes while hers glowed.

"Look, I know what I need to do."

"Tomie, talk to your dad about all of this before you make any final decisions."

"Hey, enough about this."

"To be continued… dark and light magic discussion. Let me feed Sabra, walk her, and freshen up. How about we leave in the next hour to meet up with Crow and Caya in town?"

"Sounds good. Hey, Lisette, are you still associated with the Laveau Coven?"

"I thought we were done with magic stuff for tonight."

"We are, but I'm curious."

"Yes, but indirectly."

"What does that mean, exactly?"

"I don't attend the quarterly or even the annual meetings like most, but I have a friend who keeps me in the loop."

"Cool. Should I join a coven?"

"That's completely up to you. However, you may form your own in time."

As I walked into my bedroom, I thought about that. After closing my door with a swipe of my hand, I levitated to a couple of feet above my mattress and lay there in the air with my arms folded behind my head. Staring up at my mobile on the ceiling, my mind reviewed everything Lisette told me. At that moment, I believed that dark magic was going to be my best weapon against Verlinda and whoever the five were.

Before I closed my eyes, I glanced to my right and saw Mr. Ray hovering right beside me.

# CHAPTER
## THIRTY-FIVE

"Crap!" I fell straight down to the mattress. "Mr. Ray, please give me a warning before you just pop out of nowhere."

"Oh, yeah, sure. Sorry I scared you." He floated down until he stood on the floor, and then he grabbed a chair from the desk and slid it over next to the bed. "Now, what's all this I'm hearing about you considering testing the dark waters out?"

"Who told you?"

"Really, Tomie? I always know what's going on with you. Most of your thoughts, especially the ones you're most emotional about, automatically pop into my mind. Plus, Lisette texted me," he said, waving his phone at me, and we laughed at that. "Seriously... going down that path wouldn't guarantee that the darkness would be defeated."

"Okay, tell me how I'm supposed to beat someone like Verlinda Dawn, then."

He placed his hand over my chest and tapped it three times.

"The light inside your heart will beat her and anyone

else. You don't know who you *truly* are, still?"

"I don't think so."

"Close your eyes. I want to show you something."

When I shut them, he laid his hands over them, and swirls of blue and green sparkling light danced in front of me. Those patterns soon vanished, and a beaming light shone in a spray towards me. I was standing waist-deep in the middle of a lake, but when I reached down to touch the water surrounding me, my hands and legs didn't feel wet.

Another light appeared in the form of a floating silhouette of a woman. When the figure reached out to touch my face with her glowing hands, I retreated a little, but she didn't.

"Mom?"

"Yes, Tomie. It's me."

"How can I interact with you like this?"

"Your *Mega* can create special portals to allow communication when necessary."

"You look different from when I first saw you."

"Yes, there can always be some type of alteration to my appearance. Anyway, that's not important right now."

"I have a good idea why Mr. Ray contacted you."

"Tomie, I just want to tell you a few things."

"You're going to try to convince me to steer far, far away from dark magic, right?"

"No."

"Really?"

She touched my face and said, "You're free to choose either path you desire, but remember that consequences, whether good or bad, always follow."

"I know."

"Also, keep in mind that darkness isn't necessary to conquer an enemy, as Mr. Ray told you."

"I find that hard to believe."

"Why?" she asked, as she floated higher above me.

"It's stronger, Mom."

Coming back down to my level, she said, "No, it's not. The one who possesses the magic determines its power."

"So, you're telling me I can be just as powerful as a Dark Witch?"

"Even more so because of what lives inside you."

"What're you talking about? Please, just be straightforward, without any riddles."

"Love, compassion, truth, loyalty, justice, and resilience."

"How can those things help me defeat someone who's evil, deceitful, twisted, and incredibly strong?"

"Simple. You combine any of those elements with the magic you possess, and you can conquer anything or anyone who's trying to cause you harm."

"What if I fail?"

My eyes began to fill with tears, and she touched my face with both of her weightless glowing hands.

"Tomie, I'm always with you. All of what I know, you know, too. If, for some reason, you stumble or forget because of what you may be facing, then I'll help you. Plus, you have a great team already—Mr. Ray, Lisette, Crow, Caya, and probably a few others you'll soon come to realize."

There was so much I wanted to ask—not just about the craft. Her image started to dim.

"Tomie, you can open your eyes now."

Someone repeated those words three or four more times before I responded, and when I looked up, there was Mr. Ray.

"Thank you."

"For what?"

"Allowing me to spend some more time with my mom."

"Whenever you need to connect with her, just let me know."

"Appreciate that, Mr. Ray."

"No problem."

"I thought my visits with her were limited."

"They are when you use limited magic, but there are no restrictions for a *Mega*." He winked. "I want you to think about everything, okay?" I nodded. "I'm only here to protect and warn you—not to make decisions for you." He stood up and started walking out of my room. "Enjoy your time with your dad tomorrow."

"Thank you, Mr. Ray. I want to talk to you about Opal and what she's been up to."

"I already know. I've been trying to listen to conversations between Verlinda Dawn and Mr. Fox, but somehow, she figured out that someone listened in on that first talk they had before I drove you here. Since then, she's placed a special blocking spell on all of her communications."

"Think Lisette and I can break it?"

"Not sure. I'm working on some things, but we'll talk more about that later. Just continue to focus on your training, okay? By the way, how are you and Sari?"

"That's another story for another time."

He smiled and said, "Okay. Everything will work out as it should."

As he walked out, I continued to think about what Mom had told me.

# CHAPTER
## THIRTY-SIX

**W**hen I found Lisette outside, I asked, "Did Mr. Ray give you an update on our talk?"

"He did. Was the portal visit helpful for you?"

"Yeah, it was. He keeps surprising me with all his tricks."

She smiled and said, "I'm sure he'll continue."

"I'm looking forward to it."

"Ready to meet up with Crow and Caya in town?"

"Sure. Let me grab my phone and slip on my shoes, and I'll be ready."

"Tomie, I was meaning to ask, are you and Sari okay?"

"There's a lot going on with her dad."

"Well, just know if you want to talk about anything, I'm here."

"I know, thanks."

As we walked out the door, Sabra was dozing off in her bed.

Lisette drove downtown to *Lafayette's Crab House*, which was located on the lake. The sun was about to set, so we decided to sit outside. We ordered the unlimited buckets of snow crab legs, sausage, and corn on the cob, along with a large bowl of gumbo for each.

The crabmeat was buttery and sweet and practically melted in my mouth. I probably ate about three bucketsful, and Crow ate twice that many. Double chocolate pecan pie topped it all off.

Before we completed our desserts, a few airboats sped by, and Crow waved at them. I wondered, as I was finishing up my last few bites, if he knew Caya took his out the night before.

She smiled and laughed, and I heard her phone beep a few times from texts. She glanced down at it, but then she looked away and continued her conversation. There was no need for me to check mine, but I did anyway. I was afraid I might've accidentally set it to *silent*, but the volume was all the way up.

Crow and Lisette walked towards the car ahead of us.

"Caya, stop by tomorrow to meet my dad."

She hesitated a bit before she said, "You need to enjoy your dad's company without me around."

"You won't be intruding. Hey, if you stop by, great. No pressure. Cool?"

She nodded.

Lisette was already in the driver's seat, and Crow was leaned over inside, gazing into her eyes. He touched Lisette's face with his oversized hand and kissed her on her forehead.

He then walked over to me, bent down, and whispered, "I know you still have some things you want to ask me about."

"Yeah, I do."

"Oh, thanks for being a friend to Caya."

"No problem."

We fist bumped, and I walked around to the other side

and slid into the seat. Caya and Crow stood together, and we all waved. Lisette beeped the horn, and then we pulled out of the parking spot and headed to her house.

The top of my right hand was throbbing, so I looked down and saw that it was cherry red. After a few minutes, it appeared to be back to normal.

When we got home, I checked on Sabra, and she was still knocked out.

"Really enjoyed hanging out with you, Crow, and Caya tonight. Thank you."

"You're welcome. Anytime, Tomie. We should do that more. Maybe when you have a school break, we'll drive up for the weekend."

"Sounds good. I would really like that. Night, Lisette."

"Good night, Tomie."

After my shower and brushing my teeth, I pulled the covers back and jumped into bed.

Rewinding time in my mind, I thought about the second encounter with my mom and what she was explaining to me. It has to sound pretty weird, but even though I know she wasn't physically with me, and could never hang out with me in public, being with her like that made her more real to me… as if she was alive, in a sense. At least, that was how it seemed to me. It made me feel warm and peaceful.

When I checked my phone, I saw that I had no missed unknown calls, so I laid it down. Picking my book up from the nightstand, I read about ten pages before I became drowsy, so I stopped and returned it to its original spot, as my mind drifted back to my mom and Sari. My eyes felt heavier and heavier… until I drifted off to sleep.

# CHAPTER
## THIRTY-SEVEN

The aroma of fresh cherries, sugar, lemon, and cinnamon woke me up at about 7:45. When I looked at my phone, I noticed a text from Dad.

D: **Good morning son. I'm about four hours out. See you sometime after lunch. Tell Lisette hello for me. Love you.**

T: **Hey Dad. Be careful. See you soon. Luv U 2.**

Before I got through stretching out both my arms and legs, I heard my phone beep. When I saw that it was from an unknown number, I jumped up, hoping it was my girl.

S: **Hey you. It's me. Did I wake you?**

T: **No. If you did it wouldn't matter. What's up?**

S: **Thinking of you, talking to you.**

T: **Friend's phone?**

S: **Yes. Dad won't let me have mine back yet.**

T: **Because of me?**

S: **Doesn't matter. I'm not going to stop**

seeing you.

T: Sari I don't want to make your life hard.

S: You won't.

T: I love you so much that if we needed to take a break I would.

S: I don't want a freakin' break!!!

T: Just thinking of what you're going through with your dad.

S: Instead think of us. Let me handle him. Got it?

T: Yeah. What you doing today?

S: Just working.

T: Liking your new job?

S: It's okay. Anything's better than *Pizza Beat* and the dark memories there.

T: Any cool coworkers?

S: Hmm. Well there's this one guy. He's from up north. Connecticut I think. He's silly, always joking around. Just moved here about a month ago. His name is Phoenixx Night.

T: Cool name.

S: I guess.

T: So you and this Phoenixx guy hanging out after work?

S: Not much. A group of us went to a movie last Saturday night.

T: Hmm.

S: Tomie Dupuy, are you jealous?

T: Of course not.

S: Yes you are.

In my mind, I could hear her giggling.

T: No. Okay maybe. Be honest. Is he a Zac

**Efron, Bruno Mars, or Ian Somerhalder?**

She paused for a few minutes before responding to my text.

S: **Tough question but an amazing lineup. He's sort of a combo of them with a dash of the younger Bobby Brown's attitude and swag, but nothing close to you. Since you're a Bobby B fan you two may hit it off. He knows I have a boyfriend. I talk about you all the time.**

T: **You do?**

S: **Yes. Don't be acting all surprised either.**

I felt a huge grin cover my face.

T: **Look forward to meeting him**.

S: **I bet. He'll be a senior at Frost High. I'll introduce you.**

T: **Okay.**

S: **Oh I found your love poem and I adore it Tomie Dupuy. I read it at least 10 times a day and keep it with me all the time. Thank you.**

T: **You really like it?**

S: **Yes! Hey when's that carnival thing?**

T: **It starts on July 27ᵗʰ and runs through the 30ᵗʰ.**

S: **K. I'll see you then.**

T: **How with your dad?**

S: **I'll work it out. Listen I got to go. I'll see you soon. Bye for now. Love you.**

T: **Love you too.**

She sent red, green, and purple hearts. I followed with red hearts and a GIF of *Black Panther* and *Storm* holding hands.

# CHAPTER
## THIRTY-EIGHT

**M**y morning had a good start. After getting up, I dressed in some jeans, an Astros t-shirt, and tennis shoes. I brushed my teeth and then squeezed some moisturizer into my hands, massaged it into my scalp and hair, and picked it out. Then I sprayed *Curve c*ologne all over my chest.

Once I stripped the bed, I tossed the sheets into the hamper, took a clean set out of the hallway closet, and made it up. I checked the other room and saw that it was all ready to go, so I went back and grabbed my leather bracelet from the dresser and snapped it onto my right wrist. After placing my phone in my back pocket, I picked up the hamper and carried it to the laundry room.

I loaded the large-capacity washer and added liquid detergent before pouring fabric softener into the designated slot. Touching the express setting, I started the cycle. After picking up the empty hamper, I returned it to the bathroom.

When I walked into the kitchen, Lisette was sitting at the table with the newspaper, sipping coffee from her extra-large *Wonder Woman* mug.

"Good morning," she said, as she set them down.

"Lisette, good morning. Something smells great."

"Cherry pie is baking in the oven. There's an omelet and wheat toast in the microwave for you. Just need to warm it up."

Sabra walked over to me and stretched out her paws on my leg. Reaching down, I petted her head and scratched behind her ears. She slid down and went to her bed, and I washed my hands and dried them off.

"Lisette, I just want you to know how much I appreciate everything you're doing for me, especially the training."

"Tomie, I know we're first cousins, but I see you more as my younger brother. I love you, and I'd do anything for you."

"Love you, too, Lisette, and I feel the same."

I walked over to the microwave, pressed the timer for forty-five seconds, and hit the *start* button. When it beeped, I took out the plate and sat down with my breakfast. The omelet had a spicy kick, provided by jalapenos and cayenne. The red peppers, onions, turkey, Colby cheese, and mushrooms were all tasty.

"This is really good, thanks."

My lips were tingling, so I drank a full bottle of water.

"Welcome. Glad you like it. Heard from your dad yet?"

"Yeah. He should be here around lunchtime."

She smiled and said, "Good. The beef lasagna is baking. I'll toast the garlic bread when he arrives. Salads and a tall pitcher of strawberry lemonade are chilling in the fridge."

"Man! What time did you start cooking this morning?"

"I woke up around 5:00 and got busy shortly after."

"Everything smells so delicious."

"I want him to enjoy himself and have a good visit with you."

"Oh, he will."

After washing my dishes and the others in the sink and on the countertops, I placed my clothes in the dryer and pressed *start*, then returned to Lisette.

I updated her about Sari and me.

She said, "Tomie, no matter what, there're always going to be either mortals or immortals who'll try to make your life difficult. Hold firm to your feelings and beliefs always."

"Will do."

When Lisette removed the cherry pie from the oven, the crust was puffy and golden brown. She sliced a half stick of butter, dropped it into a glass bowl, and popped it into the microwave. After she took it out, she dipped a brush into it and swept the butter across the crust as if she was painting a portrait. She placed it on a baker's rack, and the aroma from the pie filled the room. I set the table with square plates, utensils, and blue glasses.

The dryer's buzzer went off, so I pulled my things out and folded them. After I put them away, I returned to the kitchen and noticed that it was just after 12:30. Dad was going to be knocking on the door soon.

Lisette's landline rang, and she picked it up. It was Crow, so she took the cordless outside, with Sabra following on her heels. When she came back in, I heard a vehicle out front.

Opening the door with a swipe of my hand, I saw that it was Dad. He parked his truck a few feet from the house, and I walked down to meet him.

We hugged for a few seconds, as he said, "So good to see you, son."

"Good to see you, too, Dad."

"I think you've grown some."

I smiled, as he patted me on my shoulder. After he pulled his backpack out of the truck's cab, he shut the door and locked it. Taking his bag, I went inside, and he followed.

# CHAPTER
## THIRTY-NINE

Lisette came around the corner and greeted Dad. "I want you to know how much I appreciate everything you're doing for my son. Thank you."

"You're welcome, and I really enjoy working with Tomie. He's a quick study," she said, as she winked at me.

Dad pulled out an envelope from his shirt pocket, which I assumed had money inside, and handed it to Lisette, but she declined it by shaking her head. He tried again, and she pushed it away.

"If you don't take it now, then I'll figure out a way to convince you to take it later."

She grinned and said, "You don't have to pay for anything. I'm doing this, because I want to see Tomie well-prepared for anything he may encounter today, tomorrow, or a year from now… or beyond. He means a lot to me."

She came over to me and patted me on the back of my shoulder.

My dad bowed his head and sighed, "Thank you, Lisette."

"Come on and get comfortable. Tomie will show you where everything is."

I walked Dad to his bedroom, pointing out the bathroom on our way. He placed his backpack on the twin-sized bed.

"Son, I've been on the road for over twelve hours, so I'm going to take a shower."

"Okay. Everything you'll need is in there."

"All right."

Dad later joined us in the living room, and Lisette and I told him about everything she had been teaching me. His eyes widened a few times.

When we ventured into the kitchen, Dad asked, "How's Mr. Ray?"

I gave him the short version, saving the encounters with my mom to share with him when we had some private time together.

Once we ate the well-seasoned food, Lisette grabbed the pie from the baker's rack and carried it to the table. She placed it in front of us with a knife and a server utensil.

"Lisette, would you like for me to slice a piece for you?" Dad asked.

"Sure. . . and thank you."

Dad handed hers to her in a saucer and followed with ours.

"I almost forgot. Anyone want vanilla ice cream?"

"I'm good."

Dad said, "No, thank you."

The buttery piecrust, with a dash of lemon zest seeping out with each bite, practically melted on my tongue. The sweet cherries felt like little bombs popping inside my mouth.

"I take it, Opal is in a secure location?"

He placed a bite of pie in his mouth and chewed

slowly, as Lisette nodded.

"Yes, she is."

"What about Verlinda, her grandmother? Has she tried to cause any more trouble?"

"Not yet," Lisette said.

She and I looked at each other at the same time.

*How much should I let Dad know about?* I asked her telepathically.

*This can be a tricky one, because if you divulge too much, it can cause him to worry, but if you do the opposite…*

*Yeah, I know. Best to keep it simple and short.*

"We think that she's planning something because of a message Opal shared," I said.

Dad placed his fork down and glared back and forth, from her eyes to mine.

"Okay, you two, fess up. What did she say?"

"She wrote something about five coming for us soon," I replied.

"Like five enemies?"

"Probably, Mr. Dupuy."

"You have an idea who she was referring to?"

"Yes," she whispered.

"Tomie, do you feel ready to take on what may come your way?"

"I believe I am. Lisette's been teaching me some cool stuff."

"Lisette, what do you think?"

"He's excelling, but there's more I can teach him. If Verlinda threw something our way today, Mr. Ray and I are here to help him."

Dad took a deep breath and exhaled and then wiped his eyes with both of his hands.

"I'm just so glad he's here with you, Lisette."

"Wow, I never thought I'd hear you say that," she said with a delayed sigh.

She stood up and started clearing the table.

Dad said, "Lisette, we got this. Go do whatever you need to do."

"Oh, no. You're company, and you and Tomie need to catch up."

"Dad, finish your pie, and I'll help Lisette."

"No, Tomie, go!" Lisette demanded.

"It'll just take a few minutes," I said.

He picked his fork up from the side of his plate and ate the last couple of bites, and then I took it and put it into the sink. After Lisette and I were through in the kitchen, Dad and I then continued our conversation in the living room.

"I'm really learning a lot from Lisette."

"Bet you are, son. I've been protecting you for a long time."

"Why?"

"Keeping you safe has always been my top priority, but once I knew about your transformation, I realized that I could no longer protect you by hiding you from reality. You needed proper guidance from someone who knew how to teach you these skills. I just wish your mom was here."

He sighed, and I placed my hand on his shoulder, as he looked at me.

"Dad, I've talked to Mom."

As tears formed in his eyes, he wiped his face with his left hand.

"Son, you actually saw her?"

"Yeah. She wanted me to tell you that she loves you."

More tears appeared, and he asked, "Do you think you'll see her again?"

"Yeah."

"Tell her that I miss her and think of her all the time. My heart has never been the same without her."

"I'm sure she feels it."

"If I had known her parents were planning to separate us and force her to give you up, I would've figured out a way to take you both out of the country."

"Dad, why did the Dupuy Silver Slayers start targeting witches?"

# CHAPTER

## FORTY

Raising his hands, he wiped his face and took in a few deep breaths, as Lisette stood in the foyer. I glanced at her, and she looked into my eyes, before she walked into her bedroom, and then I heard her door shut.

"Tomie, it started in the early 1900s. Believe it or not, there was a time when witches and mortals cohabitated in peace."

"What happened that changed it?"

"Rosalinda Laveau was the leading teacher in Monroe Creek at the local high school. Everyone praised her. Many were aware of the secret she attempted to conceal."

"Her last name didn't help, I guess."

"You're right. People knew the Marie Laveau stories, which was one reason Rosalinda pursued an unfamiliar career. She thought people would forget what she was. Some were kind and respected her, but others didn't."

"Like who?"

"The sheriff, Patrick Dupuy—he's the one who founded the Dupuy Silver Slayers a few years later. He recruited others like him who hated witches the way he did and blamed them for all the bad things that happened. He made it his purpose to portray all witches in an awful way."

"That wasn't cool."

"No. One night, his teen daughter snuck away from the house to meet up with Rosalinda's son who was about the same age."

"Oh. I see where this is going."

"You think?"

"Yeah. Mortal girl falls in love with immortal boy. Girl's dad catches them together and forbids them to see each other. Girl then runs away with boy. Dad becomes furious and blames boy's mom, which ignites his idea to build his hateful army to cause her and all other witches harm to prevent future problems."

"Not bad, son, but that's not why the Dupuys formed their army to annihilate witches." Lisette walked in and sat down across from me with a mug in her hand. "Do you want to finish the story?" he asked her.

She took a few sips and placed the mug down on the table in front of her, as my mind raced with one question: "How do you both know this story?"

Lisette said, "Rosalinda kept a secret diary. That's how I know."

Dad added, "My great-grandmother told me the story, but I later found out the truth when I befriended a witch."

"Mom?" He nodded. "Dad, why didn't you become a Dupuy Silver Slayer?"

"I didn't like what they stood for, especially after I found out the truth."

"You're referring to…?"

"Lies and hate," he whispered.

"I'm a little confused now. You used to not care for

Lisette because of what she is."

"Tomie, I never hated Lisette. I've just been so busy being angry with your mom's family, and I blamed Lisette indirectly for being a part of what they did, but I had to realize that it was never her fault. Your mom made her own choice—one that I wish she had never made."

"So do I."

My head lowered, and the three of us were silent for a few minutes.

"Lisette, please finish the story," I begged, as I looked into her teary eyes.

"You sure, Tomie?"

"Yeah, I want to know why the Dupuy Silver Slayers despise us witches and warlocks."

"Patrick Dupuy hated Rosalinda so much that he devised a way to make the whole town feel the same."

"How?"

"His daughter came home one day, disgusted about the history of the Salem Witch Trials that Rosalinda had lectured about, and she told her dad how she felt compassion for those who lost their lives."

"This is about to get really ugly, right?"

She looked down at her hands and continued.

"Patrick brought his concerns to the school committee and convinced them that Rosalinda's lesson was inappropriate and that it was a guised attempt to recruit new witches into her coven."

"They believed him?"

"Absolutely!" Lisette shouted.

"What happened to Rosalinda?"

"The inevitable. They fired her without any warning. The police escorted her out and threw her face down into a mud puddle."

"Wow, that was so wrong. What happened then?"

"A few days later, Patrick poured kerosene all over the grounds and set the entire school on fire. He figured the townspeople would have no problem believing it was Rosalinda who committed the senseless crime, because she was scorned and bitter after the committee's decision."

Lisette paused for a while, with tears streaming down her face, before she continued.

"Patrick didn't know that his daughter and Rosalinda's son had sneaked out that night to meet up and spend some time together, and they were trapped inside the basement of the school. The propped-up metal door had closed and locked. When he heard their screams, he tried to get to them and save them, but the flames had already consumed them."

"That's pretty messed up. Did Rosalinda leave town?"

"No. She stayed, because she had to bury her son, but she didn't make it to his funeral."

"Why?"

"Patrick and his followers went to her house one night and dragged her out."

"Why didn't she stop them, Lisette?"

"She could've, but she chose not to expose herself in front of them and the angry mob that followed them there. They all cursed her, spat on her, and chanted terrible things to her face. She was taken away and thrown into jail."

"Did she go to trial?"

"If that's what you want to call it, son. Dupuy and his followers met for a few hours one evening. They decided the best way to get rid of a witch was the old-fashioned one—burn her at the stake."

"What? No one did anything to help her? Why didn't she tell anyone?" I asked.

"No one would've believed her over the sheriff," Dad said.

"So, they killed her for no reason?"

"Yes."

"What happened to Sheriff Dupuy?"

Lisette said, "He continued to build his army and spread his hate by blaming witches for anything bad that happened. He claimed to make the towns safer by hunting them down and killing them. He educated himself about *supras* in general and ways to hurt them. Word began to spread about him, and many went into hiding for a long time without practicing any magic, because they never knew when one of the sheriff's men could be lurking around them. The covens coined their title, the Dupuy Silver Slayers."

"That's awful." Lisette and Dad nodded. "The power of a lie, plus hate, equals horrific end results on an entire group of people, just because they're different."

Dad said, "That's true, Tomie. That's why I hoped for so long that you wouldn't have to deal with any of this."

"Well, I guess it was inevitable. It's time for this to end."

"You're right," Dad said. "It's going to take a genuine truce on both sides, *supras* and slayers, and I have no idea if or how that could ever become reality."

"I agree with both of you," Lisette said.

We weren't in the early 1900s anymore, and things had changed to a degree, but the mentality still existed. I also knew that I had to be a part of the solution to restore some type of peace, but I couldn't accomplish it alone.

# CHAPTER
## FORTY-ONE

Dad and I went for a walk after that heavy story and talked about Sari, Caya, Crow, and my upcoming senior year. Although Mom wasn't physically there with Dad and me, I felt that she was.

When we returned to the house, Caya was sitting in the living room, and Sabra was on Lisette's lap.

"Dad, this is Caya."

Caya jumped up and held out her hand, and Dad shook it.

"Nice to meet you, Caya."

"Thank you, sir. You have a pretty amazing son."

"I guess I'll keep him, then," Dad said with a huge smile.

We all laughed.

Caya had a slice of pie and chatted with Dad for a bit, and then when she decided to leave, I stood up and walked her out.

"Thanks for stopping by."

"Sure, Tomie. Your dad is pretty cool."

"Thanks. He enjoyed visiting with you."

"Ya think so?"

"Yeah."

I opened her car door for her and took a few steps back. When she slid in, I shut it and squatted down to talk to her.

"So, how are things going with you?"

"Okay. I have an appointment tomorrow morning with the therapist."

"That's really great, Caya. I'm proud of you."

"Yeah, me, too," she said, staring into my eyes.

"Any problems with Garth?"

"No, why?"

"I noticed you glance at your phone a lot last night."

"He's been calling, but I haven't been answering."

"Just know that you're always in control."

She smiled and started the car by waving her hand over the ignition.

"See ya around. We'll work on some stuff."

I stood up and said, "Okay."

She drove off and honked her horn, as I waved and headed back to the house. Then Dad and I talked outside for a while.

"Tomie, you and Sari doing okay?"

"I guess, but her dad hates me."

"That's his loss. You know that, right?"

"Maybe. It just makes our relationship more difficult."

"I know. I've been in a similar situation. It can be hard, but don't give up, and remember that I'm here whenever you need to talk."

"Thanks, Dad. That means a lot to me."

"By the way, about Miss Caya… I think she's a little sweet on you, son," he said with a grin.

"I don't think so. She's getting over a bad relationship. She knows Sari is my girl and that I'm committed to her."

"Just saying, what I saw earlier."

"What did you see?"

"I noticed the way she looked at you and the little things she said about you."

"Anyway…"

"Pay attention, son. Believe me."

He winked twice.

"Whatever, Dad," I said with a chuckle. "Let's go back inside. You need to get some rest."

The next morning, we had breakfast together, and then Crow stopped in to meet Dad. He convinced him to go on an airboat tour, so that was how the four of us spent the first part of our day. Dad became teary-eyed a couple of times, and I figured it was because it reminded him of Mom in some way.

Dad took a nap when we returned to Lisette's. He was leaving to go home for a few days, and then he'd be back on the road. He was going to be traveling to Tennessee and Virginia, new routes for him, the next week.

When he got up, he packed his things. Lisette made a sandwich for him, and they talked for a little while. He hugged her, and when he let her go, she stumbled back with a thunderstruck look that I didn't understand.

"Thank you again, Lisette, for everything you've done and continue to do for Tomie. You have no idea how much your dedication to him means to me." His voice cracked, as tears streamed down his face.

After a short pause, Lisette said, "No problem. Glad I can be here for him."

I walked out with him. He opened the door to his truck and threw his things onto the passenger seat, and then he pulled me into a tight hug.

"I'm proud of you, Tomie. You, continue to soak up everything Lisette has to teach you."

"Of course."

"See you in a few weeks. Tell Sari *hello* for me, and remember what we discussed."

"Sure will. Thanks for the talk, Dad. Be safe and text me soon."

He nodded, turned around, climbed inside, and shut his door.

Leaning towards the window, he said, "By the way, I left the envelope on the bed for Lisette. She'll find it soon enough. Love you, son."

"Dad, I love you, too."

He started the truck and drove off, as we waved to each other. When I walked back into the house, Lisette was sitting on the couch.

I sat next to her and asked, "You okay?"

She was silent for about thirty seconds before she responded to me.

"That's the first time your dad has ever hugged me in all these years."

"Really?"

"Yeah."

"He knows how important you are to me, and he appreciates everything you're doing for me."

"Yeah, I guess you're right, Tomie. I'm glad y'all spent time together and had a chance to talk."

"Me, too."

Later that night, Lisette went over some spells with me, and I pulled from what I had inside me from my mom's book. We stayed up late, and I tried out some for her to critique.

The next morning, when I got up and went into the kitchen, Lisette said, "We went over a lot last night, didn't we?"

Massaging the back of my head with both of my

hands, I said, "Yeah, we did."

"No practice in the next day or so. Just relax and do whatever you want. I'm going to run a few errands. I should be back in a couple of hours."

"Okay. I guess I'll just hang around."

"Sounds good. We're making great progress, ahead of schedule. Oh, and Crow's out back, working on something for me."

"Okay, I'll go and say *hi*."

Sabra popped her head up and looked at me, so I scooped her into my hand, placed her on my shoulder, and walked outside.

Crow was digging a hole to plant a tree. That was when I realized why Lisette left, and it didn't have much to do with errands. She wanted me to have some downtime with Crow. I had some things I wanted to talk to him about, since I had been reading the chapter from my book about rougarous.

When I crossed the yard, Sabra curled herself around my neck, which felt like a light wool scarf with tiny claws. When I started sweating, I unwrapped her and put her on the ground, so she could run around. Though I figured she knew how far out she was allowed to go, I kept my eye on her.

"Good-looking tree there."

"Thanks, Tomie. Did you have a good visit with your dad?"

"Yeah, it was. Thanks for taking him on the tour."

"No problem. I hope he enjoyed it."

"He did. Need any help?"

"Nah, I got it, but thanks."

As I watched, Crow continued to dig and size up the hole he was going to plant the tree in. After a few more minutes, he pulled a yellow handkerchief out of his back pocket, wiped his sweaty forehead, and drank some water. He then walked over to the tree, which appeared to weigh over 200 pounds, picked it up with one hand, and lowered it into its new home.

My mouth shot open once I realized how ludicrous it was that I asked him if he needed any help.

"Hey, close your mouth, before one of those skeeters flies in." He chuckled, as he began to fill the hole. When he was finished, he asked, "Would you mind turning the faucet on for me?"

I took a few steps backwards and did as he asked. He picked up the hose and watered the area all around the tree, as Sabra hopped along in the grass, chasing a blue butterfly. I whistled to call her in, and she ran towards me. Crow dropped the hose, walked over, and turned the faucet off.

"Let's go inside and talk," he said.

"Okay."

I picked Sabra up, and we went back into the house. When I placed her on the floor, she went for her water bowl first and then crawled into her bed.

"Back in a bit," Crow said, as he headed towards the bathroom.

"Okay."

As I sat at the table, waiting, with my left foot tapping, I wondered what to ask him first. When he returned, he pulled a chair out and sat down in front of me.

He folded his hands together and said, "Go ahead."

"What do you mean?"

"You wanted to pick my brain the first time you met me, but you didn't."

"Yeah, that's true."

"Okay, go for it."

"The stories about rougarous, or Louisiana

werewolves, wandering the swamps at night are true, not myths?"

"You know what they say about myths."

"No, what?"

"On some level, they're all based on truth."

"I never heard of them until now."

"Fair enough."

"You prefer to be called rougarou or werewolf?"

"Rougarou," Crow said, howling afterwards.

"Okay. You're full-blooded, but Caya is a hybrid of a rougarou and a witch, right?"

"You got it. My parents are both full-blooded rougarous."

"Crow, are your senses heightened during the full moon?"

"They are… you've been talking to Caya about this, huh?"

I nodded and said, "You know that I've seen a rougarou transform."

"Yes, I know you have."

"Do you have packs?"

"Some do, and others don't. I don't, because I'm a Supreme Alpha."

"What's that?"

"There's a hierarchy that exists in my world, and my bloodline is at the top. We don't require a pack to keep us safe. We're the ones who protect the others."

My eyes grew wider, as I said, "Wow, that's awesome! So, Garth belongs to one, because he's at the bottom of the chain?"

"Yeah, you pick up on things fast."

"Thanks. So, is Garth the leader?"

"No, he wants to be, but his brother is the oldest, so he is."

"You mean Ash?"

"Yes, you've met him?"

"No, Lisette told me about him."

"He's wild, full of chaos, and extremely territorial. Let me know if he ever tries to give you a hard time."

"Okay."

"Tomie, I'm serious. He's sneakier than Garth, so if you ever run into him, don't let your guard down."

"All right. Crow, is Caya part of a pack?"

"No, she's not, but I keep a close eye on her."

"Um, do you know how Garth treats her and that he's the one who put her up to taking that money from your safe? I know she already confessed that to you."

"I had a feeling about him, but I'm thinking she used some kind of spell to prevent me from picking up on certain things."

"Yeah, probably a concealing spell."

"It didn't surprise me when she told me she took the money for him."

After a short pause, I asked, "Crow, how often do you shift?"

"Depends. There're times I like to roam the swamps in full rougarou and monitor what's going on."

"Man, thanks for answering my questions. I've been reading about rougarous in a book, but you have way more information than is in those few pages."

"You're welcome. Anytime. I consider you family because of Lisette, and I'm here for you."

"Thanks, Crow. I appreciate it."

"Well, I appreciate you, too. Caya's been needing someone like you to help her open her eyes about Garth."

Just then, Lisette walked in with a few bags in her arms, and he and I stood up to grab them for her.

"So, did you two talk?"

"Yep," I said.

Later, Crow and I helped her with dinner, and while we ate, we talked about regular stuff.

As we were clearing the table, Lisette said, "Ya know, the *Deep Bayou* talent show has a prize for the winner every year."

"Hmm. You planning on being in it?"

"No, but I thought you might. You like to dance and sing. Tomie, you have some pretty amazing moves. I think you would have a good chance of winning."

"Maybe dancing, but singing, not so much."

"You could always lip-sync. A lot of the teens do it in the talent show, and the crowd loves it. It reminds me of that one show on TV, but I can't think of the name right now."

"You're joking, right?"

"No!" Lisette yelled with her hands on her hips. "I love to lip-sync!"

"Great! You might score some points with Sari. No matter who you are, having your guy sing to you will make you melt."

Grinning, I said, "I'll think about it."

"When is Sari coming into town?" Crow asked.

Since I was wondering the same thing, I didn't really have an answer.

"I believe she'll be here the day before. She'll let me know when she's sure about her plans."

"I know you can't wait to see her," Lisette said.

"You know it."

We all watched a movie that night, and then I went to bed before 10:00, which was a good change. I checked my phone, but there were no messages from Sari.

In the days that followed, magic practice, exercising, and lots of spells filled most of my time. Caya came over two or three times a week, so we could work together while Lisette supervised. Like her telekinetic skills, Caya's casting was pretty impressive. I figured that she could turn Garth into whatever popped into her head.

From what I saw in her magic, and from *glimming* her every once in a while, Caya's therapy seemed to be building her self-confidence. Garth had made several attempts to win her back, but so far, she hadn't opened her door to allow him in, and that was a big step forward.

# CHAPTER
## FORTY-TWO

Lisette practiced with me and showed me how to move larger objects. One night, she teleported me with her to New Orleans, where we walked through the French Quarter.

Light jazz, zydeco, laughter, echoes from balconies, horse hooves clanking on the cobbled streets, and rhythm and blues circulated through the air. Restaurants and bars were overflowing with all kinds of people, some dressed conservatively, while others wore much less.

"Lisette, have you ever thought about living here?"

She looked at me and began to speak, but she paused for a couple of seconds.

"I prefer my quiet little town away from here."

"Okay. Just seems like a fun place."

"It can be. It has its perks, but it also has dangers."

I stopped and said, "Dangers? What do you mean?"

She continued to walk ahead of me.

"Remember when I told you that some witches belong to covens?" When she turned around to face me, I nodded. "There are probably more diverse ones based in

New Orleans, Salem, and Pendle Hill, England than most places in the world."

"Wow. Salem wouldn't shock me, but Pendle Hill?"

"When you have some time, you should read about what happened. Very interesting history," she said.

"I'll be sure to check it out. So, we've probably walked by a witch or two since we've been here, huh?"

"Oh, absolutely. Probably more. Look up."

Above us, I saw two teen girls and a guy, leaning over the balcony rail, staring down at us. When my eyes returned to Lisette, she communicated with me telepathically.

*They're supras, and they know we are, too. Let's get out of here.*

When I glanced back up, they were still looking at us. Lisette grabbed my hand, and we dashed around the corner of the building.

"Okay, do it!" she commanded.

"What?"

"Teleport us back to the house."

"I don't know if I can."

"Yes, you can! Concentrate and close your eyes. Slow your heartrate, take some deep breaths, and envision where you want us to be."

As I tried to follow her instructions, I heard footsteps approaching. Lisette held my hand and gripped it tighter.

"Tomie, let's get out of here, like now!"

"I'm trying!"

Just as they were about to reach us, we were standing in the middle of Lisette's living room.

"That was a close one, Tomie."

"Ya think?" I asked, breathing harder than usual.

"You okay?"

"Oh, yeah. I got us back."

"You did! I wanted to see how you reacted under

pressure."

"So, that was like a test?"

"Yeah, and you passed! It's all part of your training."

"If I hadn't been able to teleport us out of there in time, would they have tried to start something with us?"

"I think they were more curious than anything else."

Lisette went into the kitchen and made some cinnamon tea with honey and brought it in on a tray. When she set it down, I saw the floral orange teapot belonged to a full set, with matching cups and spoons.

"So, there are good and bad covens in those places you mentioned?"

"Exactly. You have to be careful, especially when it comes down to any *supra*. It's good practice to *glim* or ask Mr. Ray or me about anyone new."

"What about Ranae at the shop? Is she cool?"

"Oh, yeah. I've known her mom since third grade."

We finished our tea, cleaned up, and went to bed. Before I fell asleep, I heard my phone beep. I looked and saw that it was Sari, so I bolted up and sat back against the headboard.

> S: **Tomie I'm not going to make it. Sorry.**

She followed the message with a sad emoji and a GIF of a toy bear, gushing out tears.

> T: **I kinda knew your dad wasn't going to let you come.**
> S: **Yeah. I'm so sorry.**

Several tearful emojis followed.

> T: **It's okay. We'll see each other soon.**
> S: **I really wanted to spend time with you and hang out at the festival.**
> T: **Summer is almost over and school will be starting back soon.**
> S: **I guess...**

T: **Hey it's all right. I get it. Know that I love you and really miss you.**
S: **Love you too. Talk soon. Night.**
T: **Night.**

Cell screen faded, and I laid the phone back on the nightstand. I fought the urge to teleport right then to see her, because I didn't want her to get into any more trouble than she was already in with her dad.

My heart felt like someone had yanked it out and thrown it away. I truly could relate how the Tin Man felt from *The Wonderful Wizard of Oz*, which I had read back in junior high. My tears flowed freely, as I drifted off to sleep.

# CHAPTER
## FORTY-THREE

My training continued with Lisette and Caya, but my mind was always on Sari. They both knew that I wasn't really focusing like I was before. I'd told them what happened with Sari, and they offered their support, which helped a little, but I couldn't help feeling down and wanting to spend time alone.

I read a lot of books over the next few days that I checked out from the Monroe Creek Library—not all about magic. Some were by William Shakespeare, Langston Hughes, Chanel Harry, Rachel Caine, Nikki Grimes, and Jonathan Maberry. I daydreamed a lot about Sari and continued to wrestle with the *to teleport to her* or *not to teleport to her* debate.

The morning before the festival, Caya and Lisette were baking cookies, and the aromas of raisins, cinnamon, chocolate chips, and brown sugar permeated all the rooms of the house. The two of them were talking and laughing, but they stopped as soon as I walked in.

"Hey, Tomie. Heard anything else from Sari?" Caya asked, while she rolled some dough on the counter.

"Not yet. I doubt I'll hear from her."

I shrugged my shoulders, walked over to the table, and sat down. A box of cereal and a jug of milk were already on the table, along with a bowl and spoon, so I brought them over to me with my head lowered. After filling the bowl, I scooped up a bite and put it into my mouth.

"Tomie, I've been thinking," Lisette said. "What if I teleport to Sari and bring her here for an hour or so tomorrow night?"

Almost choking on my cereal, I looked up at her.

"No! You can't."

"Why not?"

"Her dad, remember?"

"He wouldn't even know she was gone," Lisette said.

"What if he found out?"

"He wouldn't. I could put a temporary sleep spell on him," Caya said.

"Thanks, guys, but no, thanks. It's best this way."

Caya wiped her hands on the bottom of her apron and walked over to sit next to me, as I continued to chow down on my cereal.

"What are you afraid of?"

"Nothing. I just don't want Sari getting into any more trouble with her dad. He knows stuff about me."

"So, what does that have to do with anything?"

"A lot. Just drop it. I don't want to talk about this anymore. I'm not going tomorrow night, anyway!" I yelled.

After throwing my spoon onto the table, I shoved myself back, stood up, and teleported out of the room to Crow's place. Sitting on the end of the dock, I dangled my feet back and forth. As I watched two dragonflies side-by-side, darting up and down across the water, I heard heavy footsteps approaching me, and I knew it was Crow.

He sat down beside me and didn't say a word to me for what seemed like forever, but when he did, it was what I needed to hear.

"Tomie, I know how it is. You're going to be judged by others, which usually won't be in your favor, but to me, being different is a beautiful thing. I wouldn't have it any other way. You and Sari are lucky to have each other."

"I don't think she's lucky. I feel like I'm going to cause her more pain than anything else because of the way her dad is treating her, which is all about me. He's trying to protect her, and I get it. I couldn't say that I wouldn't do the same if I was him."

"I'm sure you've attempted to talk to him, right?"

"Yeah. It was like slamming into a brick wall. He's not willing to hear me out at all."

Tears started streaming down my cheeks.

"That's tough."

"Yeah, tell me about it," I said, wiping my face with both of my hands.

"Do you think it would help if you two met and talked face to face?"

"No. He already hates me, even though he doesn't really know me."

"Sorry, buddy. You're a great guy. Too bad, he's not willing to see that. You want me to talk to him?"

If Mr. Green was intimidated by me, I could only imagine how he'd react if Crow showed up on his doorstep.

"Thanks, Crow, but I'll figure it out."

He gave me a side hug and said, "Just let me know, and I'll be there." We both stood up. "You better now?"

"A little. Need to get back to Lisette's and take care of something."

"Okay. Later, man."

"Yeah, later."

He walked back to his office, and I teleported back to Lisette's. When I saw them, I knew what I needed to do.

"Lisette, Caya, I want you both to know that I'm sorry for acting like a jerk earlier."

"It's okay, Tomie. I understand," Caya said.

Lisette nodded in agreement.

"It was not cool for me to act like that. I'm just so bummed out about Sari not being able to come here to see me. I really miss her."

"I know," Lisette whispered.

"It's going to be okay," Caya said.

They both walked towards me to give me a hug.

Going to the festival was beginning to seem like a really good idea, because I needed a distraction from thinking about the fact that Sari wasn't going to make it after all.

# CHAPTER
## FORTY-FOUR

Later that evening, as Lisette and Caya were working on their costumes in the living room, I went in and sat in the chair across from them.

"What are you going as, Caya?" She stuck the threaded needle into a pin cushion, unfolded the red cape on her lap, and held it up. It had a sparkly hood. "Little Red? Great choice for you. I like it."

"Really?"

"Yeah. Where's your basket of goodies?" She leaned over the couch's arm and picked up an eight-inch by ten-inch wicker basket with a red and white checkered cloth hanging over one side. "Looks good."

"Thanks. I've been working on it with Lisette after our magic lessons these past few weeks."

"So, Garth won't be your date, will he?"

"No. Why would he?"

"Just wondered, since you're going as Red. I thought he would be the Big Bad Wolf. Perfect for him—he wouldn't even have to buy a costume. He'd fit right in."

Caya exploded with laughter, and Lisette smiled, as

they continued working on their costumes.

While I thought about the fact that they were going to shine the next night, I wondered what I could go as. With all that had been going on, especially after I found out Sari wouldn't be able to make it, that hadn't even crossed my mind.

"Lisette, didn't you say you had a chest full of costumes in the basement?"

"Yes."

I was about to go down there, but I didn't want to see Opal's face or read any of her newest riddles. Dealing with her crap wasn't something I wanted to do, especially right then.

Halfway out of the living room, I swung around and asked, "Lisette, is teleportation of any object possible?"

"Within reason. Why?"

"Watch."

Closing my eyes, I envisioned the chest in the basement—I recalled seeing it in a corner near Lisette's doll collection case. As I focused on it, I thought about where I wanted it, a few feet in front of me. Several seconds later, the bronze and black chest appeared exactly where I had pictured it, and Lisette stood up to check out my work.

Walking around it, she stared up at me and said, "Nice job, Tomie."

"Whoa! That was awesome, Tomie!" Caya shouted.

As she walked over to us, I opened the chest with a swipe of my hand. Caya and I sat down on the floor; Lisette stood over us and watched. A sheet of thick plastic lined the top, so I peeled it off. Picking up each garment one by one, I saw that they were mostly female costumes from the late 1930s and 1960s.

"Where did these come from?" I asked.

"My high school theater class, which I loved. The principal did away with it, because some super-conservative parents, who were the biggest donors, thought our performances of *Grease* and *Cats* were way too provocative, so all the props and costumes were up for grabs."

"Seriously?"

She nodded, saying, "Oh, yeah. Gotta love parents like that."

Caya and I continued to look through the rest, and I was about to give up until I saw what was folded at the bottom of the chest, wrapped in a brown paper bag. It was all black—a suit and a cape lined with red satin, along with lace-up shoes. A white button-down shirt and a folded up black cane with a silver tip were also inside.

All appeared to be in nice condition, and, to my surprise, everything was my size! What were the odds of me finding a *Dracula* costume—one of my favorite books—that would fit? At that point, I could only assume that I was fated to attend the festival after all.

When I looked up at Lisette, she winked at me and walked back to the couch to finish up the last touches on her own getup.

I held my costume up and took a whiff.

"Whoa, this needs to be washed!"

"No worries. Just leave it on the dryer. I'll take care of it for you in the morning."

"Thanks, Lisette." I high-fived her. "Okay, Caya, where can I find a set of fangs this time of year?"

"I have a bag of them."

Laughing, I asked, "Why would you have a bag of fangs?"

"My mom was giving them out last Halloween, and she had some left over. I'll bring them to you tomorrow night."

"Thanks."

She helped me fold the other costumes and put them back inside the trunk, and then she stood up and gathered her own.

"Goodnight, Lisette. See y'all tomorrow."

"Okay. Can't wait to see you all dressed up! Night, Tomie," Lisette said, as she headed towards her bedroom.

"Hold up, Caya. I'll walk you out. Give me a second."

"Sure."

After I put the plastic covering on top, I closed the chest, locked it, and teleported it back to where it came from. I took my costume and laid it on the dryer, and then I returned to the living room.

We went outside, and I opened the car door for her. She leaned in and placed her things on the passenger's side and then situated herself in the driver's seat.

As I shut the door, she said, "Tomie."

"Yeah." I squatted down. "What's up?"

"I'm sorry that Sari wasn't able to come down."

"Thanks, but it's okay. Most likely for the best, considering everything."

"You know my situation." I gave her a slight nod. "Do you want to go to the festival together? Just as friends, of course."

I paused for a few seconds before responding.

"Just friends, right?" I asked, narrowing my eyes.

"Yes, I know how much you love Sari. I just don't want to be there by myself, ya know?"

"Yeah, I get it. Okay, friend-date. See you around 7:00 here."

"Sounds good, Tomie."

"Good night."

She drove off and beeped her horn, before she pulled

out of Lisette's driveway. After waving to her, I went back into the house and locked the door. I showered and brushed my teeth, crawled into the bed, and was out.

# CHAPTER
## FORTY-FIVE

When I woke up the next morning, I checked my phone and found a text from Dad.

D: **Hey Tomie. I made it back okay. Tired. So good to see you.**

T: **Good you are home for a bit before you head back out. Enjoyed your visit.**

D: **You heard anything from Sari?**

T: **Yeah not good.**

D: **What happened?**

T: **She won't be coming down.**

D: **I'm so sorry son.**

T: **Was really hoping she could come.**

D: **School will be starting soon.**

T: **Have a feeling how that might go.**

D: **I may meet with her dad soon to talk about some things.**

T: **Please don't. That would make things worse.**

D: **It's worth a try.**

T: **Let me handle this please.**

D: **Okay. Let me know if you change your mind.**
T: **I will. I better get moving. Love ya.**
D: **Love you too son. Call me or text me anytime**.

After getting dressed and making the bed, I headed to the bathroom. Grabbing Lisette's gift from the shelf and placing it in my pocket, I glanced down at my phone to check if Sari had texted. Nothing was on my screen.

When I entered the kitchen, I saw that Lisette was cooking pecan pancakes and bacon. On a large platter, I noticed bags of cookies.

"What are those for?"

"A charity bake sale at one of my friend's booths."

"What's the charity?"

"*Lafayette's Warriors*."

"What do they do?"

"They rescue all kinds of animals and take care of their medical needs free of charge and then relocate them into adequate homes or sometimes zoos."

"That's awesome."

"I think so. I volunteer there sometimes."

"That's cool."

As we sat down at the table, she said, "Tomie, I'm sorry things didn't work out for Sari to make the trip here."

"Me, too, but it's all right. I'm going to be hanging out with you, Crow, and Caya, so I'll make the best of it."

She smiled and started digging into her pancakes. I sliced my seven into fluffy squares and poured butter pecan syrup all over them. They vanished in minutes.

"Is Crow's costume going to match yours?" I asked, as we were cleaning up the dishes.

"You'll just have to wait and see," she said with a

huge smile.

"Really?"

"Yep."

I took the bag with her sterling silver earrings in it from my pocket and held them out.

"Here."

She placed the damp dishtowel over the stove bar to dry and walked up to me to examine it.

"What's this?"

"Just a little something I picked up when we went to the shop downtown."

She leaned against the counter and said, "Tomie, you didn't need to get me anything."

"I know, but I wanted to. Hope you like it."

She opened the bag and held them up.

"Thank you so much! I love them!"

As she reached up and gave me a hug, I said, "It's not much. I got Sari something, too, but I'll have to wait to give it to her when I get back home."

"You could give it to her today."

"I know, but I want to wait and give them to her in person."

"I understand. I'm wearing these tonight!"

She hugged me again, and then she walked over to the dryer, came back, and handed me my costume on a hanger. It had a faint vanilla scent that was far better than the musty odor from last night.

"Thank you."

"So welcome. It's going to be a fun night with surprises."

"Hope it will be."

Using some polish that Lisette shared with me earlier, I shined the shoes, and they looked good. I could see my reflection in them. The rest of the day, I was thinking about Sari and all the things we could've done if she was there with me.

Later on, when I got through showering, I glanced at the clock in my bedroom, and it was 5:30. After getting dressed, I sprayed on some cologne and opened the closet door to check myself out in the full-length mirror.

My costume looked great, so I clicked my heels, grabbed my cane, twirled around, and stood up on my toes for a few seconds. The cape was sweet, flaring out as if a gust of wind entered through the room. The last thing to complete the look would be the fangs, and Caya was bringing them over for me.

When I walked into the living room, I flipped my cape up and sat on the couch. While I waited for the others, I started watching a movie on my phone. About twenty minutes into it, I heard a knock at the door. After clicking *pause*, I noticed it was 6:45. At first, I thought Caya or Crow were early, but then I remembered that they usually didn't knock and came through the back, not the front.

With my cane in my right hand, I went over and looked through the peephole. Three strangers were standing on the porch. The one on the right was dressed in a classic Princess Leia outfit—long white dress and belt, white boots, and cinnamon roll hair buns. The one on the left was wearing a Jughead Jones costume—navy blue flannel shirt, black jeans, black boots, a grey messenger bag strapped across his chest, and a crown-shaped beanie with red bottle-cap buttons.

The middle one wore a light pink dress, with pleats running down the chest and a white rounded collar, blonde shoulder-length hair, white tube socks with yellow and green bands, and tennis shoes. She was holding an *Eggo* box up to block her face.

My mind then drifted back to the movie I was

watching—when the guy answered the door, he was being hunted down by some masked lunatic.

My hand moved away from unlocking the doorknob. Stepping back, I asked myself, *What do I have to be worried about?*

Then the middle one screamed out my name.

"Tomie! Tomie Dupuy!"

I knew.

# CHAPTER
## FORTY-SIX

After swinging the door open, I took a step outside and scooped my girl up into my arms, twirling her round and round, staring into her eyes, as her box dropped to the ground.

"Sari, you're here!" I started to kiss her, but then I noticed the other two watching us, so I decided to wait and set her down. "How did you get here?"

"Luckie and Phoenixx drove me."

She pointed at both while picking up her *Eggo* box, and then she introduced us.

"Nice to meet you, Tomie. She talks about you all the time at work," Luckie said, waving her hands in the air.

Phoenixx said, "Yeah, you're pretty much all she talks about."

"Nice to meet y'all, too."

Luckie was probably 5'1" and full-figured from top to bottom. Phoenixx was about my height and looked like a combination of Bruno and Zac, with a super-thin black beard outlining his face. He wore black square-framed glasses with a light blue tint to the lenses.

"Come on in." They all walked into the living room and stood around. "Have a seat. Anyone want something to drink?"

They all declined.

Phoenixx said, "Hey, we're going to wait in the car."

"No, stay," I replied.

"Nah, it's cool. We'll see y'all later."

He walked out onto the porch with Luckie and shut the door.

"Sari, I'm going to tell Lisette that you're here."

"Okay. I'm so glad to be here with you, Tomie."

"I'm happy, but I thought…"

"Everything worked out. Let's talk about that later, please."

She stood on her tippy-toes, and I leaned down; she then wrapped her arms around my neck, as mine went to her waist. My knees felt wobbly, and my palms were hot as we kissed. It had been a while since our lips met. Hers were smooth and tasted like a cherry Jolly Rancher.

As I pulled her in closer to me, a few strands of her blonde wig tickled my nose, but I didn't care. Then I heard footsteps approaching, so I broke our kiss and stared into her eyes, until whoever it was entered. When I turned around, I thought it was going to be Lisette, but it was Caya.

"Hey, Caya" I said, while Sari remained quiet.

"Hi, Tomie. You must be Sari."

It wasn't hard to pick up on the fact that Sari was uneasy with her minimum pacing in front of me and her eyes focused on the stranger in the room.

"Sari, this is Caya. We've been training together."

"Oh… hi."

"I'm surprised that you're here. Tomie told me you couldn't make it. I know he's so happy you were able to come."

Then the silence was deafening, as we all just stood there, looking at each other.

"Cool costume, Sari," Caya said. "One of my favorite characters."

"Yeah, mine, too."

I wasn't sure which show they were referring to, but I figured Sari would tell me sooner or later.

Caya pulled out a tiny plastic bag containing my fangs from an inside pocket of her red hooded cape and dropped it into my right hand, as she said, "Here ya go."

"Thanks." I unwrapped them and put them into my mouth. Then I threw my cape up in the air and leaned towards Sari's neck. "I *want* to drink your blood!"

There was a whistle going on from the plastic fangs, and Sari laughed, though she kept her eyes fixed on Caya.

"Tomie, can I speak to you really quick in the kitchen?" Caya asked.

"Sure. Sari, I'll be right back."

I blew Sari a kiss, and she caught it in the air and held it against her chest. She then sent me one, and I did the same, as she plopped onto the couch.

As I was heading into the kitchen, I heard light jazz coming from Lisette's room, so I figured that she was still getting dressed.

"What's up?"

"Hey, the thing we talked about earlier, going on the friend-date… obviously, that's off. I'll just go alone."

"No, she brought some of her friends from work. We're all going together."

"Y'all, go ahead and have fun."

"Look, you're all dressed up, and you're going with us!"

"I don't think Sari likes me."

"Y'all just met. Why do you think that?"

"Got a feeling."

"She needs to get to know you, that's all. She's cautious about who she gets close to, even more so since the Opal Dawn nightmare."

"I'd like to hear more about that story, since I only got the short version."

"Okay, but not tonight."

"I'll be waiting in the car, Tomie."

"All right. I'm going to check on Lisette."

"She has to get all beautified," Caya whispered, as she went out the back way.

I walked to Lisette's door and knocked on it.

"Come in."

When I opened it, I saw her shadow darting around in the bathroom.

"You almost ready?"

"Yeah, I just have to put on my boots. Crow called. He's about ten minutes out."

"Good. I have a surprise for you in the living room."

"What is it?"

"Have to see for yourself."

I clicked my heels a few times.

"You sound funny. You okay?"

"It's the fangs—I'm wearing them."

"That's it. Caya must be here."

"She is."

"Was that the surprise?"

"Nope."

"Come on, give me a hint."

"Not going to give in."

When Lisette walked out of the bathroom, she radiated from head to toe. Purple and hot pink highlights on the ends of her side ponytail appeared to glow in her golden-brown hair, which fell over her glitter-dusted shoulders.

Her brows were carefully done, the arch so smooth it was perfect, and her emerald eyes were lined in black. Purple, bronze, and hot pink shimmered on her lids, and there were tiny silver dots in a diagonal pattern down the outsides of her eyes.

Lisette's sparkly bustier fit her thin and toned upper body well, and shiny silver quarter-sized geometric shapes decorated her shoulders. Her tattered black wings looked epic, with purple glitter on the edges; they actually fluttered in and out on their own.

"Are you moving those, or are they battery operated?"

"All me, but I have a dummy battery attached to it, just in case someone asks."

"You look really beautiful, Lisette."

"Thank you. You're rocking it! Okay, what's my surprise?"

"It's in there," I said, pointing towards the living room.

"Sari, what in the world?" she screamed, pulling her into a hug. "So good to see you!"

"Good to see you, too. I love your costume, especially your wings."

"Thank you. I like yours, too. A little *strange*… yet adorable."

"Eleven is one of my favorites," Sari gushed.

"Okay," Lisette said. She turned around to face me and whispered, "I thought this was a no-go."

"Me, too. I'm just as surprised as you."

"I bet! Y'all have a lot to catch up on. You'll have to tell us how this all happened."

"Yeah, later on," Sari said. "I want to get to this event that I've heard so much about."

"You okay?" I asked her.

"Of course. I'm here with you, and that's all that

matters."

She wrapped her arms around me and rested her head on my chest. The beating of her heart felt like someone had been chasing her. As I looked down, she gazed up at me and smiled, squeezing me tighter.

Just as Lisette started texting him, Crow walked into the living room. I knew he was buff and ripped, but seeing him shirtless and painted green, in jeans that were cut off at his knees, made me do a doubletake. He looked enormous, like he stepped off a comic book page, and whoever painted him did a great job.

"Hey, Sari," Crow said.

"Hi, Crow."

"Will that paint wash off easily?" I asked.

"Yeah, with a special soap and water."

"How about if you start sweating?"

"It's not going anywhere."

"Crow, you look like a real bad…"

"Shut your mouth!" We both laughed. "Thanks! Let's go have some fun."

He stared at Lisette and exhaled a few times with a gigantic smile.

As we all headed towards the kitchen, I asked, "Sari, you're riding with us, right?"

"Yeah, I'm going with y'all. My friends'll follow us."

Lisette went into her bedroom and brought out a large blue tote. She placed the bags of cookies in it, as Sabra watched us from her bed. Crow picked it up and carried it out while taking Lisette's hand, which he then lifted up to his face and kissed. As we walked out, Lisette locked the door behind her with a swipe of her hand.

"So, Sari, some friends drove you up?" Lisette asked.

"Yeah. I've been working with them part of the summer."

"Where are they?"

"In the front, waiting in the car."

"Oh, okay."

We walked out to Crow's truck, and Lisette took off her wings. He helped her in, and she placed them on her lap, as Crow set the tote bag in the camper shell. After helping Sari into the truck, I went to my side, stepped up, and slid into the seat beside her, and then we all buckled up.

When I noticed Caya's car was gone, I took out my phone.

Sari leaned over and asked, "Who're you texting?"

"Caya. I thought we were all going together, but she left already."

"I'm sure she's there."

"You're probably right."

Sari squeezed my hand. I figured that Caya was feeling left out, and that was why she didn't wait, but I was hoping we would find her when we arrived.

Crow drove to the front of the house and beeped at Sari's friends. The dude—I mean, Phoenixx—started the car up, and they followed us out.

"Sari, are Phoenixx and Luckie a thing?" I asked.

"No, they're just friends."

"Oh."

# CHAPTER
## FORTY-SEVEN

Once we arrived, Crow parked and grabbed Lisette's tote from the back, as I went over and opened Sari's door and helped her out. Lisette was already out and had put her wings back on. She touched the edge of the right one, and it started fluttering with a sparkling LED wavy light effect.

Loud zydeco music filled the air, and Sari asked about it. As I explained it to her, her friends parked and started strolling towards us. Sari introduced them to Lisette and Crow.

We all walked along the loose-graveled road towards the check-in, where a big crowd of people were waiting. Many were dressed in familiar costumes or cosplay, while others wore mashups of different characters from movies, books, or comics. I recognized most of them.

Crow paid for all our tickets, and the cashier placed blue paper armbands around our wrists loosely, but not so much that they would fall off. They were good for that night only.

The scents of roasted corn, gumbo, popcorn, pretzels,

sausage, funnel cake, cotton candy, and root beer flooded the night air. There were games, fortune-telling, rides, and huge tents with various types of entertainment.

Lisette said, "Hey, I'm going to drop off these cookies at my friend's booth and visit with her a bit before I head over to my area. See you guys later. Have fun."

"Sounds good. Talk to you later," I replied.

We went our separate ways.

My phone vibrated, and I pulled it out of my pocket.

> C: **I'm here and headed towards the talent show tent.**
>
> T: **Why did you leave earlier?**
>
> C: **Wanted you and Sari to have some time together. Figured I would see you both later on.**
>
> T: **Meet up with us**.
>
> C: **I'm going to save us seats because the talent show gets crowded fast. I know one of the workers there too so sure he'll score us some good ones.**
>
> T: **If you're sure. We'll head that way soon. When does show start?**
>
> C: **8:30. See y'all later.**
>
> T: **K**

I saw a map on the side of a food truck, and it looked like we were maybe twenty minutes away, because we were near Bayou Street, and the talent show was happening in Tent M near Swamp Avenue.

We headed in that direction. As we were walking along, I updated them about the talent show starting later. This was also a good time to learn a little more about the dude who was working with my girl.

"Phoenixx, Sari was telling me that you transferred from up North, and you'll be going to Frost High as a senior."

"Yeah, something like that."

"What brought you to Texas?"

"My dad got a job transfer."

"Oh, where?"

"Okay, Tomie, enough of the Phoenixx Interrogation," Sari said.

"I'm not interrogating him."

"Dude, you were," he snapped.

"No, I wasn't. I was just trying to get to know you— my bad. Hey, you *can* call me Tomie."

"Cool, *Tomie*. No offense, then."

"Right."

"Come on, guys," Luckie said. "Can we tone down some of that testosterone?"

Sari noticed a few fortune-teller booths and dragged me inside the one with the blue velvet curtains, where candles lit the room. Phoenixx and Luckie followed us in. When we sat down, and the psychic came in, we laughed. It was Lisette!

I said, "We didn't think we would get your booth!"

"Never know," Lisette replied with a giggle.

"You're going to use that crystal ball right here?" Sari asked, as she pointed at it and examined it with her gleaming eyes.

"I sure am."

"Do they really work?" Luckie asked. "I heard they're fake."

"Want to test it out?" Lisette asked.

"No, I'm good. I'll just watch," Luckie said.

"I read somewhere that crystal balls only work for witches," Phoenixx hissed.

"They're just a fun prop. Would you like a reading?"

"No, thanks. I don't believe in that garbage," Phoenixx

barked.

"That's fine, but please be respectful," Lisette snapped.

"You sound like you actually believe in this stuff."

"Maybe I do."

"Ya know, Sari, Luckie and I are going to walk around for a bit and then head on over to the talent show. See you guys there."

"All right," Sari said.

As they walked away, Lisette said, "Sari, I think he got uncomfortable."

"He'll be fine. I'm ready to get my reading."

"Okay, place both your hands on the glass and close your eyes." Sari followed her directions. "You can remove them now."

Lisette then put hers where Sari's were and rotated them all over the ball with her eyes closed.

"Are you running from something?"

"No."

Touching the glass again, Lisette said, "I can see that you're trying to escape, and dishonesty is following you."

Sari stood up and said, "Tomie, let's go. We'll be late for the talent show."

"Sorry, Lisette."

"No, it's fine."

When I stood and started to follow Sari out of the tent, Lisette reached out and touched my arm.

"Tomie, she's hiding something."

"What is it?"

"It's best for her to tell you."

"I'll see you later. Got to go," I said, as I dashed out of the tent.

# CHAPTER
## FORTY-EIGHT

Sari was waiting for me outside near a hotdog stand, her arms crossed over her chest.

I walked up behind her and massaged her shoulders, as I asked, "Hey, you okay?"

"Yeah. I think crystal balls are creepy now."

"Maybe so, but what's going on?"

"Tomie, I just want to enjoy being with you. Please, please, let's just have fun tonight. It's been a while since we've seen each other."

I wanted to keep pressing her to figure out what she was hiding, but I didn't want to ruin what little time I was going to have with my girl, so we checked out a few exhibits and walked over to where the talent show was about to start.

It was jam-packed. Phoenixx and Luckie were standing against the walls of the tent with other people. A hand popped up from the front row—it was Caya. She had saved four seats for us, probably the best ones in the house. Sari introduced Caya to her friends, and then Phoenixx sat next to Luckie, and I sat between Sari and

Caya.

"Awesome seats!" I shouted.

"Like I said, I got the hookup."

The MC came out on stage and told a few jokes in a crisp Cajun accent.

"Good evening, ladies and gents. It's going to be a fun night. Eighties and nineties throwback is this year's theme. No booing or clapping until the end. Let's keep it PG clean, folks."

I looked at Sari with a grin, because she knew how much I loved that era. I was familiar with all the top forty songs from back then, because my dad always had the radio playing on those stations or old CDs in the house.

There were lots of acts—magicians, ventriloquists, jumpers, dancers, and singers—and we were having fun watching them. During intermission, I asked everyone in our squad if they wanted anything from the concession stand. Sari and Caya asked for popcorn and sodas, so I stood up to go and get them.

Guess who I ran into!

Garth stood in the middle of the aisle with his mini posse of two. They were all shirtless and dressed in acid-washed blue jean overalls with colorful graffiti drawings on them. One of their straps hung loosely behind their backs. The initials *BBD* were written on the front of their jean legs in large sparkly letters.

"Where're you going, freak?" he asked in a deep voice, like he was a drill instructor.

I stopped and stood toe-to-toe with him.

"Excuse me, but you're calling *me* a freak?"

"You heard me!" he howled.

From the corner of my eye, I saw Sari and Caya look my way. When I turned my head, Caya stood, but I motioned for her to stay put. She ignored that, and then

Sari jumped up, and they started walking towards me. Phoenixx and Luckie noticed what was going on and followed them.

"Should I be scared?" Garth asked with a chuckle.

"Look, I'm here to have a good time with my girl and my friend. I don't want any trouble."

"You referring to Caya, the *slut*?" Garth whispered with a warped smile on his face that resembled the Joker.

"Hey, don't call her that!"

"So, what're you going to do about it, Tomie?"

"Recall the dock scene a few weeks ago?"

To give him a small encore, I made my eyes change to a spicy bronze, and my hands grew hot with a light blue glow. Garth looked down and stepped back. I noticed that his pupils were dilated. He stalked past me with a scowl on his twisted face, bumping my shoulder, and his posse followed.

As he was walking backwards, looking at Caya, he shouted, "Stick around—our performance is dedicated to you!"

He pursed his lips and blew a kiss at her. Then they jumped up onto the stage, which looked to be about six feet off the ground, and disappeared behind the closed curtains.

Sari asked, "Who was that?"

"Nobody."

"You okay, Tomie?" Caya asked, as she touched my upper arm.

Sari's eyes drifted towards her with one brow raised.

"Tomie, is there something I don't know?"

"No."

She crossed her arms and raised both brows.

"Really?"

"There's some stuff going on, but I'll tell you about it

later, okay?"

"Whatever."

She turned and walked back to her seat with Luckie. Phoenixx glared at me, shaking his head, before he joined them and sat next to Sari, throwing his right arm around her chair. He looked back at us and winked at me.

"Tomie, I'm sorry," Caya whispered.

"For what?" I asked, as I stared at Sari and Phoenixx.

"She's upset."

"I'll talk to her. It'll be fine."

"Thanks for standing up for me again."

"No problem, Caya. Do you want to get out of here?"

"I want to stay."

"Even after what Garth just said? If he's performing..."

"Yeah. I don't want him to think that I can't deal with what he dishes out. Anyway, he's just mad because I won't take him back."

"That's what I figured. I'll be back in a few. You sure you're okay?"

She nodded.

After waiting in line for about fifteen minutes, I returned with the snacks and carried them in a box to our seats. I handed them to Sari and Caya.

Sari looked up at me, smiled, and said, "That's why I love you so much... always watching out for others."

I sat down with my cup and took a few sips.

"I love you, too. What're you referring to?"

I already knew because of *glimming* her.

"Caya gave me the short version of the story about her and Garth."

"Oh."

After taking a few more sips, I put my arm around Sari and pulled her closer to me. Tilting my head back and looking towards Phoenixx, I winked at him. He glanced over and fixed his eyes on me until the show started.

# DOLL²: THE REVEALING

The lights dimmed, the curtains separated, and then the MC returned to the stage to announce the next act. It was Ranae from the shop. She was wearing black lace leggings, a blue jean skirt, and a big cut-off yellow sweatshirt that hung off her shoulder, with splattered purple, white, and green paint all over it. Her hair was teased out, with a large red lace bow tied on the left side of her head. She also wore red lace gloves and red skates that had blue rhinestones on the side.

Ranae played a drum medley of *Pretty Young Thing*, *Let's Go Crazy*, *The Glamorous Life*, and *Living on a Prayer*, with a raw classic rock 80s sound. She tossed her glowing purple sticks almost to the ceiling and caught them with one hand behind her back. They changed into different colors when she tapped them on the drums. She rocked it hard. When she spotted me in the audience, we waved at each other.

"Wow, Tomie. You got chicks everywhere you go," Phoenixx spat, as he leaned back in his chair, staring at me.

"You know what they say. If you got it…"

He pulled himself forward and looked away from me.

The entertainment continued, and one of the acts was a talented young comedian. Sari, Caya, Luckie, and I all laughed, and my side started cramping a bit, while Phoenixx just stared at his phone.

The MC walked out and announced the last performance of the night, and there was no more guessing when Garth's crew was going to appear.

The curtains parted, and Garth stood in the middle of the stage with his back to the audience and a microphone in his hand. His boys were positioned to his left and right about five feet apart.

When the music started, my jaw dropped.

# CHAPTER
FORTY-NINE

They started their dance routine and lip-synced the lyrics to *Poison* by Bell Biv DeVoe, *BBD*. Their moves were pretty good and followed the old video, which I'd watched probably over fifty times, but Garth's performance... super cold. Before the song ended, he slid on his knees on the smooth stage floor in Caya's direction and stopped, pointing right at her.

The crowd held their applause until the MC walked out on stage and said, after clearing his throat, "Let's give these boys a hand."

Caya's head hung low, and I knew how she felt because of some of the things Pepper Fox used to throw my way.

As Garth and his posse left the stage, overtaken by crazed hyena laughter, jumping into the air, I stood and ran up the side stairs. The MC lowered his microphone, holding his hand over it, as I whispered something into his ear.

The MC nodded and said, "Well, I apologize, folks. That was the last *official* act for the night, but we have one more performance that I think you'll enjoy. His girlfriend traveled from out of town and surprised him, and he wants to do something special for her. Let's hear it for Tomie Dupuy!"

As the crowd applauded, he handed me the microphone, and I stepped behind the curtain to ask the DJ if he had a certain song in his collection. With large headphones draped around his neck, he nodded, gave me a *thumbs up*, and told me that the music would start in about fifteen seconds.

When I walked out from behind the curtain, I said, "*This* is how you're *supposed* to serenade a *lady*. Sari, this is for you."

Looking over my shoulder, I saw Garth watching from backstage. It felt like raging flames encircled him and were about to engulf me on his command.

The room grew dimmer, and the spotlight was shining on me. When the song started, I was singing to Sari, but I hoped that Caya would find meaning in the lyrics of the song and see how a good guy can be.

I lip-synced *Every Little Step* by Bobby Brown and showcased his dance moves, along with a few of my own inspired by Bruno Mars, as I looked straight into Sari's eyes. When the music stopped, she jumped out of her seat, clapping. I rushed down off the stage, grabbed her up into my arms, and held her.

"Oh, Tomie! I loved it! Thank you!"

"Thought you might. You know you're my girl."

She smiled and rested her head on my chest.

"Well, thanks for coming out tonight. We had some great performances," the MC said. "The winner of the five-hundred-dollar cash prize will be decided in a few minutes. Relax and enjoy the music while the votes are calculated."

Phoenixx walked out with his phone to his ear, and

Luckie followed him.

Caya said, "Tomie, your performance was really great. I enjoyed it! Hope you win!"

"Thanks. It was okay."

"Yeah, whatever," she said with a giggle. "You really have an awesome guy, Sari."

"Oh, I know."

When the MC announced that Ranae won, I stood and clapped and whistled for her, as she walked out on stage to accept her prize and a bouquet of flowers.

"Hey, I'm going to check out a few exhibits. Meet up later maybe?" Caya asked.

"Yeah, sure," I said.

Sari and I left the tent and went out into the crowd. After we rode the Ferris wheel and the carousel, I played a dart game and won a stuffed elephant that was almost as tall as I was. We continued to walk around, enjoying the night, and then we found Crow and Lisette. He had a gold medal hanging around his neck.

"Hey, how'd you get that, Crow?" I asked, pointing to it.

"I won first place for axe-throwing."

"Like a contest?"

"Yeah, it's a big sport around here."

"Wow. You must be pretty good at it."

"Okay, I guess."

"That medal says you're better than okay."

"Want me to take that elephant and put it in the truck, so you don't have to lug it all over the rest of the night?"

"That would be great, if you don't mind."

"Hand her over."

"Thanks."

"No problem. You two, go and have fun."

"Catch y'all later."

As I scanned the crowd, I saw Caya and Garth from a distance at a funnel cake and cotton candy stand, and she looked like she was okay, so I didn't feel the need to step in.

The lake was located on the opposite side of the festivities, and there was a huge willow tree that looked inviting.

Taking Sari's hand, I whispered into her ear, "Let's take a walk."

When we got to the other side, we found a bench and sat down. We could see all the lights and people from where we were.

"Talk to me," I requested.

"I have been."

"No, really *talk* to me, Sari. How did you manage to get here?"

"Told you already. Phoenixx and Luckie drove me."

"I know that, but I also know that your dad wouldn't let you see me."

She looked away, stood up, and then turned around to face me.

"Tomie, my dad doesn't know I'm here."

# CHAPTER

FIFTY

**W**hat?" I yelled. "He's going to hate me even more now. He'll think I convinced you to do this."

"He won't… he'll never find out."

"You actually believe that?"

I stood up and started pacing.

"Yeah."

"What'd you tell him?"

"That I was working a double and was going to spend the night and most of Sunday hanging out with Luckie."

"Wow!"

"What?" she whined.

"You shouldn't be lying to your dad, especially about me."

"How else was I going to see you?"

"I would've been back in a few weeks."

"Tomie, I wanted to be with you now."

"Does your mom know where you are, at least?"

"No."

"Don't you think you need to call her?"

"Umm, no, I don't."

"Sari, you know I love you and would do anything for you, right?"

"Yes."

"I don't want you getting into more trouble, or us not being able to spend any time together at all, ya know?"

Then she started crying, so I went to her and took her into my arms.

"I've just been missing you so much. When Dad took my phone away, I…"

"Hey, look at me. It's going to be okay. We'll figure it out."

We sat on the bench, and as she rested her head on my chest, I told her all about my training with Lisette and more about Caya, so she would understand my relationship with her.

I noticed a few fireflies floating around between the swaying willow tree's branches. Closing my eyes, I scanned my memory and came across a proliferation spell. I focused on what I wanted to multiply and recited the words in my mind.

*Firefly, firefly… One, two, three… More fireflies, please.*

Before my eyes, the willow's vertical leaves changed to glowing bronze, as the little bugs covered them. They looked like streams of running Christmas lights. I waved my hand and commanded most of them to form *Sari, I love you!* within the shape of a heart, with others still floating around. When it was done, I tapped her shoulder and guided her to look up at the tree.

Her beautiful brown eyes sparkled and widened, and she said, "Tomie, you're amazing. I love you." She kissed me. "I'll call Mom in the morning."

"I love you, too. Good."

After looking all around to ensure no one was nearby, I levitated us several feet up into the air, as Sari held onto me tighter, and my cape rippled like waves. Following my command, my phone floated above us, as I focused on my *Sari* playlist and chose our song, *With You* by Chris Brown. She rested her head against my chest, as a few fireflies hovered around us to the beat of the song. When it ended, I lowered us back down to stand on the ground and turned off the music, as my phone went back into my pocket.

"Tomie, what can you not do? I'll never forget this."

With a wink, I pulled her closer to me. Then I looked up and waved my hand, causing the fireflies to dissipate. They went up into the dark sky and vanished as soon as we sat down on the bench. For a while, we talked and watched the water, as she leaned back in my arms.

Then a tree branch broke in the distance.

# CHAPTER
## FIFTY-ONE

Upon hearing that sound, I turned around to see what caused it. My eyes felt like they were glowing, as I saw Garth and his posse about a hundred yards away, walking up the path towards us, with Caya trailing behind them. I stood in front of Sari, ready to face what was coming.

"Tomie, what's wrong?"

"We're about to have company really soon."

"Oh, no. Garth?"

"Yep."

When Garth and his friends walked up, he said, "Hey, man, I wanna apologize for being an—"

"You don't even have to say it, because I already know."

"Tomie, let's go," Sari pleaded.

"Hold on, mamacita, I'm trying to apologize. Man, you should've won that prize tonight. Your routine was on," Garth said. He held his hand out to me, but I just stared down at it. "Come on, I'm trying here." Sari grabbed onto my arm, but I remained silent. "At least, hang out with us for a bit, and you'll see that I'm a cool guy who can have a good time."

"Where?"

"*La Fantasma Plantation*. One of the biggest after parties of the year."

"You mean the haunted place?" I asked.

"Yeah. It's not really haunted. That's just a bunch of stories told by the old-timers."

"I don't know, man. Caya, is he telling the truth about a party there tonight?"

"Yeah, they have it every year. It's like tradition. It can get pretty crowded."

Garth said, "Hey, I'll give you a tour of the old place, and I'll prove there're no ghosts."

"Tomie, let's go back," Sari pleaded.

I also felt that we should, so we turned around and started walking away from them.

"After everything I'd heard about the Dupuy family, I thought you would be up for some real fun, but I guess you're one of the weak ones, like your dead mama. Let's go, guys!"

I stopped and spun around to face him.

"What did you say?"

"Calling it as I see it," he said with an eerie smile painted on his face.

"Look, Garth, you don't know anything about my mom!"

I walked towards him, staring him down, and he backed up.

"Sorry, I didn't mean it. Just wanna have some fun and for us to be cool."

"Whatever!" I barked.

"Let's go!" Sari demanded.

"Hey, if you decide to come out, Caya knows the way.

I promise, it'll be a party you won't ever forget!"

As we headed back to meet up with Lisette and Crow, I thought more about it.

"Let's go."

"Where?" Caya asked.

"The party at the plantation."

Sari said, "Tomie, I don't think that's a good idea."

"Just want to shut Garth down, once and for all."

"He's not worth it," Caya mumbled.

Mr. Ray appeared and walked up to us.

"Didn't think you would be here tonight."

"I keep telling you, I'm always around. Hello, Sari, Caya." They both waved at him. "Tomie, you should listen to them. Don't go out to the plantation."

"It's just a party. I've already *glimmed* Garth, and I have it under control."

"You sure you saw everything?"

"All I needed to see."

Mr. Ray nodded, backed up, and walked away from me, as we changed directions and headed towards the parking lot.

"Tomie, you sure?" Caya asked.

"Yeah. Hey, where are Phoenixx and Luckie?"

Sari said, "They left right after the talent show. They'll catch up with us later."

I jumped into the backseat, and Caya started the car as she always did.

Sari said, "You and Tomie are so lucky to be able to do stuff with magic."

"Believe me, *you're* the lucky one, Sari." As Caya drove out to the plantation, she said, "Tomie, you don't have to do this."

"Everyone deserves a second chance, right?"

"I don't know if *everyone* does," Caya replied softly.

When we arrived, I saw Garth sitting on the hood of his truck, drinking something from a small paper sack. Once Caya parked, he slid off and came over to us.

"Didn't think you were going to show up. I take that back, what I said earlier." He held his hand up for me to slap it, but I ignored it. "Cool, no problem. Let me show you around. You've been here before, right, Tomie?"

"Only the outside, by boat."

"Where's everybody else?" Caya asked.

"Oh, they're on their way. A lot are still hanging out at the festival, and others probably ran into some traffic," Garth said.

The two-story house was huge. Most of the windows were broken, and a lot of the wood appeared to be rotten. The porch was caved in on one end.

"Sari, Caya, I'm going to check it out first, okay?"

They both nodded.

It was dark, so Garth pulled out a mini flashlight when we entered the foyer and walked a few feet inside. Cobwebs drooped down and swung side to side from the high ceilings, and stained sheets covered some of the remaining furniture.

Suddenly, I heard Lisette in my mind.

*Why are you there?* she asked in a stern tone.

*How do you know?*

*Mr. Ray updated me.*

*Just hanging out.*

*You shouldn't be there.*

*Why?*

*Tomie, just believe me. Get out of there now, all of you!*

# CHAPTER
## FIFTY-TWO

"Tomie!" Garth shouted.

"Yeah."

"I called your name three times, man. Where were you?"

"You know what? I'm going to check on the girls."

As the beam began to flicker, Garth started hitting the flashlight in his hand.

"Dang batteries, trying to go out on me. Sure, man. We can take a shortcut through the kitchen. It's right over there."

He pointed to his left, towards a pair of swinging doors, and I walked over, pushed them, and went into the room. I thought he was right behind me, but he wasn't.

After turning around, I leaned into the door and tried to go back through, but it wouldn't budge. It felt like someone had cemented it closed. I tried to move it physically and mentally—both attempts were unsuccessful.

When I walked to the back door and touched the metal knob, it burned me, but I didn't understand why. Jerking away, I felt blisters forming, but I knew they would go away within a few seconds.

Giving up on that idea, I headed back to the swinging doors and started beating my fists against them, yelling Garth's name, but he didn't respond. The pain was still there, so I looked down at my right hand and saw that the blisters had not faded, and it was beginning to throb even more.

A guy wearing a Yankees baseball outfit, with his face painted chalk white and a large black star over his left eye, came through the back door, which opened with a penetrating squeak. He held a bat and started swinging it around, taking small steps towards me. Then Garth stalked through the swinging doors with ease.

"Dupuy, I thought you were smarter than this," Garth said and then snickered under his breath. "I see you've met my brother Ash."

"What's this all about?"

"Oh, you'll see soon enough."

"I think I know."

"What do you think you know?"

They both walked around me in circles, heading in opposite directions.

"You're still mad about that night at the dock, when I encouraged Caya to make choices that would make her happy instead of miserable."

"Maybe… maybe not. It's time for us to teach you a little lesson, though."

"You two are no match for me."

"Really?" Ash yelled.

"Don't you find it odd that you couldn't open the door, but I could?" Garth asked.

I stepped away from them and looked at what was on the floor a bit closer, as I stooped down. Salt, mixed with something else, lined the doorway. When I touched it, my fingers began to sting. When I lifted them to my nose, I knew it was iron dust and wood shavings.

From what I read in my book, iron and salt could prevent a witch from entering someone's home, but in that case, it prevented me from leaving the kitchen area.

Crouching down lower, without touching the salt, I noticed two small holes on both sides of the doorframe. It looked like someone drilled them in order to shoot that stuff through.

I stood up and turned back around to face them.

"What're you two trying to do?"

Garth and Ash started walking towards me again. Holding my hands up, using all the power I had, I attempted to stop them, but it didn't work. I tried to think of a spell, but I couldn't recall even a simple one. With no idea what was happening to me, I tried to communicate with Lisette, but I got no response. Then it hit me that someone had *blocked* me from using my magic.

They laughed, as Ash said, "Looks like the warlock has lost his powers."

Rubbing his eyes with his fists for effect, Garth whined, "Oh, poor baby, can't defend himself now! *Boo-hoo-hoo*! We have witch friends, too, who know how to do and undo things."

Both he and Ash started changing into their rougarou forms, as I backed up several feet. Ash ripped his shirt off, and Garth yanked the overall strap away from his other shoulder. Their chests protruded, as rows of thick fur sprouted and cascaded down, and they fell to their knees, bowing their widened backs. Their shoes split open and slid off, as their feet grew a few inches, and yellowish claws emerged from what had been their fingers and toes. Large sharp spurs glistened on the backs of their ankles.

Noses transformed into snouts, and fangs appeared

with thick drool dripping onto the ground. Their ears grew to almost ten inches, with pointy ends, as they looked up at me with burning red eyes.

They howled loudly, and when they started galloping towards me, I looked around for something I could use as a weapon. When I saw a broom standing in the corner, I ran over and grabbed it. As they picked up speed and jumped towards me, I held it out in a horizontal position, my hands aching in response. Bracing myself for impact, I closed my eyes.

All of a sudden, I heard a loud crash, and the floors shook. Then lots of dust rained down on me, forming a cloud. As I coughed, I could barely make out bodies moving and flying through the smokescreen. When I wiped my eyes with the hem of my cape, I saw Lisette and Crow standing in the kitchen, and I knew she had used teleportation to bring him there with her.

# CHAPTER
## FIFTY-THREE

Crow wasn't the Hulk anymore—at least, not on the outside. He was an enormous silver and ebony rougarou with shimmering turquoise eyes, who looked to be over eight feet tall, much larger than Ash and Garth. He was holding the two up against the wall by their throats, as they thrashed and fought, trying to escape.

Lisette pulled the silver body rhinestones off her shoulders and threw them like darts at both of them, which ended their squirming and pinned them against the wall, leaving them howling even louder. What I thought were rhinestones must have been made of silver, because their fur started to smoke.

"You know the rules. Why are you two always defying me?" Crow asked in a gruff tone, fangs shimmering.

Though Crow loosened his grip around their necks, they remained against the wall. They panted and tried to get away, but instead, they were pulling clumps of their hair out. Crow yanked them down and held them by grabbing a handful of fur at the scruff of their necks. He lifted them off the floor and looked up at them.

"You'll both be dealt with by the chiefs for this," he said, his voice sounding more like a growl.

He walked them out, as Lisette came over to me.

"Tomie, why didn't you listen to Mr. Ray when he advised you not to come here? Or me, when I told you to leave?"

I thought about what she'd asked before I responded.

"I didn't want Garth to think…"

"To think what?"

She tapped her boots against the loose wood floor, both hands on her hips.

"That I was afraid."

"What's wrong with that?" I kept my head bowed down to my chest. "With you being powerless, they could've really hurt you."

"You're right, Lisette. I'm sorry."

I looked back up at her, as she grabbed my hand, and her eyes glowed while she stared down at my wound.

"You'll heal soon."

"Thanks. Please thank Crow for me when you see him."

"Tomie, you have to remember that any decision you make will have consequences. This could've had a very bad ending. . . and not just for you."

"You're right," I said, lowering my head once more to avoid her punishing and heated glare.

"Come on, let's get out of here."

"When will I get my powers back?"

"Seriously?"

"Just curious."

"It depends on the type of spell, which could be at any moment or up to a few hours. But maybe you should go without magic for an extra day or so."

"Lisette, come on. Really?"

"Yes! You need to be aware of dangerous situations. You won't take this seriously if you aren't punished. Choice and free will are fine, but as your primary teacher and someone who loves you, I need to drill it into your thick skull somehow."

I shook my head, and we walked outside. Caya and Sari were standing near the car.

Sari said, "We tried to come in when we heard loud noises, but we couldn't."

"A lock-out spell was placed on the house to keep anyone from coming inside, which is why I teleported Crow and me in," Lisette explained.

"I'm not surprised. Tomie, Garth tried to hurt you?" Caya asked.

When I looked at her, there was no need to reply—she already knew.

Sari asked, "Tomie, you okay?"

"Yeah, just some blisters."

I lifted my hand for her to see, and she hugged me.

We made our way to the car, and Lisette rode with us back to her house.

"Sari, you heard anything from Phoenixx or Luckie?" I asked.

"They're on their way back to Frost, because Phoenixx's dad was involved in a car accident."

"Is he okay?"

"All I know is that he was being admitted to the hospital."

"Man, a lot is going on tonight. I hope he'll be okay."

"I'll let you know once he updates me."

I reviewed the entire night and thought about how I came close to being slaughtered by two rougarous. Who could've ever imagined something like that? I was sure that Mr. Ray's lecture was coming soon, and I wasn't looking forward to it.

As we drove down the gravel road and approached Lisette's house, we noticed that the front door was wide open.

"Lisette, you locked that door, right?" I asked, as Caya was parking the car.

"Of course," she said warily. "Girls, stay put!"

"We know the routine," Caya replied.

Lisette and I stepped out of the car, and Sari grabbed my unblistered hand.

When I leaned back in, she said, "Be careful, Tomie."

"I will."

When I stepped in and scanned the living room, everything seemed to be in place.

Lisette pulled me back and said, "Let me go first, Tomie. Your powers haven't been restored yet."

With a swipe of her hand, she turned on all the lights in the house, and we proceeded to walk through. The kitchen looked the same except that Sabra wasn't in her bed. Lisette searched in her room, under her bed, inside her closet, and in her bathroom. At the same time, I checked everywhere on my end of the house, but no Sabra.

During those few minutes, we didn't even see the open basement door. When we noticed it, we both ran over to it and looked at each other before we began our descent.

"Lisette, let me go."

"Tomie, no!"

She slowly walked down each step, as I followed. When we got to the bottom of the staircase, we saw something that put both our heartrates into overdrive.

# CHAPTER
## FIFTY-FOUR

The little glass house was no longer on the shelf. It was lying on the floor, shattered into countless pieces.

Opal was gone.

We both ran over to it, and Lisette kneeled and ran her hands over the broken shards. They reassembled into the original shape, with several cracks remaining on the interior. She took a towel from a shelf and laid it on the table, then used her magic to move the house onto it.

She peered inside it and worked a revealing spell to show us what happened. We saw someone dressed in a dark blue hooded robe—face concealed—enter Lisette's house and open the basement door. The stranger then went down, grabbed Opal's glass house, and performed what Lisette said was probably an unbinding-release spell to allow Opal to be free from her prison.

Lisette looked at me in shock.

"Tomie, someone who was in my house allowed that stranger inside."

"What're you talking about?"

"I placed a very powerful lock-out spell around my home years ago to prevent any *supras* from entering without my permission."

"Are you telling me that someone broke it?"

"Yes! All it would take is for a *supra* who's been invited into my home to place a temporary unlocking spell, which is short-lived. Now I'll have to place a hindering spell around my home."

"The only new people who were here tonight were Sari's friends—that Phoenixx dude and Luckie."

Lisette started pacing and replied, "Yeah, but Sari was here, too."

"Hold up! Sari wouldn't do anything like that!"

"I'm sorry, but right now, I can't dismiss anyone as a potential suspect."

"Even Caya and Crow?"

"Possibly. Tomie, you need to start paying more attention to things and people. Some will deceive you when you least expect it, even those you trust the most!"

"I just don't believe Sari would do something like this. . . to anyone!"

"Hoping she wouldn't. I need to figure this out, and the sooner, the better."

"Lisette, I have an idea who might've come to take Opal out of here."

"Ms. Dawn? If so, then a big storm is coming a lot sooner than I anticipated."

"Wait, you saw something else, too, but you used a blocking spell, so I wouldn't see, didn't you?" She walked away, but I followed her. "Tell me."

"You don't want to know."

"I do. Please tell me."

She remained silent.

My entire body suddenly heated up, and when I

looked down at my blistered right hand, it was healed. My powers were reawakening. Focusing my eyes on the glass ball, I made it levitate up towards me, closer to my face.

With the tip of my index finger pointing at it, I spun it around a few times as if I was fast-forwarding past the useless scenes, until I landed on the one that would reveal the answers.

I saw much more than I expected, and when I looked at Lisette, the ball crashed to the floor.

"Ms. Dawn and Opal are recruiting their army."

Lisette nodded in slow motion, while I collapsed onto the floor to my knees.

Some other troubling images appeared to me, and it was only then that I noticed bloody pawprints to my left.

*Sabra!*

# EPILOGUE

The revealing spell also showed me their future plans as if I was right there with them.

I saw Ms. Dawn and Opal having dinner with Mr. Fox in his lavish home full of ivory, gold, silver, the finest antiques, and collectibles from all over the world. As they sat around the table, eating sushi and caviar, Verlinda Dawn spewed out more lies about all the events that led up to Pepper Fox's unfortunate demise. They painted a false portrait of how Opal had nothing to do with her death. Instead, they fed Mr. Fox their morsels of hate for Lisette, Sari, and me.

Ms. Dawn handed Mr. Fox a slip of yellow paper with some writing on it, and he escorted them out. I couldn't make out the name, but I easily read the phone number and address.

It was 713 Catawissa Drive in Salem, Massachusetts.

Whoever sent me the mystery text on my way to Lisette's, with the unknown number, mentioned that street name.

Mr. Fox walked down a long hallway, into a huge

library with lots of tall bookcases, and approached a ten-inch glass figurine of a Frost High Polar Bear crouching down, its claws stretched out. As he looked over his shoulder, he turned it 180 degrees.

Within thirty seconds, two of the bookshelves slid back, revealing a secret chamber like *Batman's* cave. He walked down a staircase; then he put on a jacket, one glove, and a pair of cushioned goggles that were hanging on hooks nearby.

Standing in front of a stainless-steel door with a glass numeric keypad on the upper right corner, he placed his bare hand over the sensor next to it. The door opened, and cold white air shot out, as he slipped the other glove on. Shivering, he rubbed up and down his arms, as he entered.

A golden coffin rested in the middle of the room, and specialized equipment and computer screens were mounted on the walls. In a clear cubicle, about a hundred feet from where Mr. Fox stood, sat a middle-aged woman wearing a lab coat and oversized round red glasses.

He waved to her, and she pushed a button on a control panel at her side.

She said in a shaky tone, "Mr. Fox, your private jet is being prepped and will be ready in the morning to load up your *precious cargo* and transport you and Ms. Dawn to Salem at 8:30."

As the top slid back, Mr. Fox nodded to her and continued to stare down at the coffin, and then he started talking to whoever was in there, but I couldn't make out most of his conversation.

Written on the side was *Frost Cryogenic Labs.*

I figured it must've been top secret, because I'd never heard of Frost having such a place.

Then everything hit me at once.

As I thought about Mr. Fox's first meeting with Ms.

Dawn and the dinner they just had to discuss their twisted plans, the revealing spell showed me what he had done. Mr. Fox had frozen his daughter's remains, and he was taking her to Salem to contact a Dark Shadow Witch to place a reverse transmigration spell on his *precious cargo*, Pepper Fox!

When I told Lisette about everything I'd seen, she confirmed that her vision was the same.

At that point, I knew that my senior year at Frost High and waiting to hear if I was accepted to the academy wouldn't be the most important things on my agenda. Keeping Sari, Lisette, and anyone else I cared for, as well as myself, alive was going to be my top priority.

The five from Opal's riddle were now obvious to me: Verlinda Dawn, Opal, Mr. Fox, Mr. Green, and the unknown Dupuy Silver Slayer.

However, she left one out, so it should've really been *six*:

**Pepper Fox**...

# TO BE CONTINUED...

**Will you be ready for the last installment of the Doll Series?**

Anticipated Release Date:
# EARLY 2019

# THE
# HATCH

# THE HATCH

A fatal motorcycle accident stole my twin brother Ryker away from me seventeen days ago. He died instantly from blunt force trauma to the head, and since then, every time I saw or heard a bike, I cringed.

My life, especially high school, meant nothing to me anymore.

Ryker and I were *fosters*—foster kids. We bounced around a few different homes, before we ended up together again last Christmas with the Dribblers. Ryker played a big part in getting me placed with them by writing letters to my caseworker, Mr. Crix.

We wrote to each other to stay in touch because I didn't own a reliable phone.

The Dribblers weren't saints, but they were much better than the Barkers, my last family, who were later banned from fostering. They were never found guilty; they were smart and knew how to squirm their way out of most sticky situations. Someone in the system told me that they left the United States once I transferred out of their home. After staying with them, I always locked my bedroom door.

Mrs. Dribbler wanted us to call her Mom, like her other three fosters—Jodie, a ten-year-old girl; Harold, a fourteen-year-old boy; and Bixie, a sixteen-year-old girl. They weren't related, but I guess she wanted to come across as the perfect mother, truly taking us all under her wing.

Jodie's parents were each sentenced to fifteen years in prison for racketeering. Harold's mom was a teen, and she decided to leave him on someone's doorstep after she had him. He was so smart that he skipped the 7$^{th}$ and 8$^{th}$ grades. Bixie never shared much about herself, and I didn't dare ask her. I figured that secrets were kept for a reason.

They all sucked up to Mrs. Dribbler, and she loved

it, but Ryker and I only felt comfortable calling her Mrs. D. Her husband couldn't have cared less. He always retreated to his mancave, which was a dilapidated shed in the backyard, after working ten to twelve hours each day at the local diaper factory. Sometimes he worked on the weekends, too. He didn't talk much to any of us, and I never witnessed him displaying any affection for Mrs. D.

Whenever she cooked—usually almost-raw slop that could barely be considered food—or bought cheap takeout, Ryker and I were only allowed to eat after all the others were finished. We usually ended up with scraps, with hardly anything left, especially after Bixie made two plates. She ate only a couple of bites before she dumped the rest in the trash.

It didn't really matter. Ryker usually had a stash of stuff for us to snack on later at our safe place, The Hatch. We came up with the code name together.

Ryker built The Hatch, a treehouse, a few months after I was placed with the Dribblers, when he figured out that we might be with them a little longer than we thought.

He found a great place in the woods, far away from the house and most of civilization. The inside was lined with several rows of battery-powered colored lights on the ceiling, zigzagging the walls, too. He painted the outside in colors to blend in with the large tree.

A stack of used comic books and an antique-looking hourglass with black sand rested on a small table in the corner. Ryker loved that thing. I think he picked it up at a garage sale a few months before we were reunited; he mentioned it in some of the letters he wrote me. He always flipped it over when we hung out in The Hatch.

When looking up at the stars from the raised rooftop, as we lay there sipping cold sodas, Ryker told me how special that place was to him.

Celebrity posters of music artists such as Ariana Grande, Rihanna, and New Edition hugged one wall, and Ryker hung all of my ballerina watercolors on the rest. The last picture of us—I was holding a stuffed lion almost six feet tall between Ryker and me, when we attended a carnival a month before—was in the center, with a flowery wreath wrapped around it.

The night before Ryker left me, he said, "Sage, whenever you feel lost or afraid, come to The Hatch."

I never knew how powerful that place was until the night of the storm.

Someone was banging on my bedroom door, and then a key rattled inside the hole. I rolled over with the covers still wrapped around me, as it swung open as if a rhinoceros stormed in.

"You got ten minutes to get ready if you want a ride! You've been in this room for almost a week now! He's gone, and he's not ever coming back!" Mrs. D shouted.

"Why do you have to say such mean things?"

"What did you say?"

"Nothing," I mumbled.

"Exactly. By the way, it's pouring down out there, and it's getting worse. You're going to school today, missy, so either get up, or I'm dragging you out of that bed!" she yelled and yanked the covers off me.

She looked fuzzy, as she walked out the door and

slammed it. My glasses had fallen off my nightstand, as well as my ballerina music box that Ryker gave me on my birthday two years ago.

Stretching out my hands, I found my glasses and put them on, and all the blurry things in the room sharpened—I could see clearly once again. When I picked up my music box from the floor, I noticed that the lower right part of the ballerina's baby blue tutu had chipped on impact, but I hoped that I could repair it later.

Ryker's funeral kept playing in my mind every time I thought of him. The service was short, and most of the sophomore class attended. His caseworker offered a small monetary gift in the amount of $125 for a suit, flowers, and food.

Mrs. D bought Ryker's suit from a thrift store, and the jacket sleeve stopped at his elbow. She plucked a few shabby plastic flowers from an arrangement in the living room earlier that day and threw them on top of his casket. I added some fresh multicolored carnations that Mrs. Meiko had given me. She was a florist I sometimes helped on the weekends.

Later that night, after the funeral, Mrs. D returned home smelling like cigarettes and beer, with a paper bag full of lottery scratch-offs. There was no doubt in my mind that they were purchased with what was left of Ryker's funeral expense money.

After school, I walked to the graveyard every day to visit Ryker's tombstone. Sometimes I brought a few of his favorite comics—*Blade*, *Captain America*, and *Wonder Woman*—and books—*The Outsiders* and the *Cemetery*

*Tours* series—and read to him.

Mrs. D contacted my caseworker and told her that I needed a psychiatric referral as fast as possible. I tried to convince Mr. Crix that I didn't need any help, but he made an appointment for me anyway. When I went, I said very little to the stuffy psychiatrist. He referred me to a grief support group and prescribed an antidepressant, which I didn't take. Instead, I hid it under my bathroom sink.

Unlike Ryker, I had no friends at school. He was the great-looking one they all loved. When the *Pops*, the popular kids, gagged or stared at me, he always swooped in at the right time. They made snide remarks about my triple-freckle patches on my cheeks or called me *Fishbowls*; my glasses were super thick. I was born with an awful eye condition, which meant that I couldn't walk five steps without my glasses, or I'd bump into something or trip... even in the shower. Regardless of those mean kids' nasty comments about my disability, Ryker always knew the right thing to say to force their piercing eyes away from me or stop their verbal daggers.

After dragging myself to the bathroom, I stared in the mirror for a bit, brushed my teeth, and took the pills out from under my sink. I set them on the counter and paced the short area a few times with my eyes glued to them. Then I grabbed the bottle, unscrewed the top, and poured them into my palm; a few fell into the sink. As I guided my hand towards my mouth, I looked up at the mirror and noticed a message that Ryker had written to me with a dry erase marker: *You're beautiful and my #1 girl! Never forget it!*

*Not today, Sage*, I whispered to myself.

I put the pills back into the bottle, including the ones that fell into the sink, and then I poured some mouthwash in, screwed the top on, shook it up, and tossed it into the trashcan under some paper towels.

Grabbing my backpack, I opened the door and walked down the stairs, where I saw Mrs. D backing out of the garage. Jodie stuck her tongue out at me, and Bixie rolled her eyes, as the rain poured down hard.

I searched for an umbrella, but I had no luck, so I went outside and headed down the street. By the time I reached my school, about ten blocks away, I felt like I was carrying an extra twenty pounds, because I was drenched.

As I was tromping towards the door, I saw Bixie walking by with some of her friends, the Bixettes. Then someone tapped me on my shoulder, and when I turned around, I saw that it was Harold.

He lowered his head and mumbled, "You better not let Bixie see you."

I paused for a few seconds, because he didn't normally say much at all, especially to me.

"Thanks, Harold."

He looked at me briefly and hurried inside, but instead of going in, I turned around and ran all the way to The Hatch. After climbing the wobbly fifty-seven steps, I untied the ribbon lock and opened the door. Inside, I found a set of dry sweats and a blanket.

After taking my wet clothes off, I changed into the dry ones. Then I wrapped the blanket around me, grabbed a few comics, turned the hourglass over, and pulled out a bag of red licorice. I'd read those things over a hundred times, but it always seemed like the first, and somehow, it made me feel like Ryker was there with me.

The hours passed quickly.

# THE HATCH

Pushing the stack of books aside, I stared out the window, and the rain was coming down even harder. Glancing at my watch, I saw that it was about 8:00 p.m. I turned on the radio next to me, and the DJ interrupted the music for a weather update.

With a trembling voice, he said, "Please seek shelter immediately. A tornado is headed towards Simararian Grove in the next thirty minutes. Please seek shelter now!"

I looked out the windows on both sides and noticed the rain was beginning to slow, but the wind had picked up. Large tree limbs broke off and flew into the air, banging against the rooftop, along with other debris.

As I backed into a corner, The Hatch began to shake, and the hourglass dropped and broke. The black sand spilled out onto the floor, but it didn't fall through the cracks in between the boards. Instead, it climbed the walls, accumulated into a pile, levitated, and blew towards my face. It formed squiggly words in the air.

*Don't Be Afraid.*

Then it flew out the window.

After checking my glasses, I saw that they were clean. It definitely wasn't my eyes—a reddish glow reflected off the broken shards. Rushing to the window, I peeked outside and noticed how the thick clouds parted for a moment.

A full blood moon!

The DJ only told half the story, because I saw twin twisters headed towards me!

I crawled towards the door, but it was stuck, and the high winds blew me back into the corner. My drawings, posters, and some of the comic books flew out the windows, but I was able to catch the picture of Ryker and me before the winds could steal my last captured memory of him.

As The Hatch shook harder, I thought I was about to fly out or crash to the ground, so I braced myself against the corner, pulled my knees up to my chest, and closed my eyes, while the twisters screamed at each other.

After spinning all the way around at least three times, The Hatch's door flew off and blew out. Through the hole it left, I saw the tornadoes fly over the house and head out of town. Then, as the winds began to cease, I looked up at that blood moon.

There was a loud crash on the roof, which collapsed, and something shocking landed in front of me in the middle of the floor. It resembled a large egg. I grabbed the bamboo stick that was lying next to me and used it to roll it around a few times.

I decided to walk over and examine it closer. Before my hand could touch it, a warm blue vapor rose from it, so I jerked away. When I heard a crackling noise, I jumped back, picked up the stick, and held it out towards the unknown thing, as more of the steam shot out from cracks in it.

Then it rolled over to the opposite corner of The Hatch, as the moon projected a scarlet glowing beam on it through one of the windows. It broke open, and something that looked somewhat human, but not completely, remained in a fetal position, as it slid out. It slowly unfolded, and four wings popped out, one of them touching my leg. I shot towards the door, flew down the steps, and ran at top speed.

Once I got far enough away from The Hatch, I stopped, looked back, bent over, and placed my hands on my shaky knees to take several deep breaths. All I saw was the night's ebony backdrop with the blood moon still hanging in the center. Then I noticed that beam from the moon was still being projected into The Hatch, which had somehow landed exactly in its proper place.

My running continued, until I saw flashing red and blue lights at the Dribblers' home.

After I walked to the back, I peeped around the corner and saw Mr. and Mrs. D standing near the cop cars, talking to one of the police officers. When I felt something twist my arm, I fell straight to the ground on my knees.

"Please, please don't hurt me!" I screamed, as tears rolled down my face.

"What are you talking about? You're crazy!" Bixie yelled in my ear. "Mom, I found her. Here she is. Get up!"

I stood up and looked behind me, and it really was Bixie, with her rainbow ponytails. She slammed her spiked bracelets down into my wrists, as she walked me around to the front of the house like a handcuffed murder suspect.

"Where have you been, missy? We thought you ran away… or worse! I almost had a heart attack! Right, Sam?"

She pulled a bottle out of her housecoat pocket. She opened it, threw a few round colored tablets into her mouth, and chewed them up, as Mr. D shook his head and walked back towards his mancave.

The cops asked me a few questions, took my statement and filled out a report, then left.

Once we were all in the house, Bixie was on the couch

with Harold and Jodie.

She mouthed, *"You're going to get it."*

Her smile reminded me of one of the creepy-looking clowns you see sitting on the store shelves at Halloween that everyone stops to look at but never purchases.

Mrs. D pulled the curtain back and peered out the window to make sure that the cops had gone, and then she turned around and backhanded me. My glasses flew off, and I fell to the floor. She stooped down and dragged me up by my curly shoulder-length hair, as I looked into her bloodshot eyes.

"If you ever pull another stunt like you did today, ditching school and having me call the cops out here, I promise it'll be your last." I could hear the muffled giggles from Bixie and Jodie behind me. "Now, go to bed! You're going to school and group tomorrow. I'll make sure of that!"

As I searched the floor for my glasses, a sharp pain shot up my arm, and I jerked my hand back. Mrs. D had stepped on it when she walked by me towards the hallway. Then I heard a crack.

"Oh, I'm so sorry. I didn't see your glasses," Bixie said, mocking me.

"Please get my spare out of my room."

"Whatever. Get them yourself! Crawl!"

After several minutes, I felt someone pull me up, and I pushed back against them.

"Sage, it's me, Harold. Come on." He helped me get to my feet and guided me up the stairs and to my room. "Where is your spare?"

"In my nightstand near the back, where my music box is."

Harold rummaged through my drawer, and then I saw something blurry walking towards me. He handed them to me, and I put them on, and I could see again.

"You okay?"

"Yeah, I'll be all right. Thank you."

Harold began to walk out of my room, but he turned around.

"You're on her list."

"What're you talking about?" I asked, squinting my eyes.

"The list to send away. I heard her talking to someone over the phone earlier about you being too much to handle now."

"That's okay. It's not the same without Ryker."

"I'm sorry."

"Thanks again, Harold."

He walked out and closed the door behind him, and I rushed over and locked it.

My mind went back to The Hatch and what I saw. I wondered if I had been hallucinating, but I hadn't taken any of the medication, and even if I had, I wasn't sure if that would be a side effect.

After taking a quick shower, I crawled into bed, tossed and turned, and ended up staring at my window most of the night. Once, I got up to make sure it was locked—it was.

As I went back to bed, I tried to convince myself that I didn't see anything in The Hatch earlier.

I probably got about two hours of sleep, before Mrs. D rattled my door with her key. Jumping up, I scooted towards the far corner of my bed.

"You got twenty-five minutes to get dressed. I'm driving you to school and picking you up for group afterwards." She walked towards my bed and leaned in close to me, pointing her finger in my face, and whispered, "I'll know if you skip today or any other day, missy."

She cut her eyes at me and started walking backwards out of my room, swishing her praying-mantis-like body around tauntingly.

"Oh, and by the way, the incident last night never happened. If you breathe even one word about it to your caseworker, things will be much worse for you here. Much!" She tossed some concealer makeup onto my bed. "Put some of that on your right cheek and blend it in well."

After taking a few deep breaths, I crawled out of bed. Looking at my face in the mirror, I noticed a slight purplish bruising on my right cheek. Then I washed up, rubbed the concealer on the area, and dabbed a powder brush all over until it was blended. I got dressed in half the time it usually takes me and gobbled down a bowl of cereal in the kitchen.

Before the rest of us even reached the car, Bixie had the front seat. Jodie was in the back. I went to scoot her backpack over, but she tried to scratch me like a feral cat. Mrs. D turned around and shoved it into her lap.

"Cut it out, you two!"

I slid down, buckled my seatbelt, and shut the door. As we rode along, no one said a word.

Before I got out of the car, Mrs. D grabbed my arm and squeezed it tight, hissing, "Remember what I told you."

When I nodded, she released her grip.

# THE HATCH

Walking into the school, I felt like everyone was staring at me and talking about me. Bixie joined her Bixettes, and they walked past me and laughed. My morning classes went by with me in a daze, and then the bell rang, and it was time for lunch.

Grabbing a ham sandwich with cheddar and mustard on wheat bread, a chocolate milk, and a banana from the cold bar, I found a window seat facing towards the woods and The Hatch. Bixie walked by and stared at me, and a few other giggles followed, so I grabbed my lunch and went outside.

Harold was sitting under a tree by himself, so I asked, "Hey, okay if I sit with you?"

He shrugged and said, "Sure."

"Can I ask you a question?"

"Yeah."

"Why are you being so nice to me lately? You hardly ever looked at me or spoke to me when I first came to the Dribblers'."

"I guess, because I know what it feels like to be a target. Since Ryker died, you're it. He protected you."

I sighed and nodded.

"How long have you lived with them?"

"Almost two years."

"Do you like it?"

"Not really, but it beats my last placement."

"How?"

"I'm not going to the emergency room anymore."

"Wow, Harold. I thought I had it bad at my last one."

The bell rang, and Harold stood and helped me up.

"Don't mention this to Mom or Bixie," he said.

"Of course not."

As we were walking and about to go to different classrooms, I leaned in and whispered, "Did you see or hear anything strange last night?"

"Nope. Just how lucky we all were for the twin tornadoes to miss us."

"Harold, you didn't notice anything different about the moon?"

"No. It was normal looking to me. Why? What'd you see?"

"Nothing. Just wondering."

Harold went left, and I went right to Algebra I.

After school, Mrs. D was parked with the engine running, so I walked over, opened the door, and sat down next to Jodie.

"You're five minutes late!"

She drove me to Dawn's Hope Center and told me that she was going to be in the waiting room, so I got out of the car.

"Hold on!" she yelled. "Come here."

When I went over to her, she pulled out some concealer and a compact from her purse and touched up the makeup on the bruise she had made when she hit me. Then I walked down the curvy sidewalk to the glass door and rang the bell.

"May I help you?" the voice on the intercom asked.

"I'm here for group."

"What's your first name and the code?"

"Sage and *red robin*."

I heard a buzz, and the door opened. A tall young lady escorted me to a steel door, punched in a code on the number pad, and pointed to *Group Room B*. When I went in, I saw the therapist's name tag in bold letters; her name was Izzie. Six other members sat in a circle. Everyone there had suffered from either an immediate or past loss.

"Welcome, Sage. Have a seat wherever you wish."

A plump green and yellow plaid pillow next to the wall attracted me, so I claimed it.

"Okay, who would like to volunteer and tell us how his or her week has been going so far?" No hands went up. "Well, in that case, I'll share. My week started off pretty rough with a load of assignments and then some new training. Today has been easier to juggle." When she was done, I raised my hand. "Sage, please go ahead."

"This is more of a question."

"That's okay."

"I was talking to my foster brother earlier and asked him if he saw or heard anything last night during the storm. He didn't, of course. Did anyone here notice anything strange?"

They all shook their heads.

"Like what?" asked Francie.

"I don't know. Forget it."

Yazmine whispered, "I've heard about weird stuff on stormy nights… strange things either heard, seen, or both. If you think you saw something, you should definitely make sure."

"Really?"

"Absolutely. Check it out again, and then you'll know for sure."

"Sage," said Izzie, "I wouldn't advise that if it's not safe. Don't ever place yourself in danger, no matter what you think you may have seen."

I nodded, still staring at Yazmine, as I mumbled, "Okay."

Someone else began to tell us about what was going on in her life, and then the talking went on and on, as my mind wandered back to The Hatch.

"My goodness," Izzy said. "It's already been forty-five minutes. Before we close, I want each of us to go around the room and share some positive thoughts or images."

Each group member participated, including Izzie.

Once we were done, Mr. Crix, my caseworker, was waiting outside to meet with me in another room. He closed the door and pointed at a chair, and then he pulled another one from a corner and sat down with his notebook.

"Sage, you really scared your foster parents yesterday by not showing up at school and being out during that storm."

"I know."

"You can't keep doing things like this and expect that family to keep you—or if you ever want to be adopted. Your past follows you. You've definitely built a reputation for yourself over the years."

"Mr. Crix, it was never my fault in those other homes."

He rearranged his tie.

"I've heard that a lot. You're at an age now that many foster parents don't want, and adoption is very unlikely for you."

Staring out the window, I took a deep breath and said, "I understand."

"All right, I'm going to be making a few surprise visits at your school and home over the next few weeks. Try to get your act together. Mrs. Dribbler has requested your transfer out of her house if you do one more thing to cause her grief."

*Really? Me causing her grief?*

I wanted to tell him everything about Mrs. D, starting from when I was first placed there to the night before, but I kept my mouth shut. I had another plan.

He scribbled something in his notebook, and then we

stood, and he escorted me out of the secure unit.

"See you next week, Sage!" Yazmine yelled out. She then walked up next to me and whispered in my ear, "You should really check it out."

She winked and then joined a few other group members and started talking with them.

When Mr. Crix opened the door, Mrs. D was there.

"Good evening, Mrs. Dribbler."

"Good evening to you, Mr. Crix. All okay here?" she asked with a crooked smile on her cracked off-scarlet lips.

A few sweat beads bubbled up on her oily forehead and ran down over her scanty eyebrows. Thick false lashes were barely hanging on to her wrinkled eyelids, which were heavily painted with puke-green eyeshadow.

"Yes, Sage and I had a little talk. Things should be better from here on out."

We all walked out of the building, and he waved as he drove away.

Bixie was texting, while Jodie was reading a tabloid, as I got into the backseat. Mrs. D started the car up and fixed her eyes on me in her rearview mirror as if we were the only ones in the car.

"You better not have mentioned anything about last night."

"I didn't."

"What did y'all talk about in that stupid group meeting of yours, anyway?"

"Not much. Just the storm last night and our fears."

"Amazes me, how much free stuff you crazies get out of the system."

Everyone went to bed early that night except for Mr. D and me.

When I got to my room, I pulled out a hundred dollars from underneath my mattress and stuffed it down deep in my pants pocket. I'd been saving up from little odd jobs over the last few months—specifically, helping Mrs. Meiko.

After wrapping my ballerina music box in a towel, I grabbed my bathroom things. Then I took out some clothes, folded them, and put them in the bottom of my backpack. I added my music box and toiletries and then zipped it up.

When I had all that done, I walked into the closet and brought out my jacket, a flashlight, a rope I made out of shredded sheets, and some batteries off the top shelf. I put on my jacket, buttoned it up, and pulled my backpack over my shoulders. After tying the rope onto the heavy bedpost of the footboard, I opened my window, threw it out, and climbed down to the ground.

When I turned around to see a shadow approaching from my right side, my heart raced.

After I saw who it was, I asked, "Where did you come from, Harold?"

"I figured you were going to run away soon."

"Take care of yourself," I said, as I patted him on his shoulder.

"You're going to your secret place?"

"How do you know about that?"

"The question you asked me earlier. . . You saw something last night, didn't you, Sage?"

"I think so. I've gotta be sure, so I'm headed there to check it out."

"Want me to go with you?"

"No. I really need to do this on my own."

"Okay. Be careful."

"I will. I'd rather take my chances out there than here. Goodbye, Harold," I said, as I hugged him.

"Here, take this."

He handed me an envelope. Inside it was a bunch of bills.

"I can't take your money."

I held it out to him, but he pushed it back towards me.

"Yeah, you can. You're going to need it a lot more than I will." He stuffed it down the side of my backpack pocket and zipped it. "When you get to where you're going, drop me a note." I nodded, as he whispered, "I'll take care of the rope in your room."

"Thanks, Harold."

As he headed towards the front of the house, I started walking into the woods. After I was a few feet away, I turned on the flashlight. The moon was out, but it wasn't blood red like last night, and there was a soft breeze. An owl hooted a few times, and I saw one perched up in a tree in front of me. It blinked its golden eyes and fluffed out its feathers, before it flew off.

When I was a few feet away from the front of my secret place, my knees began to wobble. As I was about to climb up the wooden steps, I paused. My heart was beating faster, the closer I got.

The Hatch was still secure in the tree, where it had landed when the winds dropped it. The interior looked like it had been robbed, judging by the sight of the remaining items that were tossed around or broken.

Shining the light in each corner, I searched for the mysterious winged creature, but I didn't see it.

*Just as I thought, I'm going crazy. Maybe I should've taken my prescription.*

After climbing inside, I looked for the picture of Ryker

and me. Besides my music box, it was the last thing I had left of him, and I wanted to take it with me on my journey. It was stuck between some boards near a window. When I went to pull it out, something grabbed it.

It was the creature!

The thing was transparent, and as it crouched in the corner, I could see through it like glass, which was why I missed it when I first came in.

Then it transformed into a two-tone bronze. Two small glistening turquoise-colored wings were on its upper shoulders, and two larger ones were attached mid-torso. They were folded inward and appeared to be three-dimensional, with sharp hooks at the ends. Its arms and legs were extremely muscular, and both hands and feet were claw-like. Freckles covered its body and face.

Three silver bracelets were on each wrist, and three on its ankles, with tiny golden bells adorning each one. A starfish-shaped tattoo with multiple squiggly arms was on its cheek, and it gave off a faint blue glow every few seconds.

Its eyes were angled upward, with an iridescent purple shimmer surrounding each iris. It had a wide oval face and pointy ears; silver hoop earrings dangled from each one. Its teeth were normal, with the exception of thick upper fangs and cherry-tinted lips.

Long curly ebony hair was pulled up in a ponytail, with a strand of multi-colored beads which hung down to its neck. Its chiseled chest was bare, but it wore black Kendo Hakama cut-offs—Japanese wide-legged pants. The only reason I knew about Hakama pants was because of a martial arts book I'd read recently.

I'd never seen anything like that creature—even in comics or movies—and I had no idea what it was or what it wanted from me.

It walked towards me, and I stepped backwards and fell.

Holding my arms out, I screamed, "Please don't eat me!"

It stooped down, sniffed my hair, and gnarred, "You're not my type. I'm a vegetarian."

I pulled my hands back and asked, "You can talk?"

The creature stood up and levitated into midair with its legs crossed; the roof of The Hatch had disappeared the night of the storm.

"Of course, I can talk. You humans are so easy to read… always making assumptions before you give anyone a chance."

I stood and said, "I'm sorry."

"No need to apologize, Sage. It's nothing new."

"How do you know me?"

"I know many things."

"What's your name, and what exactly are you?

"Hageshii, and I'm a *GargoJinn.*"

"What's a *GargoJinn*?"

"Short version—my mother is a genie, and my dad, a gargoyle. They fell in love when they were teens during the *Yokai Tournament Festival*, where all supernaturals— shifters, spirits, and hybrids alike—come together once a year to compete in magical games and celebrate with food and music."

Speechless, I stared at Hageshii with my mouth open and eyes wide. I'd read about supernatural beings, but I couldn't believe I was talking with one.

"I'm blowing your mind, huh?" I nodded. "Now, let's get down to business, Sage."

"Wait. How old are you?"

"The same as you, sixteen."

I blinked several times.

"Why are you here?"

"Your deceased twin made a wish one night while staring at the hourglass. He didn't even know it."

Tears poured down my cheeks, and I took my glasses off and wiped my eyes with the sleeve of my shirt, before putting them back on.

"Your brother wanted you to have a good life. So, I was sent to make it come true for you. *GargoJinns* can only travel to the human world when a storm happens during a blood moon."

"Why only then?"

"We must conceal our identity and can never be discovered. After studying your historical textbooks and our time travels over the centuries, we've seen much, especially how humans experiment without consent and destroy what your kind doesn't understand because of fear."

There wasn't much I could say to that, because Hageshii was right. I could relate a little to what he was saying because of the way people treated me, due to my eyesight disability.

He unbuckled the top of a leather satchel tied around his thigh and pulled out a clock device that displayed eccentric symbols I'd never seen before. He looked at it, placed it back in the bag, and closed it.

"Enough about my background. I must complete my mission and leave this realm soon, or I'll be stuck here until the next blood moon."

"Really?"

"Yes. Now, close your eyes and give me your hand." They were trembling, as I reached out to his claw. "Sage, I'm here to help you, not hurt you, okay? Ryker wanted you to have this last gift from him."

I nodded slowly and whispered, "All right."

"Touch my chest and think of three wishes. The only one I cannot grant is awakening the dead from their deep slumber. Close your eyes, Sage, and think now!"

Following his orders, I first felt one throbbing heart, then two. I pulled my hand away and put it back after a split-second of hesitation. As I cracked one eye open, I saw his chest begin to glow a golden-turquoise, which circulated around my hand.

"I'm going to place my claw on your forehead and transport your wishes into my hearts. Relax and don't peek."

"Wait. What's it like to have real loving parents?"

"You've never met your biological parents?"

"No. I've been in the foster system since my brother and I were born. I don't even know if they're still alive. Please tell me what it's like."

He looked up into the starry sky and said, "I can only speak from my experiences."

"Okay."

"Of course, I don't agree with my parents on everything, but I know they love me. They allow me to fly and fall on my own, but they're always there to fly with me when I need them to. Does that make sense?"

"Yes. It makes a lot of sense. Thank you."

"Ready now, Sage?"

"Yes." After a few seconds, I asked, "Can I open my eyes now?"

"Yes."

I opened them, as he stepped back and wiped a blue tear away with the back of his claw.

Looking into his eyes, I asked, "What did you see, Hageshii?"

"Your memories and thoughts are full of pain, more than the normal human teen girl." I lowered my head.

"Remember that you can never tell anyone about our encounter. If you do, then *GargoJinns* could be banned from your world forever and never grant wishes to anyone else that may need them, as you do."

"I promise."

"Will I ever see you again, Hageshii?"

"Most likely not. My work is fulfilled."

"Why do you grant wishes to humans?"

"An elder genie, Shazia Yasuragi, started this practice many centuries ago. She wanted to enhance lives by bestowing gifts to the *hopeless* to give them some happiness. There are rules, of course, the most important of which is to never tell anyone we exist. If you do, your gifts would be stripped away instantly and your memories erased."

"Has anyone ever had that happen?"

"Only a few times that I've heard about from stories passed down."

He unbuckled his satchel and rummaged through it. He pulled out a bracelet with a charm that resembled the tattoo on his cheek. It had a glass center filled with black sand similar to that of Ryker's hourglass.

"This is from my world. If you should ever need to call on me, rub it seven times and walk backwards in a half-circle. I can't promise that I'll be able to help you again, though—it'll depend upon the circumstances."

He held it up in his open claw, and it levitated from him to me, where it hovered in the air. The chain opened, wrapped around my wrist, and fastened itself.

~~~

The next morning, I woke up in my bed and heard a knock on my door, and then someone sang, "Hey, my number one beautiful girl! Time to get moving. My boss called, and I gotta go in to work in about forty-five minutes, so I can't hang out with you at the library."

After throwing the covers off, I felt on the nightstand for my glasses and put them on. I flew out of bed, ran to the door, then unlocked and opened it.

As I stood there with my mouth open, I couldn't believe my eyes. It was Ryker! I wrapped my arms around his neck and hugged him as tight as I could.

"Man, Sage, what did I do to deserve this?"

He squeezed me back.

"I'm so happy to see you!" I squealed.

"Okay, I'm happy to see you, too, sis. I gotta go soon. Come on down. Fixed your fave—chocolate chip and blueberry waffles."

Then I remembered… one of my wishes had come true, and I knew what I had to do.

Mrs. D, Bixie, and Jodie were gone to their ritual Saturday yoga class; Harold was volunteering at the local animal shelter. Only Mr. D, Ryker, and I were there. As I ate breakfast, I noticed that he was placing his stuff in his backpack. When he went outside to get the newspaper, I grabbed his motorcycle keys out of his backpack and leaned over, looking out the living room window. He was headed back into the house.

Swinging the freezer door open, I moved some frozen vegetables, placed his keys in there, covered them, and slammed it shut. Then I ran back to the table, sat down, and resumed snarfing down the waffles.

Ryker came in and tossed the paper onto the coffee table, and then he walked into the kitchen, where he picked up his glass of juice and chugged it down in one swallow.

"Okay, sis, I'm out," he said, as he grabbed his backpack and kissed me on the head. "We'll go to The Hatch later and watch a movie on my phone with some extra cheddar popcorn. Sound good?" I nodded with my mouth full, as he walked out. A few minutes later, he returned, while I was washing dishes. "Sage, have you seen my keys?"

"Nope. Maybe they're in your room."

"I know I put them in my backpack. I always do. Strange." Scratching his head, he looked all over the kitchen, and then he went into the living room. "Man, I'm going to be late. Better call in to work." He grabbed the cordless phone, set it on speaker, and dialed the number. "Mr. Tate, this is Ryker. I'm running late this morning. I'll be in as soon as I can."

"Everything okay?"

"Yeah, just misplaced my keys. Hoping I can get my foster dad to give me a ride."

"Okay. If he's not able to, I'll swing by and pick you up. Just let me know."

"Thanks, Mr. Tate."

Ryker dragged himself out to Mr. D's mancave, and when he emerged shortly after, I noticed Mr. D walking like a sloth behind my brother towards the house.

Later that day, Mr. Crix called, and Mrs. D talked to him. When Mr. D picked Ryker up later that evening, we were told to go into the living room.

Mrs. D stared at us for what seemed like forever. She

pulled out a cigar from her stained hobo purse on the floor and lit it up, blowing out five puffy smoke circles towards our faces. I held my breath until I started coughing.

"Pack all your stuff. Mr. Crix will be picking you two up—and Harold, too—on Monday morning. Looks like a young insane adoptive family in Texas passed their home study. They've been searching for three teens to adopt. Glad you three are getting out of my house. It's way overdue. I'm ready for some fresh meat!"

She stormed out, and I could hear her bedroom door slam behind her.

My eyes lit up, and so did Ryker's. This was part of my second and third wishes. Harold walked in, smiled, and went back into his room. I figured Mrs. D must have spoken to him when she first received the call.

Ryker and I hugged each other, and he knocked my glasses off by accident.

"Sorry, sis."

He stooped down to retrieve them for me.

"That's okay, Ryker."

When I put them on, everything was blurry. After cleaning them off with the end of my t-shirt, I put them on again, and all still looked fuzzy, so I took them off and scanned the room. Everything was crystal clear, like never before.

When I looked down at the bracelet, it was glowing.

In my mind, I knew and whispered, *Thank you, Hageshii.*

# THE END

# PLAYLIST

*Magic:* The Cars
*Ma Boy:* Sistar
*Dibs*: Kelsea Ballerini
*I Would Die 4 U*: Prince and The Revolution
*Poison*: Bell Biv Devoe (BBD)
*I Saw the Sign*: Ace of Base
*Roni*: Bobby Brown
*Just the Way You Are*: Bruno Mars
*No Air*: Chris Brown & Jordin Sparks
*Shape of You*: Ed Sheeran
*Lonely*: Janet Jackson
*Best of My Love*: The Emotions
*Zydeco Boogaloo*: Beau Jocque
*I Melt With You:* Modern English
*I'm in love with a Monster*: Fifth Harmony
*Mr. Know It All*: Kelly Clarkson
*Sensitivity*: Ralph Tresvant
*Take A Bow*: Rihanna
*When I'm Gone*: Anna Kendrick
*Something Got A Hold On Me*: Christina Aguilera

*Tender Love*: Force MDs
*Can't Fight This Feeling:* REO Speedwagon
*Speak To A Girl*: Faith Hill & Tim McGraw
*The Glamorous Life*: Shelia E.
*Don't You Forget About Me*: Simple Minds
*Perfect*: Ed Sheeran
*Jessie's Girl*: Rick Springfield
*There You Go*: Pink
*With You*: Chris Brown
*Free Falling:* Tom Petty
*Tin Man*: Miranda Lambert
*Every Little Step*: Bobby Brown
*Jealous*: Nick Jonas
*Weak*: SWV
*Singles You Up*: Jordan Davis
*Can You Stand The Rain*: New Edition
*Human Nature*: Michael Jackson

# ABOUT THE
## AUTHOR

Miracle Austin works in the social work arena by day and in the writer's world at night and on weekends. She's a YA/NA cross-genre hybrid author; adults also read her works. She's been writing since junior high, and *Drive* by The Cars is one of her biggest inspirations to write.

She enjoys writing free-verse poems/mini-stories and short stories. Paranormal, horror, and suspense are her favorite genres, but she's not limited to them.

*Doll* is her debut YA Paranormal novel; it won 2nd place in the Young Adult category in the 2016 Purple Dragonfly Awards.

Miracle also enjoys attending diverse book festivals and comic conventions; she has been honored to be one of the panelists on some. She hopes to present at many more teen book events and conduct school visits in the future. Texas is her home with her family and looks forward to hearing from her awesome readers who already know her and new ones too.

Visit her website to learn more about Miracle Austin:
**www.miracleaustin.com**

Email: **shadesoffiction@miracleaustin.com**
Twitter: MiracleAustin7
InstaGram: @MiracleAustin7
Facebook: Miracle Austin Author

# ALSO BY
## MIRACLE AUSTIN

Doll

Boundless